OXFORD PROOF

Veronica Stallwood

headline

First published in 2002
by HEADLINE BOOK PUBLISHING

First published in paperback in 2003
by HEADLINE BOOK PUBLISHING

10 9 8 7 6 5 4 3 2 1

Cataloguing in Publication Data is available from the British Library

ISBN 0 7553 0072 6

Typeset in Times by Avon DataSet Ltd,
Bidford-on-Avon, Warwickshire

Printed and bound in Great Britain by
Clays Ltd, St Ives plc

HEADLINE BOOK PUBLISHING
A division of Hodder Headline
338 Euston Road
London NW1 3BH

www.headline.co.uk
www.hodderheadline.com

Veronica Stallwood was born in London, educated abroad and now lives near Oxford. In the past she has worked at the Bodleian Library and more recently in Lincoln College Library. Her first crime novel, *Deathspell*, was published to great critical acclaim and became a local bestseller, as did the nine Oxford novels which followed, all of which feature Kate Ivory, and her most recent atmospheric suspense novel, *The Rainbow Sign*.

When she is not writing, Veronica Stallwood enjoys going for long walks, talking and eating with friends, and gazing out at the peaceful Oxfordshire countryside from the windows of her cottage.

Praise for Veronica Stallwood:

'*Oxford Shift* gives Colin Dexter a run for his money among the dreaming spires' *The Times*

'This is a chilling and atmospheric crime novel, with believable characters and a plausible plot' *The Sunday Times*

'Stallwood is in the top rank of crime writers' *Daily Telegraph*

'One of the cleverest of the year's crop' *Observer*

'Not only plausible but absolutely compelling' *Scotsman*

'A deceptive and atmospheric tale' *Time Out*

'For those who miss the Oxford-set crime novels of Colin Dexter, *Oxford Proof* could well be what the doctor ordered' *South Wales Echo*

'A cleverly drawn mystery . . . in a compelling series' *Coventry Evening Telegraph*

For Sarah and Simon

1

'*My name is Viola.*'

'It makes a change from Mickey Mouse, I suppose,' she says. She's got a sarcastic voice and she's standing there in a black cashmere coat with a funnel neck, swaying slightly on her four-inch knife-blade heels, looking like she owns the place. Well, maybe she owns one of the flats, at that, but I don't believe she owns the whole block. She looks like she's spent a lot of money on herself – or somebody has – but her voice is pure Essex. Some time earlier in the evening she's put on a load of make-up, but now it looks blurred, as though her face is out of focus.

But she's got the confidence that comes from downing three double vodkas, though apart from her bloodshot eyes, you wouldn't know. It's not as though she's slurring her words or anything like that.

'What's your problem?' I ask. I'm not as tall as her, and I'm wearing my favourite Etonics, which have flat soles, since they're designed for running, not for fannying around looking like a tart. Anyway, I'm standing tall and staring straight into her eyes. Hers are the pale, transparent English kind, an indeterminate brownish-green colour; mine come straight from my Spanish grandmother and are a dark, opaque brown. And I bet she'd rather be my age than hers, in spite of the cashmere coat with the designer label. You look better in good clothes – any clothes, if it comes to that – if you're thin. She isn't, but I am. That's the sort of woman I like to be, the sort whose bones you can see underneath the skin, like the actresses in American sitcoms. She could never look like one of them.

'I live here,' she's saying, cool and ladylike. 'That's why I'm here. What about you? What are you doing in this block of flats in the early hours of the morning, poking around in our dustbins? And you smell, Viola, if that's what you're really called.'

That was hurtful. I always make sure I'm clean, and wear clean clothes, in spite of my mucky job.

'Viola!' she says again, disbelieving.

I don't know why my mother gave me that name. It's not as though she was expecting a rich aunt called Viola to leave me all her money. Naming me must have been the only romantic impulse my mother ever gave into. She was a severely practical person as a rule, and that's what I was brought up to be, too: severe and practical. A place for everything and everything in its place, that's what my mother believed in. My place was in my room, clean and neat and quiet. She'd got my father acting the same way. He had his place, in the armchair to the right of the fireplace, and he stuck to it.

Where did she get the name Viola from? Was she thinking of the musical instrument or the flower? Or did it come from some dim memory of classroom Shakespeare? Whatever. I've always hated it, and when I was old enough – six, maybe, or seven – I changed it for something shorter and plainer – Phil. I perfected a blank stare for anyone – teachers, they were mostly – who tried to call me 'Viola'. Even at six you can win against them if you're determined enough. We're landed with our names, whether they suit us or not, and it's the first act of rebellion, the first rejection of them and all they stand for that we can undertake.

The first change of identity.

They put the labels on us up till then. They tell us we're pretty or plain, quiet or noisy, brainy or stupid, and we're stuck with those labels whether they fit us or not. 'Of course, *you're* not brainy like your sister, are you?' Who can answer that one? 'You'll never play the piano like me,' my mother would say. Well, why should I want to? 'Viola,' she'd trill. 'Such a *pretty* name,' she'd tell people complacently, while I stood and scowled. *Viola*.

So I gave it away. Rejected it. Rejected *her* at the same time. Viola is a shy, shrinking kind of person, don't you think? She is white-skinned and wears cotton knickers. Her blouses are buttoned up to the neck; she grows her hair long and ties it back with a narrow blue ribbon. She blinks behind the thick lenses of her glasses and if she shows her pale skin to the sunlight she comes up in a rash. That's not the sort of person I wanted to grow into, and I could see that if I stuck with Viola, that's what I'd become whether I wanted to or not. This Viola is really nothing like me.

And what happened to my father, you're wondering. He's still there, sitting in his armchair to the right of the fireplace, saying nothing. Why did he never stand up for himself? Why did he never stand up for me?

I see you looking sceptical. This woman, whatever her name is, this 'Viola', is trying to take my attention away from what she's doing here, I hear you thinking. She's trying to make me feel sorry for her, and then she's going to put pretty labels on what she's doing. How does she explain the black sweatshirt and trousers, the black woollen hat pulled low on her forehead, the black trainers, the yellow rubber gloves? What's she doing inside this block of flats in the early hours of the morning?

It's quite a nice block of flats. The lobby where the bins are kept is painted pale green, the floor's some laminate that looks like real wood, and everything is clean and fresh. The bins have white-painted numbers on them, to show you which belongs to each flat. Then there's a rack for the tenants' recycling: Paper and Cardboard, Cans, Plastic. Very nice. Very organised.

I can see you think I'm up to no good, reckon I'm some sort of criminal, even. Me, I think the bastards deserve everything they get. They ask for it. It's the waste that's criminal, the carelessness. Profligate, that's what my mother would have called it. Not that I'm asking her. I cast her off years ago, if you remember. But she was right over this.

Now me, I respect hard work and success. Everything I have, I've earned. I've worked for it. No one ever gave me anything for free, not my parents, not the school I went to, nor the people I met in the years following what they called my formal education. But I don't resent it. I learned the hard way to go out and get things for myself. No one else was going to do it for me.

Sorry. I was getting carried away there, as I expect you noticed. You're thinking that I helped myself to things that didn't belong to me.

'Who are you? How did you get in?' Her voice is more insistent now, like she really wants to know. She touches the corner of her lip, as though testing to see whether she's still wearing lipstick.

And I'm silent for a moment, because that 'Who are you?' has to be one of the most difficult questions to answer, don't you think? Have I finished inventing myself yet? Who am I? I rejected Viola, but have I completed the transformation to . . . whatever it is I want to be? Once you free yourself from the labels that other people have given you, you need never set your identity in stone again. Keep it fluid. Keep your options open, that's what I believe.

'If you don't start giving me some answers I'll call the police.' And she takes a slim silver mobile from her handbag and flips it open. She raises a digit tipped with blood red. How do people find the time to make their nails look that way? She must have an expert come in and fix them every morning for her.

The red nail stabs the nine, then pauses. 'Well?'

Time to start talking. 'How did I get in? That's easy! The door was open. Maybe it is supposed to be locked, but people are careless about pulling it shut behind them, or perhaps they think their mate's coming through in a minute and he always forgets to bring his key with him. I certainly didn't break in. You can look for yourself. There's no sign of anyone forcing that lock, is there?'

You notice that I'm talking, but I'm not giving much away. I've had more practice at this than she has, even if she's the one with the phone, and she's standing between me and the door. 'I don't know what your problem is. Anything I'm taking is what people have thrown away.' I've added a whine to my voice. A kind of don't-kick-me-when-I'm-down whine. I can see it's irritating her, but it'll force her to be nicer to me: it's the way they bring these people up. Caring. Thoughtful. Stupid. And sure enough her finger stops hovering over the nine key. She flips the lid shut, though she hasn't put the phone back in her bag yet.

Like I said, they're the wasteful, profligate bastards, and I'm not. If you want to attack someone, attack them and leave me alone. You can call what I'm doing recycling, if you like, only I'm not from the Council, I'm from the independent sector. And it's not a job you'd want, I can tell you. Even if I am wearing rubber gloves, it's no fun dipping your hands into other people's rubbish. I won't go into the worst things you find, but even if it's only the slimy remains of porridge, or mouldy vegetables and the boiled, diced kangaroo the cat wouldn't eat, I can tell you it feels disgusting and it smells. And that's no way to dispose of your dog's turds, either. Makes me puke just to think about it.

But things are a lot better since nice people like you started to separate out your waste paper and put it all ready for me in a green plastic box. Cleaner, quicker, more efficient, that's what it's made my job. You'd be surprised what printed stuff people chuck away, too. I suppose they think the binmen can't read. *Think again.*

She's coming closer now, hand stretching out to my bag. A strand of hair has fallen down across her face. It's been expensively highlighted, but as she lunges forward I can see the half-inch at the roots which is her original mouse-brown colour.

'Viola? What's your other name then, Viola? Have you got a surname?' She's trying to say I've got no father, but I know he's sitting there by the fireside, letting my mother's nagging slide off his bald head. I'm not going to end up like him. I push her away.

'Get off me! You can't look in my bag – you haven't got the right. And if you lay a finger on me or my property I'll have you up for assault. Yes, I'm leaving now, and it's no business of yours what my other name is, *or* where I live.' And if you go on shouting at me like that you'll wake up all your neighbours, and I don't suppose they'll like that at all.

Just fuck off.

I thought I was managing all right, I'd have been out of there with all my gear in another two minutes, but then the lift arrived in the basement, the doors opened and the man joined us. He must have heard us from a couple of floors away, the noise we were making. He was beautifully dressed, I remember, wearing the sort of clothes you just wanted to stroke, they looked so soft. When you looked at his face you'd change your mind about doing anything like that. He was a much tougher proposition than the woman, though he was a lot quieter. I tried staring him in the eye, the way I had her, but though his were a bright cornflower blue, like a character in a kid's book, they weren't at all friendly.

'What's going on?' he asked, in the quiet voice I grew to know well. 'Why don't you go and wait for me in the flat,' he said to the woman.

The woman in the black DKNY coat didn't want to go, but stood there staring at me, pursing her lips and scowling so that two deep lines appeared between her eyes. You want to watch that, I thought, or the wind will change and you'll be stuck looking like a prune. Come to think of it, in a year or two that's what you'll look like anyway, you bad-tempered old cow.

The man just said, 'Beverley?' and off she went, no argument, clicking away on her stupid heels, pulling her coat round her as though I might contaminate her.

Then the man turned all his attention on me. 'Now, tell me what you're doing.' His mouth smiled, but his eyes stayed as cold as before.

I could see it was no use blustering or even trying to get away. He had moved so he was standing between me and the door and I didn't rate my chances if I made a run for it.

'Just sorting through the rubbish,' I said, as cool as I could make it. 'I'm not nicking anything of any value, just stuff that people have thrown out.'

He sneered. 'Don't try that story on me,' he said. 'Just tell me what you've found. Anything of interest?'

I was going to show him, but someone else came in at that moment. The bin-room was getting as busy as Piccadilly Circus. This was another man, but shorter and stockier, with dark hair that was starting to recede, though he wasn't that old. He reminded me of a grizzly bear. Not a big, scary one, but smaller, more cuddly than that. He had a narrow forehead and a wide jaw, and heavy stubble like dark-haired people get after a few hours without a shave. He wore quite a nice jacket with a black polo-neck underneath it, and faded 501s.

'Anything wrong?' he asked. He sounded a bit nervous, but determined, as though he knew he had to do the right thing.

'Nothing at all,' said the first man.

'Well, what are you doing? You don't live here, do you?' Grizzly Bear asked me. He spoke quite sharply, but I wasn't fooled: at the worst he might have called the police, I suppose, but he wasn't going to hit me, or cut me with a razor.

'Just looking,' I mumbled. I did the trick on Grizzly where you look down and sideways, then up through your fringe. I added a shy, expectant smile. He cleared his throat and looked less certain of himself.

'Can't you let her go, then?' he said to the first man.

First Man just stared at him. I went on looking naïve and vulnerable. It didn't work on my mother, nor would it work on First Man, but I thought Grizzly might just fall for it.

'What's your name?' asked Grizzly.

'Viola,' I replied. Just for once I thanked my mother. Viola sounded arty yet respectable, don't you think? At any moment he'd invite me out for a drink and ask me the story of my life. I could see Grizzly opening his mouth to tell me not to be a naughty girl and to run away home, but First Man was having none of it.

'Why don't you go back to your own flat, old boy?' he said, and I thought he was overdoing the matey bit. 'I'll deal with young Viola here.' His hair was as artfully highlighted as Beverley's. Maybe they used the same hairdresser.

'You're sure you're all right?' Grizzly asked me, sounding anxious.

I glanced towards the other man and looked scared. 'I want to go home,' I said plaintively. 'But he thinks I'm a thief.'

'She probably is, but she's done nothing wrong yet,' said First Man. 'Don't worry, I've warned her off. She won't come back here in a hurry.'

And he stood and waited while Grizzly backed away, then turned and walked off up the stairs, glancing back at me as if to make sure I was going to be all right. He looked as though he wanted to argue, but First Man wasn't the kind you argued with. Grizzly stared at me, really hard, as though trying to remember what I looked like, and gave me an encouraging smile. I didn't really want him to remember me: there's safety in being anonymous and forgettable. But there was nothing he could accuse me of since I hadn't done anything wrong. Not then, at least. And I believed he'd have forgotten all about me by the time the results, if there were any, got back to him. I was more worried about the other man. He looked as though he knew what life was all about.

'Now, let's get back to our conversation,' he said, when the doors had closed and we heard the hum of the lift going up to the flats. 'Show me what you've been doing.'

So I opened the bin liner and let him look inside. 'I could have done with another ten minutes,' I said. 'There's a couple of recycling boxes I haven't been through yet.'

He smiled. 'Not bad, though. In fact, some of it looks quite useful.'

He didn't touch anything but shone his own torch over the contents. I looked at him properly then. Beneath the flash exterior he was like me, I realised. 'You're in the same business,' I said, understanding. I didn't even bother to make it sound like a question.

'On quite a different level,' he replied, and laughed. 'You're just a beginner.'

'I've been doing this all year,' I said. I wasn't having him attacking my professional pride. For all I knew, *he* was the amateur.

'You a freelance?' he asked. He was staring at me now. The cornflower-blue eyes were a bit friendlier, but I could tell he still didn't trust me.

'Yeah.'

'Ever thought of regular employment?'

'No.' I might as well go back and sit by the fireside with my father as do that.

'Pity,' he said. 'I'm recruiting at the moment. Varied work,' he added. 'You need to diversify.'

I shook my head.

'Suit yourself.' And then, 'I'll take them,' he said, confirming my fears. And he stuffed the papers back into the black bin liner and picked it up as though about to leave with it. I held on. He twisted it out of my hands. I opened my mouth to scream. He wasn't going to nick my night's work without a fight.

'All right, then. I'll pay you for it,' he said. I don't suppose he wanted any more of the neighbours to come running to see what was wrong. I don't think he lived in that block of flats and they might ask him what he was doing there as well as me.

He reached into an inside pocket, brought out a gold clip of notes and gave me fifty quid, which was more than I was expecting. His jacket had a fancy silk lining, just to prove it hadn't come from Marks. I thought he'd be on his way but, instead of taking the bag from me, he paused and said, 'Show me what you think is worth the money I gave you.'

I realised this was some sort of test. An entrance exam, if you like. OK. I'd show him I was no amateur and that I knew what I was about. I rifled through the contents for a moment and then pulled out six items.

'These, for a start,' I said.

My copy

Look, Phoebe, I know it's tough for

the time, but it's not so easy for me, e

agreed what I should pay you for Chloe –

back on that, you needn't worry, you know. W

to keep to our arrangements – but you can't ju

goalposts whenever you think you will. It just

never even talked about sending her to a priv

we? Have you seen the fees those places charg

made a success of it in the state system, so why

she? Yes, of course I'm 'doing all right' as you c

than all right by some people's standards, but wit

job starting, I'll have to think about relocating and

know how much a house move costs. I certainly still

remember how much I had to give you when you mo

<u>your</u> new place. Sorry, that sounds like I begrud

money, and of course I'm glad you and Chloe have a

place to live. It's just that I have some pretty subs

expenses myself just at the moment and I'm not goin

Page 1 of 2
Account Holder
Mr Neil Orson

Summary of account
On 15 March

Previous balance	£3560.13
Payments received	£3560.13
New transactions	£738.98

. . . .

Your new balance	**£738.98**

Minimum payment	**£71.00**
Payment due date	**11 April**

Credit limit

Your current limit	**£12,000.00**
Available credit	**£11,261.02**

LON

March 200
Mr N Orso

Dear Mr Or

Visit Our

For the

offici

sco

If

Thames Water

Account number
317799A-8982178

MR N ORSON
FLAT 2
APPLETON COURT
LONDON SE1

Bill date 5 November 01

Your water services bill for 8 May to 1 November 2001

Total
payable

£63.24
See Below

Service charges

8 May – 1 November 2001

Water

30.05

Wastewater

33.19

. . . .

Charges

£63.24

Flat 2A3, Normandy Terrace, London SE23

Dear Neil,

First of all I'd like to say how much I appreciate you sending the money for Chloe every month. I know it's what you said you'd do, and sometimes it's come a bit late or a bit short, but you've been really good, and not everyone does what they promise, believe me. And it makes me reluctant to ask you for more, but for Chloe's sake, I have to. It's that school. You know the problems she's been having, I've told you about it often enough. Of course the neighbourhood isn't what we could afford if the two of us had stayed together and don't think I'm blaming you for that, not really. But Chloe deserves better and I've been looking out for alternatives. She needs a place where they respect how special she is. There's nothing near this

LONDON & COUNTIES BANK
CITY BRANCH
LONDON EC1

Account No: 53-21-65-23 440765310

Dear Mr Orson,

I am writing to confirm that we have increased the
overdraft limit on your current account to £4,000. I should
like to take this opportunity to remind you that we do not
expect you to be permanently overdrawn to this extent, but
that you should aim to clear your overdraft every month.
Any long-term borrowing should be dealt with by means of a
bank loan. Of course, given your credit record, I or one of
my colleagues would be very happy to discuss such an
arrangement with you, should you find it desirable.

FOREWORD PUBLISHING

You are cordially invited to attend,
with a partner,
the Annual Staff Party
which this year will be held on
Friday 7 December at 7.30 for 8 p.m.
at the Randolph Hotel,
Beaumont Street, Oxford

'Not bad,' he said. 'But you've wasted your time on inessentials, haven't you? Why've you bothered with the whingeing letter from the ex, and his sod-off note back to her?'

'They show he's middle-class and loaded,' I told him. 'And you can tell from what *she* says that he's not really organised about his money. She says it sometimes comes late, or short of what she's expecting. I bet he doesn't check his bank statements properly – or his credit-card ones. He wouldn't notice any mistakes for months, most likely.'

'Good. But you can tell he's worth some time and effort without that. I've already made up my mind about this one. The bank and credit-card stuff gives us what we want, and the recent utility bill. It's lucky for us he didn't tear that bill across. And the invitation to the staff party gives us his employer's name – we'll soon find out the detail on that. You need a bit more discipline, a bit more focus, but you're showing promise, Viola.'

I pointed to the water bill. 'People don't realise you can use them to establish your identity. He says he's thinking of moving house,' I went on. 'Or "relocating" as he calls it. He might just be having the girlfriend on, of course.'

'Well, I think we should arrange for his mail to be redirected to a new address, don't you?' He was bolder than me. I've never tried that one. 'And we'll make sure he's on the electoral register of his new address. We're thoughtful people, don't you think?'

We both laughed, I remember.

'Where are you going to move him to?' I wanted to know how this was done. I like to learn new things and improve myself.

'An old people's flat.' I must have looked surprised because he added, 'A young friend of mine will visit her grandmother and pick up his mail for him. And if anyone comes asking questions, they won't get much joy out of the old woman. She won't understand and she's as stubborn as a concrete block.'

He was feeling pleased with himself for being so bloody clever. He wanted to show off, prove he was better at this than I was. But I didn't want to stand chatting much longer. For all I knew, the police might be on their way. That kind of over-confidence can get you into trouble. I turned towards the door.

'I'd better be going,' I said.

'And I mean it about giving you a job,' he said.

It was tempting, certainly. I was getting tired of going out nights, sorting through other people's rubbish. Maybe he could offer me something different. He certainly had enough money in his pocket to make me take him seriously. 'What did you mean by "diversify"? What sort of job are you offering?' I wasn't going on the game, that's for sure, but from what he'd been saying, he had a fair-sized operation. There could be opportunities for an ambitious person.

'Just what you've been doing here, to begin with, though you may need to move to another district.'

'I'm used to moving on. It doesn't do to get your face known anywhere.'

'Good. I'm glad you understand. Well, after a spell in a new place, we'll see how much talent you show. If you're as good as I think you might be, you could go right to the top. What did you say your name was again?'

He didn't believe I was really called Viola, and who could blame him. I gave him the name I usually went by – Phil – and he nodded, as though he'd known it already, though he couldn't have done really. It was all part of his act, I realised later, when I thought about it.

'How old are you?' he asked next.

'Twenty-three.'

'I'd have put you as younger than that.'

'I can look my age if I have to,' I said. I was in my working clothes. You don't expect to look sophisticated dressed like that.

'And you've got a good voice. Do a bit of work on your accent and you could be anyone. Where are you from?'

'London.'

'Big place. You look like you're from a good home, so what are you doing here?'

I don't like talking about myself. If you give too much away, people think they have power over you. But he just went on looking at me, expecting me to answer, until I grew tired of listening to the silence. 'I come from Bromley.'

'Parents?'

'I suppose my parents still live there – they wouldn't have the imagination to move away. They're still sat there staring at the wallpaper.'

'And you didn't fancy that?' His voice was friendly, encouraging.

'My mother wanted me to go to college and learn Business Studies. Word processing and spreadsheets, shit like that. She liked the idea I'd go off every morning wearing a navy suit and carrying a briefcase. I wanted to sign up for the foundation course in Art. I liked designing stuff, making things. I was good at them. But she wasn't having any of that. "You're just messing around, Viola," she said. "It's time you got serious about your future." I could see what that led to all right, the examples were right in front of my eyes. She'd bullied my dad into being serious since the day they got engaged. And she'd bullied my sister into a serious marriage. You never saw *her* crack much of a smile after that. I tried telling Dad what I wanted to do, but he just said you had to give up stupid dreams and settle for reality, the way he had. Facing up to things, he called it. Settle for being miserable all your life, more like.' I thought I'd forgotten all about this shit, put it behind me, but now even I could hear the bitterness in my voice and feel the words pouring out of my mouth like vomit.

'So you got away,' he prompted.

'We had rows, and I went off with my mates when Mum thought I should be studying. Anything to get out of that stifling house. She locked me in my room, so I climbed out the window on to the garage roof, and down to the ground. After that, she stopped my allowance, so I got a part-time job.'

'And?'

'Oh, the usual. She took my clothes away, and when that didn't keep me in, she started hitting me. She's not a big woman, but she put all the force of her own disappointments into hurting me. I think she was just fed up that I wanted to do something she hadn't, like enjoy myself. She thought I should stay there while she told me what to do all the time. She thought we were back in the twentieth century, and that I should obey her just because she happened to be my mother. Well, she was wrong. I'd had enough and one Saturday morning I went off with my mate Dean. He was having a hard time with his stepdad and we reckoned we'd be better off on our own. He knew some people who shared a flat up in Shepherd's Bush, and we moved in with them. I've never been back home and I don't think I ever will.'

'But you'd still like to be an artist?'

'You're joking!'

'There's room for creative people in my business,' he said, but I reckoned he was being sarcastic. 'What happened to your mate Dean?'

'We split up after a bit. He contacted his mum and agreed to go to college to study catering or something. I liked living the way I was.'

'And now you want to screw all the people who remind you of your parents,' he said.

'That's rubbish. I never think of them. I put all that behind me. I'm my own person.'

'If you say so.' He took a small silver case out of an inside pocket and removed a business card from it. Then he drew out a pen and wrote something on the back. 'This is my mobile number,' he said. 'Take the coach to Bristol tomorrow morning and give me a ring when you get there.'

He was a high-handed bastard, and cocky with it. He was quite sure I would do as he said. But he was right about the relocation part. It was time I moved on.

'I'll give you some work to do, teach you my methods. I'm sure you'll catch on fast enough.' And he smiled at me. He was too old for my taste, but he was quite fanciable when he smiled.

'I'm a quick learner,' I said.

He put his hand on my arm, like a friend would. 'Good,' he said. 'You come to Bristol tomorrow and in the evening I'll take you out for a decent meal. We'll go somewhere special and celebrate. We'll paint the town if that's what you want.'

And that's how I met Baz and started my new career.

2

'Kate? I have some lovely news for you.'

Kate Ivory put down the mug of coffee she had been drinking. Estelle Livingstone, her agent, was on the line, sounding unusually enthusiastic.

'Lovely news?' Kate's first-floor window looked out on to Agatha Street, where the trees were just starting to show a haze of tender green in the March sunshine. But in spite of this, not to mention the chirping of the birds and the profusion of daffodils in the gardens opposite, Kate's head was full of plans for selling her house and moving away from Fridesley – so much so that it took an effort for her to realise what Estelle was talking about. 'About my book, do you mean?' She had been hoping to leave thoughts of work to one side for a few weeks.

'That last novel of yours . . .'

'*Spitfire Sweethearts*,' prompted Kate helpfully.

'That's the one,' said Estelle.

'Set in World War Two,' Kate added, as much for her own benefit as Estelle's. It was amazing the way the plot of a book disappeared from her memory once it had been printed out, consigned to a Jiffy bag and posted to her agent.

'Stop interrupting,' said Estelle, returning to her customary sharp style. 'If you remember, last time we spoke I told you that now Fergusson's have accepted *Spitfire Sweethearts*, you've completed the two-book contract we had with them. And I said we could be a little more ambitious in placing your next work.'

She was speaking as though addressing a rather slow child. Now she mentioned it, Kate did remember something about her plans for the new novel. It was just that her mind was on getting away from Fridesley at this precise moment. She moved the coffee cup a couple of inches to the left so that she could read the details of a house for sale in Fridesley Lane. How much were they asking for it, she wondered. She really needed to move: Agatha Street was getting her down since the recent tragedies. When Edward and Laura Foster were killed in the house on one side of her, and then Jeremy Wells, her neighbour on the other side, died in a car crash shortly afterwards, she had started to feel uneasy. Empty houses on either side of her ... though she wasn't normally superstitious, it had seemed like an omen. And the street was changing. Familiar peeling paintwork and rusty fences had been replaced, while the tussocky, overgrown front gardens had been transformed by low-maintenance coloured gravel and miniature Japanese maples. Young professional couples, too busy for a conventional marriage and children, had taken over from large, noisy families like the Venns, whose messy lives had spilled on to the street and in through Kate's back door.

'I need a breathing space,' she said, as much to herself as to Estelle. 'I can't face writing another first chapter. Not yet.'

'This is no time to go all moody on me,' said Estelle. 'This is a great opportunity for us, and I'm not going to let you blow it. You must pull yourself together, dear.'

Dear? Had Estelle ever called her that before? Maybe, Kate thought, it was indeed time for her to pull herself together after all. 'Don't worry,' she said hastily. 'I've got plenty of ideas buzzing around in my head, not just the outline I've already sent you, but another story along the same lines as *Spitfire*

Sweethearts. I've set it in the forties and fifties since I've already done so much background reading.' This might be an exaggeration, since she had read only two or three books while writing *Spitfire Sweethearts*, but it was no good being modest with Estelle – if you weren't careful, she'd take you at your own evaluation. 'Have you sent the outline to Fergusson's yet? Are they interested in it?'

'Of course they are, but—'

Kate turned the page of the *Property News*, wondering if there was a house for sale that resembled her own terraced one in Agatha Street. She wanted an idea of the price she might get for it. 'Did you manage to push up the advance?' She was keen to redecorate before she put the house on the market, and she really needed to do something about the patch of yellowing grass at the back. Pink gravel, perhaps? If she bought large terracotta pots and filled them with . . .

'You're not paying attention,' snapped Estelle.

'No, really, I am.' Kate turned her mind from weeping cherry trees back to the contract for her next book. 'You haven't mentioned whether Fergusson's have offered a decent advance this time.'

'I've been trying to tell you – I'm not talking about Fergusson's. This is a much better proposition. I said I'd show your outline to three or four top editors, and one of them has made an offer. You're going up-market – at last!'

'I am?' Kate looked down at yesterday's washed-out T-shirt and the jeans she'd meant to consign to Oxfam and quickly imagined herself into a smart black suit and crimson silk top to project the right classy image to her agent.

'I have an offer from Foreword,' continued Estelle.

Kate added a string of real pearls and a pair of black pumps from Charles Jourdain. 'On the strength of half a dozen pages of A4?' On reflection, she removed the pearls and replaced them with a flame-printed scarf in finely-pleated silk.

'They liked what they've read and they believe you have a future with them.'

Kate repressed the urge to jump up and down with pleasure, and tried hard to sound cool and sophisticated. A company like Foreword would expect sophistication. 'They're the people who really know how to market their authors, aren't they? They sell millions of books.'

'They're good at marketing, certainly, though they're not the biggest in the fiction market. But they've been looking to expand their list, which is why I sent them a couple of your published books as well as the outline for the new one. I really think they're just the right people for you.'

'Classy. High-profile,' suggested Kate.

'They've always had a very good reputation, of course, and now they want to sign up some bright new talent to enhance it further.'

'And aren't their offices here in Oxford?'

'Yes, not far from the railway station, I believe. Pity about that. I expect they'll have to move to London with the big players if they grow the way they want to.'

'Oxford's convenient for me, certainly. But tell me more about the deal.'

'They're talking about a three-book contract,' crowed Estelle, unable to conceal her own jubilation.

'How much?' asked Kate, voicing the serious novelist's primary concern.

Estelle gave her a figure which was more than double Kate's expectation. 'For each title,' she added.

'Sounds acceptable,' said Kate as calmly as she could manage.

'So I'm taking it that you'd like me to accept the Foreword offer?'

'Yes, Estelle. That is a definite yes.'

'Excellent.' And Kate could hear her agent smiling into the telephone. 'I'll tell them to draw up a contract, but meanwhile you can go ahead with the next book. Your new editor, Neil, will want to meet you, Kate, to discuss your future career.'

Future career? Even more promising: this might mean an end to her hand-to-mouth existence. 'I assume we'll meet here in Oxford. Will you be joining us?'

'Of course. Oxford is only an hour away from London. I'll arrange something as soon as possible. How are you fixed?'

'I'll check the diary,' said Kate, knowing well that the days stretched ahead with nothing to look forward to except an appointment with her dental hygienist.

Estelle mentioned a few possible dates a couple of weeks ahead and Kate agreed that she could make herself free for any of them. Estelle was well aware, of course, that an author will always clear her diary for a free lunch with an editor. But the two weeks gave Kate time to try on expensive clothes and spend some of Foreword's generous advance. If she put her purchases on a credit card she would only have to pay interest for a month or two before the cheque came through. And she mustn't forget to book herself into her hairdresser for a new cut and a session with the foil strips to freshen up the colour.

'You'll like your new editor,' Estelle was saying, breaking into Kate's daydream. 'A delightful young man.'

Delightful? Young? Warning bells sounded. Kate hoped this didn't mean that Estelle was about to embark on another unsuitable liaison. She had a penchant for delightful young men and when the relationship broke up – as Estelle's relationships invariably did – Kate might well find herself with a cancelled contract, looking for a new publisher.

'He's one of the bright new generation,' continued Estelle. 'He's joined Foreword only recently from a major London fiction house, so he's used to dealing with best-selling authors. He's already found one promising new author for Foreword, but he's not just looking for blockbusters, he's sensitive, too, with a real love of books and good writing.'

'You mean you want me to watch my spelling?'

'He'll be more interested in your style and original use of language than your orthography.' Orthography? Estelle was practising for going up-market too, it seemed. 'But he does love your natural gift for storytelling. And now you'll be able to go deeper with the psychology of your characters and their motivation. Neil and I think that Fergusson's demand for historical romances has been holding you back. But with Foreword you'll be able to let your true talent shine out.'

Kate leaned back in her chair and tried to keep the smugness out of her voice. 'He sounds like the ideal editor. Does he have a surname?'

'Orson. Neil Orson.'

Kate wrote the name in her diary. 'I look forward to meeting him,' she said.

'I know the two of you are going to get on really well. And one more tiny thing.'

'Yes?'

'Why don't you quickly draft the first chapter of the new novel, to show him what you can do when you put your mind to it? You could let me have a copy a couple of days before our lunch, and I'll pass it on to Neil when he's poured the first glass of white wine.'

'I'll give it a try.'

She had planned to start washing down walls and paintwork later that morning, but now she would have to go to her workroom and sit down at her computer instead. After she'd done what Estelle asked for she would find out more about selling her house and looking for somewhere new to live. It was a number of years since she'd moved into Agatha Street and she was sure that things had changed since then. Although she was itching to move, it felt like a reprieve for the house that had been hers for ten years. And although it would be hard to cut her ties with Fridesley, she would make sure that the delivery date for the first of the new books took into account a house move. She would be quite firm with Estelle and Neil over that.

Her life was moving ahead on the career and house fronts. All she needed now was a good relationship with a reasonable man. For a moment she remembered the man she had met the previous year, Jon Kenrick. For a short while it had seemed that they might be an item. But the timing was all wrong. She realised now that at that time she hadn't fully recovered from her break-up with George Dolby. And she had met Jon as a result of the gruesome local murders. She just wanted to get away from those memories and everyone associated with them. Jon, unfortunately, was one of the people she had had to leave behind.

3

Neil Orson would have enjoyed hearing Estelle's description of him, and would have agreed with every word of it. Of course she was delighted to have netted him as editor for her young protégée, Kate Ivory! Kate, as she passed through her thirties, would have been equally pleased at the modifier 'young', but Neil wasn't to know that.

While Estelle was speaking to Kate on the phone, Neil had bolted himself into the en suite bathroom that was one of the perks of his new job at Foreword, and was staring at his face in the mirror. The bathroom was tiny – in fact he could hardly turn round in it, let alone swing some innocent small feline – but he was the only editor to have such a luxury, and he felt sure it was because he had been marked down for early promotion. They'd been keen to get him to move down from London, of course, and had been rewarding him with these little sweeteners. He knew it couldn't last: for the moment he was in the honeymoon period with Foreword, but one day another star would join them and then he would be taken for granted. It was up to him to make his mark on the fiction list before that happened.

What concerned him at this moment was not the originality (or otherwise) of Kate Ivory's prose, or even the accuracy of her spelling, but rather the exact stage of development reached by the small boil in front of his left ear. If he squeezed it now, would it crumple up and die, or would it explode into angry red life so that Roland Ives would stare at it during their meeting? At the moment it was quite inconspicuous, (or so he thought) and it was probably safer to leave it alone, but it was itching slightly, and the yellow, pus-filled point was protruding in a way that told him it was almost certainly ripe for squeezing.

His dilemma was solved by the abrupt ringing of his telephone. He unbolted the bathroom door and returned to his desk.

'Yes?' He looked with approval at the receiver in his hand: it was the colour and texture of a Granny Smith apple and matched precisely the wall-to-wall Wilton. He would have liked polished wooden boards and an antique rug, but he could see that it would not be practicable on the fourth floor of a modern office block. It was a pity, too, that they hadn't given him one of the corner offices, which boasted windows on two sides, but at least he wasn't consigned to one of the claustrophobic boxes in the centre of the building, which had no windows at all and were strictly for losers, he considered.

The office was nearly perfect. He frowned at the 'nearly', but it was only imperfect in the sense of incomplete. He had brought one or two things from his flat in London, and had his eye on one or two more that he would purchase when he could take an afternoon off. Where other people personalised their office or work station with a spider plant in a plastic pot, a whimsical fluffy toy and a couple of wacky cards pinned to a partition, Neil placed on a shelf two heavy glass vases in smoke-blue, shaped like large raindrops. On the wall he had hung an original Rainer Kleemann, with that same smoke-blue predominating. He had thought about a pale chair from Rolf Benz to seat his visitors on, but he hated to think of what might happen to it in the casual ambience of a publishing office. And how many of his visitors would recognise its designer's name without prompting?

No, he thought, as he said, 'Neil Orson,' into the phone and looked around him. This room wasn't imperfect in the way that the living room in his flat was. There, in spite of the desirable furniture and objects he had collected, the effect was spoiled: the white leather sofa was ruined for good.

He should have known that Cassia was a smoker, but at the time he was too taken with the amazing length of her straight black hair, the opacity of her tanned skin and the expensive simplicity of her dress (cream silk, with a gravity-defying neckline) to notice her tainted breath. She smelled faintly of peppermints. How was he to know that she had popped a Polo into her mouth before taking the lift to his apartment? She had guessed that he was an anti-smoker – immaculate surfaces and the lack of ashtrays would have given her the message – and once he had descended into a deep post-coital sleep she had slipped from his bed and returned to sit on his bone-pale leather sofa. There she had smoked a cigarette, unaware, apparently, that the smell would linger and give her away to Neil's sensitive nose.

The next day, after she had léft, he had found it. He had dusted the low table and was rearranging the cushions when he saw a raised and puckered black burn, like a slug, defiling the surface of the leather. She knew what she had done, that was plain, for she had tossed a grey suede cushion on top of the mark to hide it. Then she must have dropped the stub into her Gucci handbag and taken it away with her. Meanwhile, his sofa was ruined. He kept the mark covered with the cushion so that no one else could see it, but he knew it was there. He was always aware of it, that curled slug of a burn mark on his Saporiti sofa.

He had got his own back, naturally. There was no way he would forget something like that, or let it pass. Cassia worked in Publicity, and he started to put around a rumour or two about the gaffes she had made. He said he would prefer someone else to work for his authors, since Cassia was so *unreliable*. 'Lovely girl and all that, but you don't want her spilling red wine down the posh frock of a literary editor, do you?' And, 'She managed to lose the photos we commissioned from an expensive American. Poor old Cassia, seems to be losing it, doesn't she?' Cassia left before she could be 'let go', and he'd heard she was working for a supermarket chain now. He doubted whether she could still afford the designer dresses she'd been used to wearing. A feeling of self-righteousness warmed Neil's heart and brought a smile to his lips.

'Mr Neil Orson?' a voice was repeating in his ear.

'Yes.'

'This is Tracey from the Customer Services department at London and Midland,' the voice continued. Tracey had an ingratiating tone and a mild Midlands accent.

'I don't need another pension plan,' said Neil, preparing to replace the receiver.

'Oh, no! It's nothing like that!' trilled Tracey, sounding almost like a real human being. 'I'm not selling, Mr Orson, I'm trying to give you something.'

One part of Neil's brain told him that the likelihood of his bank's giving anything away to one of its customers was small, but another, more primitive part – remembering perhaps the financial deprivations of his youth – put in quickly, 'What are you offering?'

'A small number of highly valued customers have been carefully selected to receive completely free for the next six months our Accident and Sickness Cash Plan,' Tracey recited, apparently reading from a prepared script.

'How much?' he interrupted.

'I'm sorry?'

'How much will you pay me to break my leg or catch pneumonia? That's what you're talking about, isn't it?'

'Benefits are related to the customer's income, averaged over the previous six months. In your own case this would result in a payment in the region of five hundred pounds per day of incapacity, as certified by your own GP.'

'And you're giving me all this free of charge?'

'For the first six months, yes. Only after that period would you pay our low monthly premiums which would be deducted from your account by direct debit.' As Neil hesitated she added, 'And you may cancel your cover at any time during the first six months and pay absolutely nothing.'

'You're telling me I can't lose.'

'Exactly that, Mr Orson.' For a moment it sounded as though she might have departed from the script.

'Then you'd better sign me up,' said Neil. 'Just send on the bumf.'

'Fine. Just one more—'

'Isn't that all? I have to leave for a meeting in a few minutes.'

'For your own protection, I should just like to run through a few simple questions in accordance with our security procedure. Can you give me your Visa account number?' As Neil hesitated, she added, 'You'll find it printed on the front of the card, Mr Orson.'

'Oh, yes,' and he fished in his pocket and gave her the number.

'Right. And that's a company card, is it?'

'Yes,' confirmed Neil, running his finger along the gold-embossed *Foreword Publishing* underneath his own name. 'And I hold a MasterCard for my personal use.'

'And the credit limit on the Visa?'

'Look, I really do have to leave for my meeting.'

'This will only take a few seconds more.'

'Five thousand pounds,' put in Neil proudly.

'That's correct. Now, I'd like your full names, please.'

'Neil Geoffrey Orson.'

'Date of birth?'

'Fourteenth March, nineteen sixty-nine.'

'And, finally, if you could give me your mother's maiden name?'

'Budleigh.'

There was two-beat pause. 'I didn't quite catch the name. How are you spelling that?'

Neil obediently spelled it out for her.

'Thank you so much for your co-operation, Mr Orson. Your Accident and Sickness Cash Plan cover will start immediately, though the paperwork may take a week or two to complete and send on by post.'

Neil replaced the apple-green receiver. It was almost worth falling under a bus to get five hundred a day, though it might be prudent to read through the policy's small print before doing so. He might have wondered why Tracey, if she had his details in front of her, had needed to ask the spelling of his mother's maiden name. But he had the meeting with Roland in three minutes, and he only just had time to pick up his document case and take the lift to the top floor. It didn't do to keep the Managing Director waiting.

When Neil reached Roland Ives's office, slightly out of breath from racing down the corridor, he found the Managing Director waiting for him, standing by the window in his office.

There was a blue-suited woman in her forties sitting in a chair near to him. She looked as though she belonged in the Accounts department.

'Neil,' said Roland, 'so glad you could join us.' Ives looked as though he had just that moment left the hands of his valet. Neil even caught a whiff of minty toothpaste as he spoke. Though Roland, as he knew, had endured a long, frustrating journey in from a picturesque, but distant village that morning, and rumour had it that he ironed his own shirts since his wife refused to do so and the au pair was too busy keeping three strong-willed children under control. The mental image of Roland standing at the ironing board in his vest while his wife dipped manicured fingers into a box of dark Belgian chocolates was dispelled by the Managing Director's next words.

'I've invited you to my office because you've just given away the details of your company credit-card account to an outsider.' Ives didn't believe in wasting time with small talk.

'She wasn't an outsider, she worked for the bank!' exclaimed Neil.

'How do you know?'

It seemed ridiculous to say, 'Because she said so,' so Neil stayed silent.

Roland Ives waited for a couple of seconds then continued, 'I should like to introduce you to Tracey Evans, who is a security consultant.'

'How do you do,' the blue-suited woman said primly.

'But we were just speaking on the phone,' said Neil, recognising the Midlands accent. Tracey smiled at him but didn't reply.

'Remind me again what the credit limit on your Visa card is,' added Roland into the silence.

'Five thousand pounds,' mumbled Neil.

'And someone could be running up bills on the company account in Warsaw or Hong Kong at this very moment with the information you gave away.'

Neil studied the floor. Slate-blue Wilton stared back at him.

'Look, Neil, I'm sure you've got the message now,' said Roland Ives more kindly. 'You don't give your details away to anyone. And don't think you've been singled out – everyone in the company at your level and above has been tested like this. We had some trouble a couple of years back and we decided that this rather brutal method was the best way of ensuring that people became more security conscious.'

Ives reminded Neil of his father when he had just finished reading a less than complimentary school report and had delivered one of his little homilies about doing his best, and working harder in future. 'Do you want to add anything, Tracey?'

'Just to remind Mr Orson that he shouldn't give any of his personal details – his date of birth, mother's maiden name, name of his pet hamster – to anyone. And watch what you throw away: tear correspondence and account statements into small pieces before putting them in the bin.'

'Yes, of course.' Neil only just managed to avoid saying 'Miss'.

'Well, thank you for your co-operation, Neil.'

Neil gathered that he was free to go. He half-expected Ives to tell him to run back to his Latin class and be a good boy in future, but his boss was asking how he was finding the journey to work, and whether he'd thought about relocating now that he'd settled in at Foreword.

'Property in this county isn't going to lose its value,' he said.

'Really?'

'You'd be sad to leave London, I can see that. My brother Julian and I are trying to convince the rest of the Board that we'll have to move the company to London if we want to be major players in the fiction league. They can't see it, of course. Well, they're all older than Julian and me, and what was good for their grandfather is good enough for them. We'll talk them round in the end, I know, because we're right. But it will be a good while before we're ready for the move. Think on, Neil, think on.'

They chatted about it for a minute or two, then Neil slipped thankfully away to his own office.

At first, as he walked back down the corridor, he was angry at the way he had been humiliated by Ives and Tracey. It was all very well saying that they put all new senior staff through this same test. He wondered for a moment how many of them had failed it. Was he perhaps the only one? What kind of company was this? Had he really made the right move in taking a job with Foreword?

He'd been wary about working outside London – he didn't want to lose touch with all the people who mattered in the business, after all – but the package Foreword had offered him, and the freedom they had given him to sign up new authors, had swung it in the end.

Neil knew already that there had been talk of Foreword's moving to London at some point in the future. The Ives family had built up a solid academic publishing company in Oxford over the past hundred years or so, but it was the younger generation who had decided on the move into fiction publishing – and had been successful. London was where it all happened, they told the Board, but Neil knew it would take time and heated discussion before they managed to shift Foreword away from their home base.

By the time he reached the stairs he was thinking that his dressing-down had all been a great deal of fuss about not very much. Anyone could have believed that Tracey was really employed by the bank. And as for all that shredding and tearing – who had time for fussing about like that? Then, by the time he walked from the lift on the fourth floor to his office, he was feeling humbled again as he remembered how he had fallen for Tracey's sales pitch.

'Might have made a bit of a fool of myself there,' he said ruefully to Amanda as he passed her desk. His Editorial Assistant was attaching a covering letter to the proof of a dust jacket.

'They didn't catch you with their credit-card scam, did they?' she asked cheerfully.

'Yes. I was thinking about other things, and fell straight into it.'

'That's the way it works. You were set up. I shouldn't worry about it. I believe that Ben Mitchell in Marketing was the only one who saw through it.'

Neil started to cheer up.

'Ives is a bastard, isn't he?' added Amanda.

Neil was about to agree with her, then wondered if it was really a good thing to slag off your Managing Director to one of the other staff. 'He's only doing his job,' he said lamely. 'I don't suppose you know who it was who made the mistake that cost the company thousands?' he asked her.

'I do believe it was Julian Ives,' she said.

Neil looked a lot more cheerful. 'His own brother? The head of the Design Department – really?' He would remember that the next time he was carpeted for some minor fault.

'Great cover this, don't you think?' said Amanda, slipping the pages into a board-backed envelope. 'The author should love it.'

'Let's hope so. They usually suggest at least one "improve-
ment", I've always found.'

Amanda fixed on the address label, wrote *First-Class Mail*
on the envelope and placed it in her Out tray. 'I'll bring you a
coffee and swipe one of Zoe's doughnuts for you,' she said. She
was a kind girl, and Neil recognised that she was trying to
make up for his humiliation in Ives's office.

On the other hand, thought Neil five minutes later, as he
dropped powdered sugar down the lapels of his dark suit, when
it came to the question of where he lived, Ives had a point.
He could probably buy quite a nice little property in rural
Oxfordshire for the sum he'd get for his London flat. Prices
here were rising all the time, and it might be a canny investment.
But was he ready for the life of the country gentleman? He
liked to escape from the provinces and back into the capital.
London had a buzz that was missing from Oxford, though
three or four hours spent commuting each day was a high price
to pay. Should he live in Oxfordshire and spend weekends with
friends back in Town when he felt like a change? Maybe he
should look for something in Oxford itself and get used to life
in the provinces before settling for a cottage with roses round
the door, a car permanently spattered with mud and life in a
village with an expensive pub, no shops and no public transport.

Certainly it was no use relying on a rapid decision by the
Foreword board on a move to London. He could see years of
heated argument ahead over that one. He opened the bottom
drawer of his desk and took out his clothes brush. By the time
he asked Amanda to book a copy editor for a promised
manuscript, he was looking quite immaculate again.

4

It wasn't until a couple of weeks after I'd joined Baz's workforce that he sent me off on my own.

I'd been living in Bristol for those first two weeks, sharing a room with one of his employees, and going out with another of them to learn Baz's own bin-diving methods.

'Think of yourself as a trainee,' he told me. Trainee? Sounded like the sort of thing my mother would suggest. I suppose I was doing OK, but I wasn't earning any more than I had when I was freelancing. Still, if you're a trainee, then one day you get qualified, right? And after that, you get promoted. I had to hold on to the idea that I had prospects in the organisation.

Lyn, the girl I shared with, was working a different scam, in a restaurant. What with me working nights and sleeping days, and her doing the opposite, we didn't see a lot of each other to compare notes. I think Baz liked it that way, and anyway, Lyn had a boyfriend and spent most of her time off at his place. I thought he was a waste of space, but there's no accounting for taste, is there? Lyn was a drippy sort of girl, too, with one of those voices that sounds like she's always asking a question. I didn't think she'd last long. Or if she did, she wasn't going to get promoted, like me.

For my own work, Baz put me with a man called Scott; he told me to keep my eyes open and watch what he did. Certainly Scott wasn't much of a talker, so anything I learned, I learned by using my eyes. Scott called me Phil, which is what I preferred. I liked to think that in my dark tracksuit, wearing trainers and with a hat pulled low on my forehead, I could pass for a boy as easily as a girl.

Scott and I had a funny relationship – if you can call it that. We hardly exchanged more than half a dozen words during the night's work, and then it was a case of, 'Shine the torch here,' and 'Eyeball this for me.' I never even found out whether Scott was his first name or his last, and whether he lived alone or with his mum. And since he wasn't interested in me, he learned nothing in return. Again, I sense that Baz prefers it this way.

Scott knew what he was doing, though. He was quick and thorough, and he left nothing behind him that would raise people's suspicions – no litter of paper, no empty cans in corners, no fingerprints. He always wore gloves and his clothes were as clean as mine. I liked that. I can respect a man who's careful in his personal habits. He checked that I was wearing gloves of my own, and that my hair was hidden under a woollen hat, every time we went out. No one caught us at work, no one came after us.

Still, after two weeks of this, I was getting fed up. I'd just decided that I was a loner after all, that I'd rather go back to being a freelance, when Baz told me I could move on, act on my own again. He sent me to some town north of Bristol called Worcester, though still in the western part of the country, over near the Welsh border.

'I've never been anywhere like that,' I told him. I hardly knew such places existed.

'That's good,' he said. 'No one will recognise you, will they? Keep a low profile. Don't stand out. Don't give anyone a reason to remember you.'

The town seemed so small after London and Bristol. The countryside pressed in against the concrete and brick of the buildings, and the weather was always wet. Every day I woke to the same depressing sight: thin, persistent rain falling out of a low, leaden sky. The clouds were so thick there was no telling whether the sun was to left or right of you. And it was all very well trying to fit in, but the people spoke with a nasal twang that was a bastard to copy.

Baz had a place for me to live all prepared, though. I liked that about him. He did look after his workers. Probably had a sickness and pension plan for us, but no one I knew ever got sick, and we were all well short of retirement age.

'Bin-diving!' I grumbled. 'I thought I'd be moving on from that.'

'Stick it for a couple more weeks. Things will get better after that.'

Throughout my life I've found that good times always are a couple of weeks away. Meanwhile, at least I had a warm place to live, food to eat and money in my pocket.

Then came the night I struck gold.

I'd pocketed my Maglite and laid a firm hold on my zip-top bag before entering the neat little lobby containing the residents' bins. When I switched on the torch and flashed it around I saw freshly painted walls, a well-swept floor and uniform, scrubbed-looking bins. It reminded me of the place where I was working the night I met Baz. It was even painted the same green, though the floor was of a patterned vinyl this time. And that night's work had yielded at least one worthwhile mark.

Baz didn't often tell me what happened to the papers I collected for him. But when he'd done the necessary work on the identity – applying for a driving licence, putting Orson on the electoral register at the old people's flat, checking Orson's date of birth and mother's maiden name – that time we went off on a spending spree together. I asked him how he'd got hold of

45

Orson's details, but he told me I'd learn stuff like that later. I think he must have been paying someone in Orson's bank, but he didn't want to let on about it. There was no point in pushing it; once he'd decided he wasn't going to talk, there was no persuading him.

Certainly in these flats I was dealing with similar clean, organised people as in the London ones. Professionals, by the look of their rubbish. I didn't need to scrabble through the mess of takeaway cartons, muesli scrapings, hair combings and rotting fish that usually met my eyes when I lifted a dustbin lid. It was the part of the job I hated most, but I was determined to persevere with it so that I would succeed in the end. One day I would find a document that would make Baz's fortune and I would share in his riches. I was destined for great things in his organisation – Baz had told me so.

Most of the residents in this block had torn their paper up before stacking it in their boxes. Two had even used a shredder. Although this was disconcerting in a way, it did mean that I was in the right block of flats. Who would bother to shred their paperwork, by hand or machine, if there wasn't something worth protecting?

It was the contents of the final bin that were the most promising. I saw that the bin-owner hadn't bothered to recycle anything as soon as I shone my Maglite in, so I got on with sorting through his rubbish. I found an empty jar of smoked oysters, a couple of wine bottles with French labels telling me they were château-bottled. Even the smell of this bin was superior: rich and yeasty, with an undertone of fish. This was a bin worth diving into. I moved the top layer to one side and shone my light down so that I could see what was there.

Not bad. The tenant ate out a lot, I guessed. He cleaned his teeth, if the empty tube of toothpaste and strands of used floss were anything to go by. But apparently he didn't eat fresh fruit or vegetables, for there were no mouldering peelings or apple cores. There weren't too many papers or letters, though.

Then I saw the gleam of white and reached my hand in to see what it was. It was awkward, wearing gloves, to get it out without smearing it, but I was becoming practised at this.

Oh, yes. Very careless of you, Mr Karl Church. I do believe Baz will be able to do a lot with this letter from your bank. It quotes the sort number, your account number and the name of the manager. Just what we wanted to know. Thank you. It also tells me your overdraft limit. This is the sheet of paper that is going to ensure my promotion. Someone will walk into another branch of your bank and con the counter clerk into parting with your money. Wish I could be there to see it happen.

I nearly gave up at this point, but then I lifted an empty cereal packet and struck gold again: another envelope. Karl Church hadn't even bothered to open it, he'd just flipped it into the bin along with the empty muesli packet.

I pulled it out and opened it, then skimmed through the contents. It was an invitation to apply for a credit card, offering a low interest rate, promising that his application had already been approved. Karl Church might not want it, but I was sure Baz would send it in in Church's name.

I couldn't wait to get back to his place and see what he made of my finds. I left quietly and unobtrusively, as usual, but by the time I'd got back to where I'd left the motor – well away from the targeted flats and parked quite legally so that no Neighbourhood Watch busybody would take my number and report me – I was feeling on top of the world.

'Oh, I can use this one all right,' said Baz when he came to pick up my week's haul. 'Well done.' And he gave me a bonus as well as my usual pay.

'Can I help you milk his accounts?' I asked.

'I can hardly send you into a bank pretending to be Mr Karl Church,' he said, 'but I'll show you how I build an identity. You mustn't rush into it, you see. Give yourself time to do it properly.'

'Why do you register the name of the punter to vote at a different address?'

'Because that's how credit companies check that you're who you say you are and that you've got a good credit rating – they check your name and address against the electoral register. When they check Karl Church against the address we'll give him, they'll find him at home. I use blocks of flats, or retirement apartments. It's easy enough to pick up the electoral register form and add a name to it. A small sum passed to the postman, just to encourage him to hand over useful correspondence, that's good, too.'

He's clever, Baz, don't you think?

Soon after I'd found Karl Church for him, he sent me to another small town in the West Country. I was still diving the bins, but he was showing me other stuff, too. He'd discovered what a good memory I've got. I only have to look at something when it's printed out, and I can remember it. It's like a photograph in my brain. Names, addresses, numbers – they're imprinted on my memory and I can read them off again when I get home. And people leave stuff like that just lying about.

So I go into some small business premises – garages are really good for this – and I make an excuse for the owner to leave the room.

'I'm interested in buying the blue car on the other side of the forecourt,' I say. 'Can you tell me how many miles it's got on the clock?' And he goes trotting dutifully off to find out. Meanwhile, I read all the stuff he's got lying around on his desk, and I commit it to memory. If he looks disorganised, the sort who won't miss a piece of paper missing from the heap on his desk, then I lift a sheet or two and take it back to Baz.

It's odd how men – and garage-owners are mostly men, you'll find – don't suspect that women are up to no good. This applies particularly if the woman is small, and slightly built, and smiles at them and looks up through her eyelashes. They all fall for that one. I suppose their minds are on sex, not money, which makes it all the easier for me to fool them.

It makes me laugh.

But give it another month, and I'll be putting in an offer on that motor for real.

When I look in the mirror these days I see a different Viola from the one I knew a couple of months ago. I see a face that's fuller, skin that's smoother and less pale than before. I'm looking prosperous, that's it. I'm better dressed, too, and more confident – you can see it in the way I'm standing. You can hear it in my voice when I speak to you.

I haven't spent too much of my new money, mind. I've bought a new T-shirt or two, a couple of pairs of jeans, a pair of shoes. I like to think I can move on at any time, and travel light, taking no more than a backpack and a suitcase with me.

Baz said that the next time he had a woman's identity covered, I could try out my new skills on blagging my way into the bank. He told me how to go about it: I was to choose a busy time, and pick on a friendly looking cashier. I had to spin a good story about needing the cash right there and then – something about a business deal and how I'd lose it if I couldn't make an immediate cash offer. When they asked me for details of the account, I could give it to them straight away, no hesitation. Baz warned me to watch it. Most people can't come up with their own details quite as quick as I can. But I can do the honest face and the open smile.

I've done it twice, now. I walk up to the counter, then I pretend I haven't got my cheque book with me. I need to draw out a few hundred pounds, maybe even a few thousand, in cash. I'm trading in antique dresses, you see, and there's this collection I have to pay cash for. I need four thousand for that, and right away. I've got the overdraft facility, haven't I?

They give me the money. The fools.

Baz thinks my face may be too distinctive to play this game too often. He had to move me on again after that in case I got caught.

And so now I'm in Oxford. It's all right, I suppose, if you like old buildings and dozy people. I've got a whole flat to myself, not just a room. And I've got several girls under me. OK, so it's three girls, if I'm honest. I tell them what to do, and then I collect their information. This is automated, it doesn't involve memorising facts and figures. High-tech. It's hard work, and the girls can be a stroppy lot, but it's better than spending my nights going through other people's rubbish.

And when I go round visiting the other girls, taking their information off them, I know I've moved up into management, even if I have to spend some of my time waitressing at Chez Édith. Odd thing is, I quite like it in the restaurant. I find I'm really good at balancing trays and at persuading people to eat more than they intended. But the important work starts when I take off my apron and get out on my rounds.

There's no stopping me now.

5

Kate was sprawled on the floor, a mug of coffee in one hand, her cat, Susanna, resting companionably against her hip. All around them were spread pages from the local newspaper, house details from agents and A4 pages that Kate had printed out from the Internet.

'The problem is, Susanna, location. That's what they all say, don't they?' The cat had closed her eyes and was breathing through her nose in a way that might have been interpreted as a snore. 'Are you paying attention? I need some input from you, since you are likely to be my only house-mate.' She put the mug down and pushed the papers around a bit. 'When I say location, I mean that I don't know where I want to live,' she confided.

The only decision she had made was to stay in or around Oxford. In, preferably. She hadn't really taken to life in a village, the one time she had tried it. The villagers hadn't really taken her to their hearts, either, if she was honest. She wasn't yet ready for the slow tempo of life, or the way the village street was deserted during the day, or the lack of a post office.

She had to leave Fridesley, that much was clear. The houses on either side of her were still empty, though she had seen one or two couples looking in through the windows, as though they would like to find out more about them. But even the arrival of new neighbours wouldn't dispel the memories of violent death that lingered in the very paving stones.

'Am I overreacting?' she asked Susanna. 'No,' she concluded, since Susanna failed to answer. Jeremy's death, at number 8, had ostensibly been an accident, but the murder of the Fosters, at number 12, had made the national news, and was still spoken about, in doom-laden tones, in Mrs Clack's shop. Would anyone want to buy that house and live in it? Maybe someone would buy it to let. And would the deaths affect the price of her own house when she put it on the market? It seemed callous to consider such things, but she had to be practical if she was to afford another house in Oxford – or anywhere else in the south-east, if it came to that. So, where?

It would be lovely to live right in the middle of Oxford, within spitting distance of Carfax, but most of the property in the centre belonged to the colleges and, even if they pleaded poverty, they weren't likely to give any of it up. Anything central was likely to be well out of her price range, anyway.

She liked the idea of living in east Oxford, but her mother, Roz, had bought herself a house there and, though they were getting on quite well these days, Kate wasn't sure that living in the next street would be a good idea. They both needed space. North Oxford? But it was stuffed full of academics, and bossy women with precocious children and unhygienic kitchens.

'Did you say something about my prejudices?' she asked Susanna. 'You could be right, but then again this might be an accurate assessment of the place.'

Headington, then? Very nice. Some of it up-market, but other parts full of ordinary people like herself. However, Headington was where George lived, and Emma and Sam Dolby and all their children. She didn't fancy bumping into *them* every time she popped into the supermarket for a pint of semi-skimmed. Not that she minded Sam and Emma, it was George she didn't want to meet on a morning when she was wearing a faded T-shirt and her most unbecoming jeans. Although she was the one who had broken off their relationship, she would hate him to think that he wasn't missing anything.

Where else? Botley? Cumnor Hill? Kate shuddered at the thought of the traffic queues to get into Oxford along the Botley Road. She shuffled through the scattered papers again and wondered about Rose Hill. So when the phone rang, she was really quite glad of the interruption.

'Hello. Is that Kate?'

'That's right. Hello, Emma. What's up?' Emma Dolby sounded tense and worried. At any moment she was going to ask for Kate's help with a member of her numerous family and Kate wasn't sure how she was going to respond.

'What makes you think something's wrong? Really, my husband and children are quite normal. It's not as though we have any more problems than any other family, do we?'

'Of course not. It's just that you have, well, quite a lot of children, as well as just the one husband, and even if each of them only has one problem a year, that does make for a pretty regular series of problems, doesn't it?'

'You're talking rubbish again. Why can't you listen to what I'm trying to tell you?'

'OK. Tell me.' As well as bringing up her numerous offspring and looking after her husband, Emma wrote well-thought-of children's fiction and taught creative writing.

'It's Sam.'

'I thought that was all sorted.' Emma's husband never really left the straight and narrow, but occasionally Emma suspected him of doing so. Privately, Kate thought Sam was far too busy attempting to earn a living for his ever-expanding family, and anyway lacked the imagination.

'No, not Sam. I'm talking about *Sam*.'

'You'd better explain.'

'Little Sam, only don't let him know I called him that, will you? We used to call him Samson, just for fun, so that we didn't mix him up with Sam, but when he reached thirteen he objected to that name, so now we call him Sam, instead, but it does get confusing. Sam calls him Sam Junior, but I haven't got used to it yet.'

'I think I'm following you. But I'll copy Sam, though, to save the confusion. So what's up with Sam Junior?'

'It must be him. None of the others would understand what it was all about,' said Emma, starting in the middle as usual. Kate waited for her to get far enough into her story so that she could pick up a hint of what she was talking about. 'Yes?' she encouraged.

'It was when I got my credit-card statement. I don't use it much, and I try to pay it off every month, but sometimes it is useful for paying for concert tickets, or for buying necessary bits of school uniform just before the end of the month. Only this month's statement didn't make sense. I'd only paid for a new swimsuit and goggles for Abigail's swimming lessons . . .' Here we go again, thought Kate wearily. Once she starts on the details of her children's crowded lives she'll never get to the point. 'Ammie wanted a tennis racquet,' Emma was saying now. 'Jack's trainers . . . Tristie's T-shirts . . .' Tristie, wondered Kate. She couldn't bring his face to mind at all. '. . . so I knew it must be one of the older children,' ended Emma.

'What must?' asked Kate, who seemed to have missed out on the kernel of this narrative.

'Why, the charge on my credit-card statement, of course.'

'He borrowed your card?'

'He must have done it without asking me.'

'Very naughty,' said Kate. But what did Emma expect *her* to do about it? 'I'm surprised a shop would accept a credit card from a thirteen year old, though – especially if the name on the front was Mrs E. Dolby. You'd think that would be a bit of a giveaway, wouldn't you?'

'He's fifteen now. And it was on the Internet,' said Emma, and now her voice was rising again.

'Books or CDs from Amazon?' hazarded Kate.

'I wish. No, it was a twenty-five pounds charge to a company called something forgettable, like Ugdip or something.'

'I'm not sure I believe that.'

'Oh, you know the sort of meaningless name they give companies when they're up to no good. It was one of those.'

'And what were they selling?'

'Pictures of women with silicone breasts, collagen lips and no clothes on,' said Emma, succinctly for once.

'Why are you blaming Sam?'

'Sam?'

'Could we stick with calling him Sam Junior, do you think? Maybe Sam J for short?'

'Sam J – right. That's quite a good idea. Well, Sam J's the one with the computer. He's always stuck up there in his room, playing on the damn thing. I wish we'd never given it to him, but he argued that he really needed it for his schoolwork and so we bought him one for his birthday. I haven't got one, and neither has Sam.'

'You write your stories longhand?'

'Yes. And then I type them out on my electric Hermes. It was state-of-the-art when I bought it,' she added.

'You wouldn't get much of an Internet connection with that, certainly,' said Kate. 'What about the other children?'

'The next two after Sam J are Abigail and Hugo. I don't think they're interested in silicone yet.'

'Have you asked him about it?'

'I didn't quite get to the point where I accused him of borrowing my credit card, but he did tell me he wasn't really interested in purchasing items from the Internet.' From which Kate gathered that Emma hadn't got even close to confronting her son about the matter.

'Does he usually tell fibs?'

'No. We always talk things through when he has a problem.' But perhaps, thought Kate, that was before he was fifteen.

'I've told the credit-card company that the charge is a mistake, that I couldn't have made a purchase from the Internet, but the man at the other end of the phone didn't sound convinced. It had taken me twenty minutes of pressing buttons on my phone and listening to some dreadful canned music before I even spoke to a real human being, too. What do you think I should do?'

'Surely they've put a hold on the charge while they look into it? That's what happened when a wine merchant charged me for a case of wine and then didn't dispatch it.'

'Well, yes. But I had the impression that they thought I might be fibbing because it was a porn site. It didn't feel very nice while I was trying to explain it away.'

'I imagine that's what they calculated when they charged your account.'

'You think I should fight it?'

'Certainly. You know you're in the right. If you're sure that none of your children is borrowing your credit card, then write the company a letter. And keep your card locked away some-where safe.' The trouble with the Dolbys was that they put such a high value on respectability, they were easy game for a scam like this one. But Emma mustn't simply pay up, she must argue for her rights. And then forget all about it, Kate thought, as she rang off.

The phone rang about ten minutes later and she was half-expecting it to be Emma again, so there might have been a note of weariness in her voice when she said, 'Hello.'

'Kate?'

'Yes, it is. Who's that?' A male voice, but not one she'd heard for a while. She'd been so difficult the last time they'd met that she hadn't expected to hear from him again.

'It's Jon. Jon Kenrick.' He paused, as though waiting for a reaction from Kate, though she knew he wasn't a man who usually doubted his reception.

'Jon. I'm really pleased to hear from you.'

'How have you been?' He sounded relieved by her response.

'I'm fine. I'm really fine.' They both knew that she meant more than she was saying.

'I'm glad—'

'I was acting—'

They spoke at the same time and then both paused to allow the other to continue.

'I'm sorry for the things I said last time we met,' Kate told him. 'After everything that happened last year, I wasn't be-having very rationally, I'm afraid.' It was awkward, apologising over the phone like this. It would be easier face to face, so that she could read his response to her words.

'You seemed so unfriendly, I thought maybe you didn't want to see me again.'

'You can blame it on all the things that happened. The deaths, the betrayals, the lies. It felt as though the whole world was unreliable. I wasn't ready to trust anyone at all.'

'Especially all the men,' suggested Jon.

'I did say I wasn't being rational. But yes, that's how I felt.'

'You're feeling better now, you say?'

'I've decided to move house, so I'll get away from this street and all its memories. My agent's found me a new publisher, so my career's taken an upward turn. And now I really think I'm ready for a fresh start.'

Jon laughed. He sounded relaxed for the first time in the conversation. 'Trust you to take on everything at once! Will you have time for a friend or two as well, do you think?'

'I might manage to cope with an intelligent male friend, one with a good sense of humour and a forgiving nature,' she said.

'I'll see what I can manage. Tell me, how far have you got with selling your house?'

'I'm about to put it on the market, but I have some work to do on it first. You know the sort of thing: painting walls, cleaning woodwork, tarting up the front garden.'

'You've lived there quite a while, haven't you?'

'Nearly ten years.'

'I don't suppose you'll have much trouble selling it, not in Oxford. Where are you thinking of moving to?'

'I can't decide. I think I'll stay in Oxford, but not in Fridesley.'

'I can understand that.' He didn't bring up the question of the murders again, she was relieved to hear.

'I'll put my furniture and most of my belongings in store if I can't find somewhere else by the time it's sold.'

'Is that wise? Aren't house prices in Oxford rising every month?'

'Maybe. But I want to move out as soon as possible. I've spoken to a few of my friends and I think I can find enough spare rooms to camp in for a few weeks till I find something new.'

'I'm glad I've caught up with you then. You will keep me posted as you move around the country, pitching your tent in strange gardens?'

'I think the supply of spare rooms will last for a few weeks. I won't be reduced to tent-pitching quite yet.' There was a pause, and for a moment Kate wondered whether he was going to offer her the use of his own spare room. She said quickly, 'And how about you? What have you been doing for the past months?'

'I've been spending too many hours stuck in front of a computer,' he said. 'I need a break – preferably in the country.'

'Somewhere like Oxford?' she suggested.

'I was hoping you'd say that. How about meeting up again soon? We could go out for a meal, or go to a concert or a film, if you like.'

'I'd like that. And this time I promise not to be so aggressive.'

'That sounds promising. Shall we make it one evening next week?'

'Yes, but—'

'There's a "but"?'

'I'm meeting my new editor one day next week, and I don't yet know which day.'

'Why don't I give you another ring in a few days' time?'

'That's a good idea. I look forward to it.'

Kate felt quite pleased with herself when she rang off. The last time she and Jon had been out together she hadn't been able to disentangle him in her mind from the sight of those two broken, bloodied bodies at the gate, just a few feet from her own front garden. He wasn't a policeman, he worked for NCIS, the National Criminal Intelligence Service, but still she associated him with men in blue uniforms, and guns, and danger. She knew it was unfair, but when he invited her out soon after the tragedy, she had been at her spikiest, keeping him at a distance.

When he had given up asking her out, or even phoning, she hadn't been surprised, and thought she would never hear from him again. Now she realised that she was glad that he'd got in touch once more.

6

'Hello, Kate.'

'Estelle. You're sounding very cheerful.' And friendly, too, thought Kate with surprise.

'I've arranged the meeting with your lovely new editor.'

'I look forward to it. Which date did you choose?'

'The fifteenth.'

'I'll put it in the diary,' said Kate as though she would have to squeeze it in among the myriad things she needed to do that day.

'Why don't we meet in the bar at that big hotel in central Oxford, at twelve, say?'

'The Randolph?'

'That's the place. And we'll go on to the restaurant together to meet Neil.' If Estelle was actually coming all the way to Oxford, this was a really big deal!

'Fine. And I'll put the chapter you asked me for into the post.'

'You've finished it?'

'Just about.' She'd finish it later that day. There was nothing like a deadline to get her moving.

They met Neil in Raymond Blanc's small restaurant in Walton Street, which made Kate realise that she really had gone up in the world.

Neil was just as Estelle had described him, only nicer. He was not very tall and not very slim, and the back of his hands were hairier than Kate usually found attractive in a man, but he had a wide and genuine smile, and was prepared to listen to what the others said to him. He was dressed to emphasise his creativity in a designer jacket, T-shirt with a high v-neck, and jeans, but impressed Kate more by his ready laughter when she was being witty. He laughed in an uninhibited way, showing half a dozen fillings in his teeth, and drawing looks from other customers, but which broke down any reserve there might be at their table.

Most impressive of all, in Kate's view, was the fact that he had actually read her novels, not just the blurbs on the jackets.

Estelle was saying, 'And I'm sure you're going to like Kate's books, Neil.'

'Like them? Of course I like them!' he said, forking in a large slice of duck and chewing with gusto. 'They're so full of energy and humour. And this latest one of yours is the best yet. I just loved the first chapter Estelle sent me. It's great to know you're getting on with it so well, Kate. I'm impressed.' He washed the duck down with a mouthful of red wine, then dabbed at his mouth and chin with his table napkin. 'It has a depth to it that's new for you. I think you've just begun to hit your stride, and I'm delighted that Foreword have recognised your talent at this stage in your career.'

Kate wanted to say, 'Go on! Go on!' but restrained herself and merely leaned forward a little and looked interested.

'There's a warmth at the heart of your novels which is most appealing,' he said. He used a chunk of his pommes frites to mop up the dark red sauce from the duck, and popped it into his mouth. Kate liked people who enjoyed their food, even if they were a bit splashy about it. Estelle, she noticed, was picking at her fish and nibbling on a green leaf or two from her salad. Kate would have liked to help her remove the bones from the mullet, but didn't think she'd be popular with her agent if she did so in public.

'Yes. You have a truly original voice,' Neil was saying. And he was smiling at Kate as though he found her altogether delightful.

With this kind of encouragement, Kate knew she could produce as many heartfelt, warm and original novels as he required. She could see that her career was entering a new and happier phase. Estelle might even remember her name and the title of her book next time she phoned.

Over coffee, when the agent had removed herself to the Ladies to reapply her lipstick, Neil said, 'So, would you recommend living in Oxford?'

'Why? Are you thinking of moving?'

'I'm getting tired of commuting every day from London.'

'I expect it will be a bit of a wrench, though, moving out to the sticks, if you've been used to life in the big city.'

'I'm committed to Foreword now, so it's time I found a place to live closer to the office. It was giving out the wrong signals when I pointed my car bonnet towards London every evening. Well, yesterday I rang an estate agent to get some idea of the market. He seemed to think my London flat would sell in just a few days for a very handsome sum.'

Lucky man, thought Kate, and wondered whether to suggest he bought a dear little terraced house in Fridesley, so close to the station, so convenient for the town centre, but decided against it. She would have to tell him why she was moving and didn't think he'd fancy living so close to three recent murders.

'I'm moving myself soon,' she said, thinking it would be odd if she sent him a change of address card out of the blue without mentioning it beforehand.

'Really? Why's that? You're not leaving Oxford, are you?'

'No, I don't think I could do that. I love my little house,' she said truthfully, 'but it's time I moved a rung or two further up the property ladder.' This was true, too, but it was hardly the reason she was selling her house.

'Good move,' said Neil, then laughed at the inadvertent pun. 'That's been my thinking, too.' He leaned across the table and spoke more quietly. 'I was brought up in a small semi in the depths of South London,' he confided. 'It may seem superficial of me, but I've always wanted something much, much grander.'

'And why not? I have my dreams of a country estate, too. In France, perhaps. Or Italy. I could spend my mornings at the word processor, my afternoons tending my olive trees, and my evenings eating al fresco with my friends and family.'

'You make it sound like an olive oil commercial.'

'Perhaps I'll settle for a vineyard instead.'

'I've always rather fancied Umbria,' said Neil. 'A view across the valley to a medieval hilltop town. All painted in sepia and green, with sky of an unlikely blue.'

'Yes. We could be sitting in the mellow autumn sun, sipping wine from our own grapes, speaking Italian . . .' For a moment she had been tempted to drop Jon Kenrick into the middle of this fantasy.

'Can you really speak Italian?'

'No, unfortunately.'

'We'll have to sign on for lessons.'

They both laughed and Kate had to admit that her dreams were still extremely vague. Still, with Neil on her team, as Estelle might say, the dreams could one day soon be a reality.

'Here's to success and very large houses,' she said, raising her glass.

Estelle returned with fresh scarlet lips and they finished off the wine, all of them in a happy, relaxed state.

'Now, Neil, tell me more about yourself,' said Estelle. Oh dear, thought Kate. Here we go again! She'd nearly forgotten that Estelle preferred younger men. 'Are you married?'

'No. Divorced.'

Even Estelle felt the emotional temperature drop ten degrees. 'Oh well, we all make these little mistakes from time to time,' she said in a masterly understatement.

'You must let me know if I can help you with your house-hunting,' put in Kate, eager to change the subject and put the smile back on Neil's face.

'I'll probably rent a flat to begin with, till I've got the feel of the place and found which are the desirable areas.'

'You wouldn't want to end up in Blackbird Leys by mistake, certainly,' said Kate.

'It sounds delightfully rural.'

'In fact it's a large housing estate on the eastern outskirts of the town.'

'Definitely not your sort of area,' said Estelle firmly.

'Headington or Summertown – they're more your level. Or Boar's Hill, perhaps. You can look down on the dreaming spires from there,' said Kate.

'We'll have to find you a nice little house, too, Kate,' said Estelle kindly. 'Somewhere in a pleasant area, with restful neighbours, where you can get on with lots of work.' No view of the dreaming spires for her then, noticed Kate.

Neil, whose good humour had returned, smiled at Kate and said, 'Here's to successful house-hunting!' And soon after this they parted, feeling very pleased with themselves and each other.

* * *

Next day, Estelle phoned Kate. 'You did splendidly!' she said.

'I'm glad you thought I behaved myself.'

'Of course you did! Neil and I shared a taxi to the station afterwards and we both agreed what an asset you'll be on the Foreword fiction list. I told you you'd be a success one day, Kate, didn't I! Perhaps I never said so in so many words, but I always had confidence in you.'

There was silence at the other end of the phone, as if Kate was completely overcome.

'And don't worry about the deadline for the next novel. Neil has enough in the first chapter and the outline you gave him to compose the copy for the catalogue. We've allowed you plenty of time to write it. You just concentrate on finding a comfortable place to live and work, Kate.'

Kate said goodbye and Estelle felt pleased with the encouragement she'd given her. Mostly you needed to nag your authors into producing anything at all, she had found, but this time she felt her kind words were justified. People said that you got better results if you were encouraging rather than critical, but she believed in being bracing and positive rather than nannying her authors along. Those who survived the treatment were usually successful in the end.

Estelle had made this phone call from home, and now she visited her cactus and succulent collection, checking that each plant had what it needed in terms of sunlight and water. They were spread along every windowsill in her house, those on the south side shielded by blinds. She spoke to them in a gentle tone that few of her friends or even her lovers had ever heard her use. The plants responded by blooming for her, sometimes quite spectacularly. Other people might find them dull, or even unattractive with their gaudy, alien flowers, but Estelle was deeply attached to them and gave them all the care and attention that other people lavished on their pets, their offspring, or even their authors.

At home in Fridesley, Kate was still looking at the latest batch of house details sent to her by an estate agent. Her mug of coffee was cold, so she made herself a new one and returned to where Susanna was waiting for her to decide where she wanted them to live.

'We need shops, and a cinema. A theatre would be nice, too. And it must be close to the station so that we can get to London, or the airport, when we want to get away, don't you think?'

She bundled up the papers and stuffed them in the magazine rack. Maybe it would be easier to put her own house on the market first, then she'd know how much she had to spend. She looked around the room, trying to be as critical as a would-be buyer, then she walked slowly round the rest of the house. She picked up a notebook and biro in her study and started making notes. Susanna had remained curled up on the sofa, but she addressed her anyway: 'Clear out the cupboards, wash all the paintwork, paint the bedroom . . .' The list went on down to the bottom of the page and then on to the next. She would put everything else to one side and get it all done. She'd feel a lot better when it was finished, and ready to start a fresh phase of her life, not to mention a new novel.

She calculated that it would take her five days, seven max.

Three weeks later Kate was beginning to see that there was still a lot of work to be done if she was going to get the price she needed for her terraced period house. Once she'd washed down the bathroom tiles she could see that she would have to give them an anti-fungal treatment and then repaint the walls. She'd better buy herself a couple of sets of new towels, and a bathmat, and clean every lampshade in the place. She hadn't realised, either, just how many possessions she had managed to accumulate over the past ten years, either. What on earth had possessed her to buy a canvas printed with a design of primroses, for example, together with skeins of tapestry wool in thirty-four different colours? She'd be blind by now if she'd ever completed more than the square inch in the middle of the canvas. She didn't think Oxfam would be interested in it, either, so she chucked it into the open maw of the tenth black plastic bin bag.

She hadn't even started on her wardrobe yet.

After another week she rented a storage space and started packing her remaining belongings into cardboard boxes. There were still too many of them, but at least she had thrown away half the contents of her filing cabinet and desk drawers. She had put the papers out in her green box and watched one of the binmen reading the top pages as he was carried down the street on the back of the truck. She hoped he was enjoying her ten-year-old correspondence with the electricity company.

7

Next day Kate was passing the end of Bartlemas Lane, remembering her time at Bartlemas College one summer a few years ago, and the visits she had made there the previous year, delivering a computer disk for Jeremy Wells. It was that favour which had led her directly to her current situation: selling her house, moving away from Fridesley, she reflected.

'Hello, Kate.'

It seemed inevitable somehow that it should be Faith Beeton, a Fellow of Bartlemas, who interrupted her thoughts.

'Faith! How are you? What are you doing these days?'

'Staring into the same estate agent's window as you, apparently.'

'Was I?' She had been too deep in thought to notice that she had automatically stopped in front of a display of houses for sale.

'Are you moving?' asked Faith.

'Yes. And you?'

'I'm toying with the idea. I've put my house on the market, but I'm not convinced that I'll ever actually move. I'm allowing myself to be overtaken by events. If it sells for enough money, I suppose I'll look for something else to live in.'

That was academics for you, thought Kate. Useless at the practicalities of life. She said, 'You're just off St Clement's, aren't you? I should have thought that a house so near the centre of town would sell in a couple of days.'

'You could be right. But I'm not seeking a new place quite as eagerly as you are, I imagine.'

'Actually, I was taking an hour off from the hard graft of sorting out my house and belongings. I must have been on automatic pilot when I stopped here.'

'I don't think I've ever seen your house,' said Faith, following her own line of thought as usual. 'Whereabouts is it?'

'Fridesley.'

And after that it seemed natural to invite Faith back to Agatha Street for a coffee, since she, too, was at a loose end.

'We could exchange ideas on buying property,' said Faith when she'd accepted the invitation. 'I bet you know more about it than I do.'

'I doubt it. It's ten years since I last moved house.'

As they walked back to Fridesley, she remembered that Faith was one of those women with an insatiable curiosity about other people's lives. Faith was already telling her about the houses for sale that she had visited. It seemed as though she was less interested in the properties for sale than she was in the intimate details of their occupants' furniture, clothes, curtains and the contents of their bathrooms. She could imagine the stunned expressions on the owners' faces as they finally ushered Faith out of their front doors.

As they entered the house in Agatha Street, Kate feared that her own belongings would soon form the subject of some witty conversation at Bartlemas High Table. She was glad that she had already packed away a large proportion of her life.

Sure enough, after Kate had made the coffee, Faith proposed a tour of the house.

'Oh, it's not very interesting, and anyway, I'm trying not to drip coffee over the floors. They've taken me long enough to clean. Why don't we go down to the study? I've left it till last so

70

that I can still write a page or two a day, just to keep my hand in.'

They went downstairs and Kate indicated a place on a side desk where Faith could safely put down her mug without fear of its spilling on papers or machines. The room looked much as normal, except for the sad-looking, half-empty bookshelves with volumes leaning drunkenly against each other, or stacked in heaps. An open carton showed where Kate had started to remove those not currently in use. A thin film of dust on the top books showed that this was not a job Kate was pursuing with any undue haste. But as though to prove that she was serious about the task, she picked a book, seemingly at random, from the nearest shelf and put it into the carton.

'Packing away one's books is one of the hardest jobs, don't you think?' said Faith. She had taken the revolving chair behind Kate's desk and was swinging gently round in an arc. Kate had the queasy feeling that she had already been supplanted in this room and that she was a visitor, or a ghost, perhaps, in her own study. 'Though in your case perhaps it will be even harder to pack away your unfinished manuscript.'

She sipped delicately at her coffee, making Kate wonder whether she should have used the proper china mugs instead of the thick green pottery ones with the name of her stationery supplier stencilled on the side. She cradled her own mug in her hands and leaned against the filing cabinet. Faith's eyes were roaming avidly over the notes and papers spread across the desk. 'Is this the new book? What's it called?'

'It doesn't have a title yet,' said Kate, who hated anyone to look at her work before it was ready to be shown to agent and editor.

Faith picked up a piece of paper. 'So this one's set in the present, is it? I thought you liked to write historicals. Is this a change of direction?'

It felt like a take-over. As though, by touching and reading, Faith would start to own Kate's ideas and her work.

'Nothing's settled yet. I can't get down to any proper work until I've moved house. Those are just a few scribblings to keep my hand in. It's like practising scales for a pianist.'

'Shall I throw them into the bin?' asked Faith.

'No. Please. Just leave it all as you found it.' Kate was beginning to regret asking Faith back to her house. She was discovering that Faith might, if unchecked, take over her work, her life and even her thoughts and opinions. Perhaps her undergraduates appreciated what she would most likely describe as 'care and concern', but Kate most definitely didn't.

'Why don't you come and sit over here?' she said, indicating the only other chair in the room. 'I really don't like people looking at my work before it's finished.'

'I thought you said these were mere scribblings,' said Faith, but she did at least get up from the desk and take the chair that Kate had offered.

'I've moved to a new publisher,' said Kate, attempting to take back the initiative. 'I've given up the historicals and now I'm writing modern literary fiction.' Not quite a fib: her new work was certainly more literary than it used to be.

'Who's that?'

'Foreword. They're here in Oxford. You may have heard of them.'

'Of course. They've had a reputation as academic publishers for a hundred years or so. I've offered them my latest work.'

'And they've spent the past few years developing as a major fiction publisher, too,' said Kate proudly. 'But weren't you with OUP before?'

'We're not discussing an academic book. I've been trying my hand at something lighter.'

So that was why she was showing such an interest in the odd pages lying around in Kate's study. Maybe she was fishing for ideas.

'Were you successful? Have they offered you a contract?' asked Kate, trying not to feel jealous.

'We're still negotiating,' said Faith.

Yes, thought Kate, that's the sort of thing I used to say in the days before I had an agent. 'Tell me how you're getting on with selling your house,' she said, deciding it was time to change the subject.

'I think you're right that it won't take long to sell. Keeping it immaculately clean and tidy, with all my personal belongings out of sight, is a bit of a bore, but they tell me it's essential. It's finding a new place that's proving more difficult.'

So Faith wasn't really drifting through her life, after all. That was another of her acts. 'Have you decided on an area yet?'

'I quite fancy Fridesley.' She looked over at Kate as though a brilliant idea had just come to her. 'Do you think I could look over your house, since I'm here? It might suit me very well.'

Kate had a vivid image of Faith sitting at a desk just like hers, in her study, with that amused smile on her face. Her computer would be on a desk like this one and Faith would be writing a novel based on the notes she had just been reading. She would then sell it to Foreword for even more money than they had offered Kate. It was a ridiculous thought, but it wouldn't go away.

'I don't think you'd like it here,' she said lamely.

'But I think I might. And consider how much time, effort and money it would save if you didn't go through an agent.' Faith had finished her coffee and was leading the way out of the study and into the kitchen, to rinse her mug under the tap

73

and place it upside-down, precisely in the centre of the draining board. 'Why don't you show me round?'

'Are you sure you want to live next door to those terrible murders?' asked Kate, opening the door to the living room.

'What a lovely view!' said Faith.

'Only of Agatha Street.'

'But I love watching the world pass by. And yes, I did read something about a shooting in Agatha Street, but it wasn't in this house, was it?'

'Next door.'

'I expect most houses have something nasty in the background if you look closely enough at their history. Can I see the bedrooms and bathroom?'

'The second bedroom is very small. Hardly more than a boxroom, I'm afraid.'

'A room for keeping my boxes in will come in very handy,' said Faith. 'But I suppose it is likely that some people might well be put off by the idea of living next door to a murder. Have you found that? "Brutal slaying" – isn't that what the papers called it?'

'Only the tabloids. I believe the broadsheets referred to "an unexplained shooting in quiet Oxford street".'

Faith laughed. 'I like that "only",' she said.

'Have you seen enough?' asked Kate, watching as Faith opened the wall cabinet and appeared to examine the contents in detail. In a moment she'd ask her why on earth she'd bought that tube of blue mascara.

'Yes, I think so for now. I'll let you know in a day or two if I want to make you an offer.'

'Perhaps I should come and look at your place,' suggested Kate. 'I quite fancy living in St Clement's.' She suppressed the thought that it was really too near to Roz's place. 'Think how convenient it would be if we made a straight swap.'

'I don't think so. I'm bursting out at the seams of my little house. I don't think you'd fit in at all.'

That was the trouble with people who knew about words. They could always come up with the right ambiguous phrase when they needed it.

Sam Alexander Dolby sat in his bedroom and stared at his blank computer screen. Around him lay the usual debris of a fifteen year old's life: jeans worn once or twice and not dirty enough for the linen basket, empty Irn-Bru cans, crumpled crisp packets, half a dozen socks, all of different colours and, balanced precariously on every heaped surface, mugs that might once have contained coffee but which now sprouted greenish, moss-like growths. A smell of unwashed feet and, strangely, of stagnant ponds, permeated the room. From beyond the closed door of his room came the cries and thudding noises that were so much part of the ambient Dolby sound that Sam no longer noticed them.

Sam was listing his current grievances against his family. First on the list came the question of his name. He was tired of being defined in relation to other people, and in particular, his father. Baby Sam, Little Sam, Samson, Sam-Son, Sam Junior. And while they were naming him in such an unimaginative way, they hadn't even thought about the embarrassment of his initials. Sad Sam. When he looked in the mirror he saw the same undistinguished round face as his father's, the same muddy hazel eyes, the same unmanageable curling brown hair. In a few years he'd be able to add the same beard, the same pouches under the eyes. It was time he made a stand against this inevitable descent into Samdom.

Maybe he should insist that everyone call him Alexander. The trouble was, there were already three Alexanders in his class at school and he could see that the move might be unpopular with the teaching staff. No that that mattered, but they'd probably insist he was known as Sandy, or something equally horrible, to differentiate him from the others.

Sam pushed a button and the computer flashed its lights and invited him to log in. As a blow against globalisation he had installed Linux on his hard disk and he watched screens full of white characters scroll past. When he finally reached the desktop he clicked on to Netscape.

And that was his second grievance. Why should his mother accuse him of using her credit card to buy stuff on the Internet? Not that she had accused him outright, of course. That wasn't her way. She'd hinted and started to creep towards the subject, and then one of the smaller children had claimed her attention and she'd disappeared, leaving an atmosphere of generalised disapproval behind her.

He'd found her credit-card statement on her desk and skimmed down its sparse entries. He'd seen immediately what she'd been trying to question him about. He'd interrogated Hugo and Abigail about it in his turn, in what his mother would have considered an insensitive and even brutal manner, and they were just as positive as he was that they weren't interested in doing any such thing either. 'Gross,' said Abigail, and went back to applying a sticky grey preparation to her face that promised to improve her patchy complexion.

Sam entered 'credit card fraud' into his favourite search engine and started to sift through the hits. There were more than 530,000 of them and it was going to take him a very long time.

8

Three months later...

It was a dull and rainy day and nothing out of doors held any attraction for her, so Roz Ivory was drifting around the top floor of Debenhams, on the excuse that she was looking for a set of towels for her newly painted bathroom. She rather fancied soft, fluffy, virtuous white. Or perhaps waffle cotton. Or that rather smart anthracite shade? Nutmeg? Given the state of her current account, she should be searching out the special offers or finding something at an open-air market. But she hated cheap towels – the way they became sopping wet long before you were properly dry, and then went grey and slimy after you'd washed them a few times. She returned to the thick, imported American ones she couldn't afford. Actually, she told herself, someone with an artistic nature like hers really couldn't get worked up about mundane objects like towels. Her eye had just caught a three-foot high wide-necked vase with a flame-coloured glaze. She could fill it with tall lilies in the summer, and with branches of beech leaves in the autumn.

'Roz? Roz Ivory?'

The voice came from over on her right. She straightened up and looked to see who was speaking. She thought she remembered the blue-black hair; wasn't so sure about the fragile figure wrapped in layers of fuchsia and purple wool; felt that someone wearing those marvellously soft suede boots must be an old friend of hers. They were just the shade of rust that she had been thinking of for her beech leaves.

'It's . . .' But the woman's name escaped her.

'Leda. From California. Don't you remember those parties on Don's houseboat?'

'San Francisco?'

'Sausalito. On the other side of the bay. Blue skies, flowering shrubs, that lovely little fish restaurant with the bronzed hunks for waiters. Surely you haven't forgotten them, not to mention the thick fog rolling in every morning?'

The only fog Roz remembered was a haze of aromatic smoke from the joints that Don rolled so sensuously in his long, tanned fingers, and a languorous sense of well-being – no wonder she'd forgotten the woman's name, along with most of the other practical details of her time in California. For a moment there, as her memory of Leda's name failed her, she'd wondered whether her age was catching up with her, but there was no need to worry yet, after all. She could still blame the grass.

'And so very different from cold, grey Oxford.'

'The weather may be hell, but you get a better class of man here, though,' and Leda laughed.

By her accent, she was no native-born Californian. That was surely the sound of the Home Counties underneath the flattened vowels and drawl.

'I'm no expert on men any longer,' said Roz.

'I can't believe that! But I suppose we all move on. What do you think of these?' asked Leda. She had an armful of silk flowers in shades of blue and mauve.

'Bit bourgeois for your taste, aren't they?' suggested Roz, eyeing Leda's asymmetrically chopped hair and the butterfly tattoo on the hand clutching the delphiniums.

'It's my latest enterprise.'

'Buying artificial flowers?'

'They're for decoration.'

'I think we'd better retire to the coffee shop while you tell me about it. I feel in need of a large slice of carrot cake at this time in the morning, and my caffeine level needs a top-up, as well.'

'I do like people who enjoy their food,' agreed Leda. 'I can't stand to see them picking away at a designer lettuce leaf and leaving some decent charcuterie on the side of their plate. And I've never seen the point of decaffeinated coffee. Where's the buzz in that?'

They chatted on as they parked themselves at a table with their coffee and cakes. Then Leda said, 'I'm opening a restaurant,' and waited for Roz's reaction.

'I hadn't realised you were so keen on cooking,' said Roz carefully, remembering the unremarkable reddish stew that was served in generous portions on top of a bowl of steamed brown rice whenever she'd been on Don's houseboat.

'Don't worry. I've learned a lot since our Sausalito days.'

It was possible, thought Roz. Sausalito was twenty years ago, when they were all young – or at least when they could do a passable imitation of youth. Leda's speciality, as she remembered it, was making cocktails – the sort that involved a frosted glass, thin slivers of exotic fruit, and alcoholic liquors in unlikely colours. This could be useful if you were running a bar as well as a restaurant, she supposed. But why was Leda taking on such a strenuous new career? She might be a few years younger than Roz, but not all that many, and as Roz understood it, running a restaurant was one of the most tiring and cut-throat things you could do.

'And you've run a restaurant before?' she asked.

'Not exactly. But I am good at organising things, so why not a restaurant?'

It sounded like a recipe for financial disaster to Roz. 'What sort of enterprises have you run before?'

'Oh, I've organised quite a few events,' said Leda airily. 'Charity dinners, parties of businessmen going to the races, that sort of thing.'

'Hm,' said Roz. 'But—'

'I need an income,' interrupted Leda. 'I didn't come out of the last divorce quite as well as I'd hoped.' She made it sound as though getting divorced had been her main livelihood up to that point in her life. Maybe it was.

'I did loads of business entertaining for my husband, so I thought I'd use my accumulated experience and invest what loot I'd managed to extract from him in a business enterprise of my own.'

'You're not talking about Don?' enquired Roz cautiously.

'Good Lord, no! Don sold out: he took off for a copywriting job in New York, leaving me with the damp, leaking house-boat.'

Don sounded as though he'd finally come to his senses, thought Roz. 'Tough luck,' she said.

'Yes. He took his stash with him.' Leda's voice was brittle, but Roz heard the pain behind the flippant words. Leda pushed her hand through her hair in a youthful gesture so that the overhead light lit up the golden streaks. The movement drew Roz's attention to the way the gold was designed to blend in the natural silver at Leda's temples.

'You're looking terrific,' she said. 'I can't believe that California was so many years ago.'

'You really think I look all right?'

'Great. And so that was divorce number one?'

'I'm not sure Don and I ever bothered to get round to a formal marriage ceremony.'

It wasn't the sort of thing they went in for in those days at that place, certainly. One or two of their friends had had some kind of do-it-yourself event on a hillside, or at the beach, involving readings from Kahlil Gibran and the singing of something expressing environmental friendship by Judy Collins, before they returned to their bottles of Californian Chardonnay and the sweet smell of grass. 'The pillars of the temple stand apart . . .' murmured Roz.

'You can say that again,' said Leda, with feeling. 'You could have driven a tank through our pillars, I can tell you.'

'And now you've come out of divorce number—'

'—three. Or possibly four.' She was counting on her fingers, but then hid her hands when she noticed that Roz was watching. But wasn't it more enterprising of her to be a divorcée three – or four – times over, than to be a widow just once, like Roz?

'Three, four. Whatever,' said Roz tolerantly. 'And now you've got a load of dollars in your pocket and an itch to open a restaurant.'

'I've always loved food.'

'Haven't we all!' A good reason for visiting a restaurant rather than buying one, Roz considered. 'How are you doing this? Are you investing in a going concern, or starting from scratch?'

'I've signed the lease on a little place at the bottom of the Woodstock Road. It's been running as a greasy spoon and it's taken a fair bit of money to bring it up to scratch, but I'm investing the remains of my capital, and I'm really enthusiastic about it.'

Roz raised her eyebrows. 'No need to sound defensive. I'm

impressed by your enthusiasm, let alone by what you're going to be doing.'

Hard slog, she thought, feeling pleased that she wasn't the one who'd just signed that lease. Washing up. Scrubbing down surfaces. Peeling vegetables. Chopping. Peeling more vegetables. Shopping at food markets in the early hours of the morning when you should be getting your beauty sleep. 'I'm sure it's going to be a great success,' she said, without any real conviction.

'I do hope so. Have you finished that enormous slice of cake, by the way?'

'Yes. Even I can't get through any more of it.'

'Do you mind if I polish it off for you?'

'Be my guest.'

The fact that Leda was slim to the point of fragility was just another of life's injustices. After another twenty minutes of reminiscences, Roz waved goodbye to her rediscovered friend and went back to contemplating economy lines in towels. Sod it! She picked up the tall, flame-glazed pot and took it to the till. She was sure her credit card could stand one more outing, though her daughter would doubtless tell her that she should be thinking about the interest rate the card company would be charging her.

Back in her house she thought what a beautiful pot it was as she placed it in the empty fireplace, and what an excellent purchase she had made. It would look even better with a couple of well-chosen stems in it. Maybe she should go back and get some of the artificial flowers that Leda had been buying.

9

'Not bad at all. In fact, it's very tasteful, young Viola.'

That's what Baz said when he saw the place I'd found. It's funny how something isn't real until I hear someone else say it out loud. I remember once, when I must have been about thirteen, I was sitting on a bus and I heard the woman behind me saying, 'I hate Christmas,' and at that moment I knew it was true for me, too. It was as though that thought was waiting somewhere in my head for someone else to express it. Yes, I thought. I hate the fake jollity, the shop assistants in Santa Claus caps, with bells hanging from their ears. I hate the sanitised carols pouring out of loudspeakers, the plastic mistletoe, the hand-me-down decorations in the streets. I hate the way our family always had their worst rows on Christmas Day so that no one ate much of their dinner, and those who did felt it lying like a lead weight in their stomach for hours afterwards.

How did I get on to that subject? I was talking about my new flat, wasn't I?

I thought Baz might let me have a room of my own this time, rather than sharing with someone like Lyn, but I wasn't expecting much. I'm used to moving around and making do with whatever rooms I can find. He'd sent me to places like Worcester and Hereford that you'd never normally think of visiting. And when I'd learned my craft, he moved me here to Oxford. This job is cleaner than the bin-diving, and it doesn't feel as risky, not if you keep your wits about you and don't get careless. I don't suppose the job will last for ever, not in the same place, but this time I'll have some regrets. Like I said, I'm actually quite enjoying working in Chez Édith. I like the company and watching the people who come to eat there. Baz is paying me enough money so that I can carry on having a whole flat to myself, and I won't be so keen to move out of it again.

Am I getting soft? I'll be looking for a job description and arrangements for a pension next if I'm not careful. Back into the bourgeois society, five years after I swore that it wasn't for me. Bourgeois or not, I can't help walking round this place, feeling the space, knowing it's mine, enjoying what I've got.

One living room. Large enough for a bed against the far wall and a built-in cupboard where I can hang my clothes. I spread a green cover across the bed during the day so that it looks like a settee. Maybe it wouldn't fool anyone, but I like it that way. Then there's a couple of easy chairs pulled up in front of the telly – wide-screen – video recorder and DVD on a shelf underneath. It looks like I could invite a friend in to watch a video with me on my evening off, if that's what I wanted.

Through one door and there's the kitchen. Bit small, but I've got a kettle, a microwave and a couple of electric hot plates, a fridge and some cupboards for plates and mugs. Through another door and I've got a shower and a toilet.

So you see, it really is a flat, not just a room like I've had before. A proper studio flat. Lovely words to roll around in your head and savour. And all mine. I walk through the front door, bolt it behind me, and I'm at home.

It looked very bland and boring when I first moved in. The landlords do that on purpose, apparently, so that you can impose your personality on the place. I think they're just lazy, myself. Anyway, it reminded me of my parents' house. That was beige, mostly, with a bit of grey added here and there as an accent colour. Story of their miserable lives.

There's not much I can do with the curtains or the sofa and chair, but I've stuck some bright pictures on the walls. I don't care if it does make marks on the paintwork. Sue me for it, OK, if that's the way you feel. I've added a couple of cushions, and every time I walk through the market I buy a bunch of flowers. There's usually something they're selling off cheap, and I bought a bright blue vase to put them in. They really help to cheer the place up.

Tonight I'm watching the telly. I have to go out working later, but for the moment I can sit in one of the blue chairs, lean back on the striped cushion, drink a beer and eat a ready-meal from Tesco's. While I'm doing that, I can watch the people who want to be someone else. *Stars in their Eyes*, it's called. It's my favourite programme.

Who doesn't want to be someone else, someone more glamorous – a celebrity? We all think about it some of the time, I reckon. But this lot have taken the idea seriously. They spend their lives making themselves sound and look exactly like someone else. Then what? Five minutes in front of the cameras, singing on a few million screens, and if they do it well enough, do it better than anyone else, they win. They don't get any money or anything, just the glory of knowing they're the best. If they're lucky, they get offers of work so that they can go on being someone else, someone glamorous, someone who isn't them, for the rest of their lives.

That Dusty Springfield lookalike, she won't come back to a room like this, you can bet, not once she's been a winner. And when she's out there, in the spotlight, does she really believe that she's no longer little Jane Nobody from Croydon, but a superstar instead? I think that's the trick of it, believing you really *are* the other person so that it's not an act, or even a performance, but you really change into someone else when you're out there.

I'd go in for it myself if I could sing, but I've got one of those little croaky voices and I'm never sure which note I'm supposed to be aiming for. Anyway, I don't think I'd like to come out through those doors on to a stage, into the lights and the applause. I'd be sick in front of them all, puke my guts up on the stage, I'd be so nervous. They say the nervous ones do best, that they can make their own personality disappear and pull on someone else's, like it was a glove or a pair of shoes.

Me, I like to stay obscure when I do my pretending. And then again, I earn money at the end of the day, money that pays for this flat, and the friendship of a man like Baz. 'You're the best,' he tells me. 'You go on and show 'em, kid. No one can do it like you.' And that makes me feel good. If Baz tells me I'm the best, then I know that's what I am.

I don't walk through a door into the limelight, but I'm a winner, all the same. I take over some other woman's name, I dress like she would, and I walk in and I become her. My stage is a department store or a bank. My aim is to look ordinary, just like any other normal woman, not like a star. If I lose, they'll call the police. If I win, no one will applaud, and my set will last for a few minutes, max, and there'll be no encores, no repeat performances. But it will last long enough to change my life, and hers too, I suppose.

Baz is different. He doesn't often go out there and perform. (Of course there are those who consider that his whole life is a performance.) In the time I've known him, he's only done it twice. I expect there have been other times for him, but those two were when we were Baz and Phil and we were on top of the world, fooling everyone, making ourselves thousands in just a few hours. The first was when we spent all that money for Neil Orson, and the other was when he cleaned out the accounts belonging to the man in Worcester. The man called Karl Church. Playing the arty types from the publishing world was fun, but taking all that money off Karl Church was even better.

'You found me this mark,' Baz said, 'so you can help me spend some of his money.'

'You want us to paint the town red?'

'If you like.'

We dressed up and went to London again. It was my first time back after several weeks in the provinces and it felt like coming home.

'This is how to do it, Phil,' he told me. 'With style.'

He drove, in a big new Peugeot he'd just bought – on someone else's credit, naturally. He left it in an underground car park and we took taxis after that. It was in and out of the major stores in Regent's Street: up in the lift to the Accounts department, and then they were falling over themselves to give 'Mr Church' a store card.

'This is why it works,' said Baz. 'All these banks and credit-card people are desperate to lend money. They just see the APR, the money they're going to slam on to the account every time we spend. They're greedy bastards and they deserve to be taken for a ride.'

And so that's what we did. We took them for a ride, and we enjoyed ourselves while we did it.

You should have seen us in Regent Street! Baz looked really good. He was wearing an Italian suit and a beautiful silk shirt and tie. His hair was recently cut, he smelled of aftershave, and when he flashed his cufflinks you could see they were sapphires set in platinum. I was wearing jeans and T-shirt with a short leather jacket, but all my clothes had designer labels and I think the shop people believed I was his daughter. At any rate, if they thought I was his tart they were too polite to let on.

If you'd been there, you'd have offered us a couple of thousands' worth of credit, too, believe me. They asked for identification, of course. And Baz had it. Good quality stuff, as well as the credit card he'd received when he sent in Church's application. That and his honest, perma-tanned face were all they needed.

Then we went shopping. Some of the stuff was for us, but mostly he bought with an eye to reselling. He was enjoying himself, like a kid on a day trip, but he always had his mind on the profit. That's why he's so successful. It's no good just thinking about the fun you're having, you have to keep your eye on the profits. I've learned a lot from him.

That little pink and turquoise rug in the bedroom came from Liberty's, courtesy of Church, that afternoon. Pretty, isn't it? I've got my eye on another big print in the same colours in the art shop in Broad Street. And I might buy myself some silk-covered cushions next time I'm in Liberty's.

I really enjoyed the times we spent together, when it was just the two of us. Somehow, while we were pretending to be someone else I felt we were truly ourselves. We put on the clothes, we adopted the voice and manners, and then we were no longer Baz and Phil, we were our real selves, with different names that were known only to us. I know it's Baz, I know that's an act he's putting on, but those moments when we're going through the swing doors of some big department store, we're as close as this. And I know what's in his head, just as he knows what's in mine, and we play our parts, bouncing our ideas from one to another like actors in some fine West End play.

Well, that's how it seemed to me.

He'd string me along, make believe I was special, and all the time I knew he had a woman he went home to at night. I bet she was some ageing tart, nothing glamorous, but probably a good cook. It's something I've noticed about Baz: you'd think he'd go for someone really young, but he doesn't. He seems to prefer them older, what he'd call mature. He told me once he liked his women as much for their conversation as for the sex, but I didn't believe him. I dunno though. Maybe it's true. Anyway, I don't suppose he and the one he lived with were married, and I don't suppose he was faithful to her, but I didn't fool myself he'd ever care about me that way. He'd never take me seriously.

But she didn't know the Baz I did. I'm sure of that, just as I'm sure she never had the fun that I did.

10

Kate Ivory had sold her house, though when it actually came to the moment when she said 'yes' to the offer being made, she found she did have some regrets, after all.

For one thing she had painted and scrubbed and tidied to such a high standard that the house looked just as desirable to her as it did to the people who came to view it. But then, it wasn't the house that she wanted to leave, only the street where it happened to be situated.

The second thing was that she hadn't actually found anywhere else she wanted to buy. With house prices rising daily she knew she shouldn't wait around too long, but after the stress of the past couple of months she felt she never wanted to move house again. This was going to be it. Definitely her final address. So it was a case of finding the perfect house, the perfect location. Second best and compromise just weren't an option.

Meanwhile she had filled her rented storage space with her furniture, her books and the extensive range of belongings she had managed to acquire during the past ten years. Even after ruthless sessions where she filled a dozen black bin liners and took them to the tip or to the charity shop, she still had enough to fill a substantial three-bedroomed house, she calculated.

But at least now she had reduced her immediate needs to a couple of suitcases and half a dozen cardboard cartons. With care she could squeeze everything into her car. She was mobile, she was free. She felt several years younger. Is this what had attracted Roz when she decided to leave her teenage daughter and set off on her travels? Is this how she had felt when she stayed away for so many years? Kate could understand the appeal of the footloose life. It amused her to think that for the present they had exchanged lifestyles. Roz was settled in a respectable terraced house in east Oxford while Kate was looking for a floor to sleep on and a desk to work at – metaphorically speaking, of course. She had no intention of living quite as frugally as that. She had fully intended renting a small flat, even a single room, while she looked around for a house to buy. But several of her friends had rallied round and offered her a room, or even the loan of their house while they went off on holiday.

She was glad that the new owners of 10 Agatha Street were newcomers to the town: a professional couple with no children, both in well-paid jobs. They approved of the cream paint she had put on the walls and woodwork, the uncluttered look of the place, and were going to keep it that way, with the addition of nothing more than a well-chosen *objet* or two on their shelves. She couldn't see them lining the walls with books, the way she had.

And now it was time to forget that the house had ever been hers, she told herself. What they did to the place was their business, and none of hers any longer.

She packed away the last of her belongings in her suitcases while humming various sixties tunes that expressed the lyric-writer's love of freedom. Though, as a matter of fact, she was perhaps exaggerating just how completely she had escaped from Fridesley.

'Where will you be living? Have you decided which of your

friends to stay with first?' asked Jon when she rang him for one of their regular phone conversations.

'With my friend Camilla, in Fridesley Lane.'

'About five minutes' walk from Agatha Street? Isn't that the house where we first met?'

'Oh, you're right. I was staying with Camilla then, too.' She could think back to that first meeting with Jon and its circumstances with hardly a twinge now. 'It feels as though I'm making a break for freedom, but it's hardly that, is it? It's a brisk five minutes away, but it's still in Fridesley.'

'That's all right. Just as long as you're not tempted back to check on Agatha Street too often.'

'I don't think so. It doesn't look like my house any more, with all that cream paint. And they tell me they're going to put down gravel in the front garden as it's so much less bother.'

'Time to concentrate on finding your own place, do you think?'

'Yes.'

'Tell me about Camilla. Isn't she the one who sounds like a headmistress?'

'She looks like one, too, these days – possibly because she *is* the headmistress of a classy girls' school who bullies her pupils into achieving frighteningly good exam results. But she's an old friend and I think we'll get on all right.'

'So she'll be away during the daytime?'

'And busy during the evenings, too, so I'll be able to get down to my writing if I feel like it.'

'And you can get on with your house-hunting.'

'If only I could decide *where* I want to live.'

'Keep looking. I'm sure you'll find something soon. How long do you reckon you'll be staying with Camilla?'

'I calculate we can get along for about a fortnight. We'll both cope with that without ruining our friendship.'

'And she'll allow male visitors occasionally, will she?'

'Camilla has a very unbuttoned side to her character that few people know about.'

'I look forward to meeting her.'

Camilla stood in the spare bedroom, chatting to Kate while she unpacked. 'I see you've brought your running shoes with you,' she commented.

'And a couple of baggy T-shirts.'

'You think you'll need to get away from me from time to time?'

'I think we're both used to being on our own. And anyway, I need to keep fit. Running's a great way to get oxygen to the brain.'

'I think we both need regular doses of solitude. And unlike me you have no office to escape to, after all.'

'It's true I haven't shared a house with anyone since I left George last year. Solitude seems more important with the passing years.' She wondered what Jon's views on the subject were. She must ask him next time they met.

'Well, I admire you for sticking with the fitness programme. I find that putting my running shoes on is easy enough, it's getting out through the front door that's the difficult bit.'

Kate had forgotten that Camilla was once nearly as fond of running as she was, though she thought it was more for its health-giving, weight-controlling properties than any pleasure that it gave.

Kate had e-mailed all the friends and even acquaintances in her address book with her movements over the next few weeks. She didn't want to lose touch with anyone. And she wasn't sure how long it would be before she was settled again.

A couple of days later, with her friend ensconced in the Headmistress's study at the Amy Robsart School for Girls, Kate was trying to find enough enthusiasm to walk into Oxford to register with yet another estate agent. But the skies were tipping torrential rain down on to the pavements, the garden was a sea of mud, and Kate couldn't seem to get focused on anything for any length of time. She'd been drifting through the rooms of Camilla's house, straightening already-straight objects, drinking endless cups of coffee and getting twitchier by the hour. She didn't want to walk into the town centre in the downpour, let alone look at houses. A generalised dissatisfaction had descended on her and she couldn't think how to dispel it, when the phone rang.

'Hello, Kate?' It was Jon.

'Oh, Jon. I'm so glad you've rung.'

'Really? Are you going to tell me you've found a house to buy?'

'I wish! There doesn't seem to be anything promising on the market at the moment. Nothing I can afford, anyway. I thought it would be liberating to be footloose, with just a couple of suitcases and no responsibilities, but it doesn't seem to be working out that way. If I see another cheerful yellow kitchen, avocado bathroom suite or Laura Ashley bedroom, I think I shall scream. I even dream about patterned wallpaper.'

'Sounds like the standard response to house-hunting. By the way, I meant to ask you. What did you do about your cat?'

'She's fine – happily installed with my mother. She won't be coming back till I've found her a suitable home.'

'You sound as though you think she should be poring over house details, or out there in the rain, pounding the streets.'

'Quite right too. And what about you? Aren't you due for a visit to Oxford soon?'

'As a matter of fact, I have to be there tomorrow. That's why I rang.'

'I could make you lunch,' she suggested.

'I was planning on driving down this evening, and I hoped you could come out for dinner with me.'

'That sounds an even better suggestion.'

'Seven-thirty?'

'Suits me fine.'

Kate threw away the rest of her mug of coffee and went to choose something to wear for the evening. She thought about preparing Camilla's supper for her, but found that Camilla's freezer was full of nutritious meals that needed only to be placed in the microwave for a few minutes, so her contribution to food preparation was really not necessary. She didn't need to worry that Camilla would miss her company, either. They would be spending many more evenings together, and anyway, Camilla was just as independent as Kate herself, and enjoyed nothing so much as her own company, or that of a good book.

Kate hummed as she looked through her attenuated wardrobe. It was a cool day, and if it ever stopped raining she would wear her plum silk jacket, she decided.

Camilla arrived home while Kate was in the middle of transferring the essential contents of her large, practical handbag into a tiny, decorative one.

'It's amazing how little you really need,' remarked Kate. 'Only about five objects to define yourself. Though, of course, I couldn't manage for long without a notebook and pencil.'

'Yes, you'd have to include those in your definition: *Kate Ivory, Novelist.*' Camilla looked at the pile of objects left over from the transfer. 'Not to mention the fact that you need your mobile phone, driving licence, cologne spray, paperback novel for when you're bored, enough loose change for the car park and . . . what on earth is *this*, Kate?'

'It's one of Susanna's toys. I must have forgotten to leave it with Roz.'

'So she's fostering the cat for the time being, is she?'

'Yes. They get on well together and I didn't want Susanna to get more neurotic about the house move.'

'And you think Roz will be a calming influence?'

'I think she can manage to look after one small ginger cat, don't you?' She wasn't much good with a daughter, but a cat, after all, was an independent creature.

'So who's the lucky man?' asked Camilla, taking in Kate's spruced-up appearance. She had removed her coat and hung it on a hanger in the hall cupboard, changed from outdoor to indoor shoes and placed her briefcase on the floor next to her desk in the study. Kate quickly removed her discarded handbag and its contents from the room and placed them on the bottom stair, ready to take upstairs on her next journey to her room. She didn't want to irritate Camilla with less than perfect tidiness so early in her stay.

'Don't worry, Kate. I'm not really a perfectionist. Your usual standard of tidiness is quite adequate, really.'

But Kate saw her eyes flicking to the book she had laid down on the table that wasn't quite in line with the edge. She would have to watch it, living here.

'Now, tell me about this man,' said Camilla.

'Jon. Jon Kenrick. I don't think you've met.'

'No, but I do remember him. We spoke on the phone when you were staying here once before. We didn't meet because I was at school, but didn't he come to the house then, too?'

'Yes, that's right. I think you'll like him,' Kate added.

'I remember speaking to him. He sounded like a solid and reliable man in his forties.' It wasn't always clear whether Camilla's schoolmarmish manner was a joke or not. Kate had the feeling that it had started as an amusing act but that now it had been fully integrated into Camilla's character.

'He's a quietly good-looking man,' said Kate. 'An intelligent and amusing dinner companion. He and I are slowly developing a rewarding relationship. But he is somewhere in his forties, certainly.'

'I go for something younger and more exciting, myself.'

'Roz is like that, too.'

'Sensible woman, your mother.'

'You think? On the other hand, not one of us has done very well at long-term relationships,' pointed out Kate.

'So what? We've had fun, haven't we?'

They were both laughing when the doorbell rang.

'Come in,' said Kate. 'This is my friend Camilla. You've spoken to her in the past, on the phone.'

'I remember it well,' said Jon. 'How do you do?'

Under the hall light he was looking tired and more drawn than last time she had seen him, only a week or so before. He cheered up at the sight of Kate in the plum silk jacket, though.

'I've booked us into a quiet country pub with decent food,' he told her after they had spent a few minutes in polite conversation with Camilla and were seated in his car. 'I'm sorry it isn't somewhere more exciting, but I wanted a place that didn't look too much like a restaurant and that had been in the same safe hands for at least thirty years.'

Kate raised her eyebrows at him.

'The week's been rather demanding so far, and I felt the need to relax,' he said, as though worried that she'd think he was just a little *too* solid and reliable. Probably he'd read Camilla's judgement of him in her face when they'd met.

'It sounds just right,' said Kate. If she felt the need for bright lights and music she wasn't going to mention it.

He had chosen well. When they reached the pub – taking a narrow, winding lane and driving through a village where all the inhabitants appeared to have retired for an early night – Jon parked in the car park and they walked back to the front of the building. The pub was built of that grey Oxfordshire stone that looks dreary and uncompromising under cloudy skies, or in the rain, but which glows pink and gold in the sunlight. Luckily the rain had stopped pouring down a couple of hours previously and the sun was just sinking behind a nearby copse, bathing everything in scarlet. There were roses clambering over the front of the pub instead of the usual line of hanging baskets, and on the gravel stood rustic benches and tables for when the weather was hot.

Indoors, the seats were grouped around a couple of huge stone fireplaces. At this time of year they were filled with pots of dried flowers. Kate and Jon sank into chintz-covered sofas while they studied the menu. Jon, since he was driving, was drinking mineral water and Kate, who didn't want to get too uninhibited too early in the evening, settled for something only mildly alcoholic. Eventually they moved through into a dining room with a barrel-vaulted roof and gentle lighting. The conversation around them was loud enough to give them a sense of privacy.

'So, what brings you to Oxford?' asked Kate when their starters had been served.

'Let's forget about talking shop,' said Jon wearily. 'This is my first evening off this month. Tell me about house-hunting, instead.'

'I think we covered it pretty comprehensively over the phone. I've found nothing new since we spoke, I'm afraid. It might be easier if I could decide which part of Oxford I want to live in, and concentrated on it. But I can't really afford the areas I like, and the places I can afford don't appeal.'

'The ones that have man-eating wallpaper?'

'And are defended by large, fierce dogs. I really don't want a house covered in dog hairs and smelling of mouldy pet food.' Kate forked in a mouthful of salmon mousse. 'Why don't you tell me about yourself, instead?' she said. 'I still know very little about you.'

'Where shall I start?' Jon didn't look uncomfortable exactly, but he gave the impression of someone who was unused to talking about himself. And although they had seen one another half a dozen times or more, Kate knew little more about him now than she had at the beginning. She didn't think he had anything shameful to hide, just that he was a very private person.

'I can't guess where you were born from your voice, though I think you're probably from the south rather than the north.'

And so they exchanged the information about themselves that they hadn't had time to learn when they'd met a few months previously. Yes, he was born in Surrey and had had an ordinary childhood, followed by a degree from Sussex University. He told her about his parents, and his sister and brother. His parents still lived in the same house where he had been brought up. He visited them about every couple of months. His brother and sister had both moved on, to Canada and Scotland respectively. They exchanged news by e-mail and telephone, but he didn't know when they'd all meet up again, though of course his sister and Scottish brother-in-law and his four nieces and nephews usually met up over Christmas every year.

'It sounds like a pretty solid family to me,' said Kate. She had always envied people with families like Jon's, but it did occur to her for a moment that she might find the reality a little claustrophobic.

Kate in turn told Jon about her father, who had died when she was a child, and about Roz – 'But you've already met her, haven't you?' He frowned, and she remembered that the circumstances of their meeting weren't the happiest. Roz had been at her most irresponsible and irritating. 'And you didn't like the man she was with,' she said slowly.

'No.'

'Barry Frazer,' she said.

'Not a nice man.'

'I can't say I like him much myself. He's always charming and attentive around Roz, but I'm not sure he's quite what he seems.'

'I should trust your instincts.'

'The trouble with Roz is that she decided she'd had enough of the respectable, bourgeois life and she just took off when I was seventeen, as though she was a teenager herself. She was an ordinary housewife and mother while I was a kid, but then she seemed to regress. She's got no sense of responsibility! It's as though she'll make friends with anyone, just as long as they're not respectable. She doesn't want to see how worthless Barry is.'

'You think it's time she grew up and behaved like your mother again?' asked Jon gently.

'Something like that. Is it so unreasonable? But I'm not being entirely selfish. I think some of the people she's hung around with in the past have been dropouts and spongers. She's never been rich, but more than one man in her life has walked out taking a large chunk of her money with him.'

'You're afraid that Barry Frazer will do the same?'

'Oddly enough, no. I think he's the opposite. I think he's persuaded her to stop gambling on the horses and to invest her money in something more sensible.' She was more worried that Barry had actually been helping her mother out with money, but she didn't want to say that, even to Jon.

'You think the relationship's serious?'

'They have a good time together. He takes her to the races, to the theatre, out for expensive meals. I think they find each other amusing and entertaining. Roz isn't exactly an intellectual, you know, and neither is Barry.'

'And she likes to shock her daughter, and some of her friends, by being seen around with a criminal like Barry Frazer.'

'I don't think she knows he's a criminal. She described him to me as "an entrepreneur". But you're not here in Oxford because of Roz, are you? You're not going to arrest her?' asked Kate, her worries about her mother and her shady friends surfacing at last.

'I have to keep reminding you that I'm not a policeman.'

'But you investigate crimes.'

'Large-scale crimes, bigger than the sort of thing Frazer's involved in.'

'People like Fabian West, do you mean? Are you still looking for him?'

'Other people are doing the looking. I'm more interested in his latest ventures and how they work.'

'Will he ever be found, do you think?' Fabian West had been behind the murders of her neighbours and so Kate had a vested interest in his capture. If she was totally honest, she might admit that she had been responsible for his escape just before the police arrived at his Worcestershire home to arrest him.

'Eventually he'll make a mistake, I suppose. We believe he's still in the country, though we could be wrong about that, too.'

'You know what he looks like, though, don't you?'

'No one's seen him for the best part of a year, so he may well have changed his appearance. His most recognisable feature is his eyes – they're different colours. One's grey, the other a light brown. But I'm sure he can find coloured lenses to disguise the fact. He won't find it so easy to disguise his height, but the world seems to be full of tall men these days.'

'Has he given up forgery?'

'The police arrested his team of experts, so he had to abandon that enterprise. Now they think he's discovered the possibility of making another fortune on the Internet, which does concern me. But it means he could be anywhere at all.'

'It all sounds much higher-powered than Barry Frazer.'

He hesitated. 'Fabian West has always had visions of grand, international crime. Barry Frazer may be running a large operation, but it's localised. I can tell you he is under investigation, though – but not by me.'

'Can I tell Roz that?'

'You can warn her off Frazer, but don't tell her why.'

Kate stared at her plate and didn't reply.

'Please,' he said. 'It would be awkward for me if it got out that he'd been warned off by someone I knew.'

'OK.'

'And just in case you're wondering, I didn't come down to Oxford to question you about your mother's friend.'

'No, no, of course not.' Kate was suddenly very sorry that she'd brought the subject up. 'You didn't want to talk shop, did you? It's my fault for mentioning it.'

'We could let the subject drop and return to stories of our childhood,' suggested Jon. 'You could tell me all about your young life, when Roz was at home with you.'

'She's not a bad person,' said Kate. 'And just because she can be irritating – or even reckless – doesn't mean I don't love her.'

'I don't doubt it.'

'Shall we look at the dessert menu?'

'If it would help.'

'I've always believed that a really good chocolate pudding can make you forget your problems,' she said. 'At least while you're eating it.'

'Let's give it a try, then.'

But in spite of the good food they finished the evening with both of them in a subdued mood. Jon dropped her off at Camilla's at a respectable hour and refused Kate's half-hearted offer of coffee.

'I'll give you a ring tomorrow,' he said, as Kate took out her front-door key.

'Yes.'

'Maybe you'd like to come to London one evening next week? I might even cook you a meal at my place,' he said.

Kate looked at him. This was the first time he'd suggested she visit him at his home. She recognised it as a step forward in their relationship. She was still feeling sore about the subject of Roz, but she said, 'Thank you. I'd like that.'

Camilla had apparently already retired for the night and after half an hour, Kate decided to follow her example. She picked her bag off the floor, hung her jacket on its hanger in the wardrobe and made sure that the glass she had used for water was washed up and replaced in its correct place in the kitchen cabinet. She was getting the hang of Camilla's ways. She hoped they wouldn't take long to discard once she had got her own place again.

11

Sam Dolby was sitting in his room, the door firmly closed, staring at the page on the computer screen. This was worth printing out and studying carefully, so he clicked on the printer icon and waited while the pages emerged from the machine. As he did so, he realised that his mother was shouting to him from the bottom of the stairs. She so often shouted at one or other of them that he automatically switched off when he heard her voice. He knew that this habit irritated her, but he reckoned it was an effective survival technique and not one he was willing to give up.

'Sam! Are you on the Internet again?'

The words finally penetrated his mental armour. So what? She was always on at him about something or the other.

'Just think about the phone bill, will you?' The voice came from right outside his door now, but he didn't think she'd actually turn the handle and enter. It was against her principles, after all. If she respected her children, they would respect her in return. It didn't seem to occur to her that the bargain was one-sided. 'You're costing me a fortune!' she shouted. 'I think you should get off the line now. The girls want to speak to their friends. And anyway, I want to make a phone call myself.'

If she'd said that to begin with, he might have done what she wanted. But the print-out was complete, anyway, so he cut the connection. He could carry on with the rest of his research later in the evening, when everyone else was in bed. For the moment it would be enough to read through what he had just found.

He opened the door and shouted, 'Phone line's free!' but from the thundering footsteps that followed his announcement he guessed that Emma would again be unlucky in reaching the phone before Abigail or Amaryl monopolised it for the next hour or two.

He picked up the print-out. The first sentence that caught his eye stated that it was not against the law to obtain a service by deceiving a machine, which made it difficult to prosecute those who used other people's credit cards to order stuff over the Internet. Where did you get credit cards from, he wondered. In spite of his mother's suspicions, he wouldn't help himself to hers. And he didn't fancy actually stealing one from someone's wallet.

The next article told him how. He would have to send a load of spam to every e-mail address he could get his hands on. The theory was that you offered some appetising benefit, but requested identifying data in return, including credit-card details.

Sam spent the next few minutes sketching out a plausible message. It would be no good sending it out from his own account, however. He'd have to register under a pseudonym and maybe use one of the machines in the library so that the messages couldn't be traced back to him.

For a while Sam lay sprawled on his bed and dreamed of embarking on a life of crime. The idea of sitting in his bedroom and making huge sums of money while his boring family carried on with their own virtuous lives, unknowing and uncaring, in the house around him, really appealed. On the other hand, he conceded, even someone as impractical as his mother might notice if large parcels started to arrive at the door, addressed to him. And where would he dispose of the items? His contacts in the world of fencing stolen goods were nil. It would surely be more profitable to get his hands on actual money. He skimmed through the rest of the material he'd downloaded. 'Net-PI' would provide him with software to find out anything he needed to know about absolutely anyone. Armed with the right info, he could obtain convincing ID from yet another site, he found. And it was absolutely legal. Could be useful.

When he logged on again later in the evening he would find out more.

Neil Orson was feeling pleased with himself. The flat in Appleton Court had sold less than a month after he put it on the market. And quite right, too. He knew he'd chosen the location well, and the flat was in impeccable order. He congratulated himself on having made another excellent decision in his life.

With property prices still going up, he didn't want to stay in his rented flat in Oxford for long, but he'd made enough of a killing to be able to afford to look around and decide where he really wanted to live. He didn't want to jump at the first house he was offered and then find he was in quite the wrong part of town. He could have asked Kate Ivory's advice, of course, but he wasn't sure that she had quite the same ideas on upward mobility as he had. He could find himself living in the arty, Bohemian part of town if he wasn't careful, and that wasn't quite the image he wished to project.

Maybe there would come a time, too, when he would want to buy a house in the country where he could live with a wife and children – though he hadn't met any likely candidates for the former role since he had moved to Oxford. For a moment he thought of Phoebe and Chloe, left behind like his parents' South London semi. If he had them with him now they'd be littering the place with clothes and toys, and whining because it was raining and the view from the windows showed nothing but sullen, muddy allotments and dull, suburban houses.

No, Chloe and Phoebe belonged to the past. Even Chloe seemed hardly to be related to him now. She was Phoebe's child, and he had no influence on her life. He paid a modest amount of money for her upkeep, but after that his responsibilities were at an end.

Neil had been walking back to his office after a pub lunch while he was thinking these thoughts, and he noticed that he was passing the local branch of his own building society. If he was going to start looking seriously for a house to buy in Oxford he might as well pop in now and agree a figure for a mortgage.

A well-groomed young woman in a navy-blue skirt and pink shirt typed his details into her computer. 'Could you confirm your previous address for me?' she asked. He gave her the Appleton Court address, and she typed that in, too.

'Ah,' she said.

'Is there a problem?' asked Neil, trying to interpret her tone. It had moved from warm and friendly to wary, and even suspicious.

'I'll have to make some checks and get back to you,' she said, this time keeping her voice professionally neutral.

Neil left her his office phone number and returned to work. He was only mildly disturbed by the clerk's response, and turned back to the manuscript sent in by Beavis Kingsley, who was supposed to be a top-flight agent.

'You'll love Roddie's writing,' he'd said. 'It's just your sort of thing.'

But the first chapter was truly dreadful. Not only could Roddie not write, he had laid his manuscript out in single-spaced blocks, separated by an inch or two of white space, and used a very large and eccentric type-face which gave Neil the impression he was being shouted at. After a page or two, the lines were wavering before his eyes, the lack of pace was making him drowsy, and he wondered whether it was worth persevering for another chapter. He carried on for a further half-hour of this torture, by which time he had forgotten all about his visit to the building society.

At four-thirty, as he returned to his room from the coffee machine, his phone rang. He put down the paper cup on the coaster he kept for the purpose and answered the call. It was the building society. And it was no longer the polite young woman dealing with his enquiry but someone older, male, more senior.

'I'm afraid we are unable to offer you a mortgage at the present time,' he said. Definitely unfriendly.

'Why not?' Neil wanted to shout that he had lots of money in his savings account – thousands, in fact. He could offer well above the minimum deposit on a property. And he had a well-paid job and a brilliant future. He was a solid, law-abiding citizen who always paid his bills on time. Why wasn't the building society clamouring to lend him money?

'There appears to be a problem at your former address, Mr Orson.'

'Appleton Court? What sort of problem?' For the first time, an alarm bell rang in Neil's head. This might turn out to be more than a slight clerical error, after all.

The polite (but unfriendly) voice said, 'It appears to be a question of financial commitments which you have failed to honour while you were living at your previous address in London.'

'But I've always paid my bills. What are you talking about?'

'It seems that your current financial commitments are such that we couldn't lend you anything like the sum you're looking for at the present time.'

'There really is a mistake,' insisted Neil. 'I've sold the flat in Appleton Court, and even after I paid off my mortgage, there was plenty left. And apart from the few hundred pounds I owe this month on my credit card, I don't have any commitments.'

'Why don't you come in and see me tomorrow morning, Mr Orson. If there's been a mistake we can soon sort it out.' The voice had, perhaps, thawed a little.

When he had replaced the receiver, Neil pushed the manuscript to one side, not caring that he had promised to let Beavis know by the end of the day whether he wished to make an offer for it. He really didn't care if this was the next sure-fire bestseller that he was rejecting. What was concerning him was that someone had made a mistake – *over his financial standing* – and *that* was something that sparked off too many painful memories.

When he had confided to Kate Ivory that he had come from a small semi in Croydon and now he wanted something bigger and smarter to live in, he had told her only part of the story.

He had never told anyone about his father's tragedy. At least, Neil corrected himself, the *mistake* had been his father's, the tragedy had been Neil's. And while he was blaming people, he might as well blame his mother, too. It was her brother who had come up with the crackpot idea, after all, and approached Neil's father for money to back it: a free service for people who were job-hunting. A forum for those looking for work and those offering employment. A weekly newsletter, free of charge, delivered to your house. It would contain interesting articles, written by his uncle himself, giving hints about applying for jobs and how to make a career change. All the costs would be covered by the advertising revenue.

For such a cautious man, Neil's father really didn't look too carefully at the figures. Neil seemed to remember that his parents were going through a thorny patch at the time, with many accusations on his mother's part and excuses on his father's. Perhaps he had jumped into the scheme merely to get his wife off his case. Whatever the reason, Neil's father handed over several thousand pounds to his brother-in-law. And he was far from being a wealthy man.

The plan had escalated by now, and when the first newsletter was published, the cover was glossy, and in colour. The helpful articles were written by professional journalists. Neil's father paid the bills, since they never did raise any advertising revenue. Who thought the unemployed would make good customers, after all? And the employers preferred to advertise their jobs in the newspapers, the way they always had. However, Neil's uncle persevered. The breakthrough would come any day now, he said. It was a shame to give up just as they were about to succeed. His brother-in-law paid the printer every week, and the people who pushed the newsletter through letterboxes. 'The signs are good. We'll soon be making money.'

They didn't, of course. In the end, Neil's father paid off his brother-in-law and all his creditors – there were a surprisingly large number of them, including a wine merchant. The sum he gave his brother-in-law was intended to persuade him to leave the country, but even in that he failed.

The atmosphere at home deteriorated, Neil remembered, with his mother's accusing voice following his father from room to room as soon as he arrived home from the office until the moment he went to bed after the ten o'clock news. When the National Lottery started, some years later, Mr Orson was quite sure that this time he would be a major winner and he 'invested' much of his remaining nest egg in his lucky numbers. He did once win ten pounds, and a further two pounds on a scratch card, but nothing more.

Neil had a sneaking suspicion that he took after his father, and he was absolutely determined that he would never make such stupid financial mistakes himself.

Next morning, Neil went into the building society to hear the bad news. Loans had been taken out in his name, using his credit rating, for thousands of pounds. Someone had applied for credit cards, and store cards, and maxed them all out. He had no idea how it had happened.

'Why didn't I see the statements? Didn't they write to me?'

'Someone changed your address for you, Mr Orson. The letters and statements would all have gone to this new address.'

'Well, why can't the police call there and arrest whoever is responsible?'

'It's an accommodation address. A block of retirement flats. Mail addressed to you could quite easily have been picked up from the hall without anyone taking any notice.'

'The police could put a surveillance team on to it, surely.'

'The criminals will be long gone by now. They'll have moved on to another victim.'

'What can I do?' He was almost in tears.

'You need to report this to the police,' he was told. 'It will all be sorted out, but for the moment we can't consider offering you a mortgage on any new property you might wish to purchase, I'm afraid.'

Neil's next stop was at the police station. He found himself repeating his story to an impassive policeman and explaining that he was not a con-man, and that someone else had bought thousands of pounds' worth of goods in his name, without his knowledge.He received a crime report number which he could quote to the finance house who had lent the money to the thieves, to the credit-card companies and the West End stores who had given them credit.

'Will you catch them?' he asked.

'We'll look into it, sir.' But it wasn't a priority, apparently. There had been no physical violence against him. This kind of crime had not been made a target, like car theft or street crime. It hardly featured in the crime statistics. And anyway, the untangling of this kind of fraud required detectives with specialist skills who were in short supply. Details would be passed on. The unit concerned with such matters would be informed. Neil had the impression that 'the unit' consisted of three overworked officers in a crowded office somewhere in a distant London suburb.

'But why did those London shops hand out their store cards so easily? Didn't they ask for identification?'

'They'll have had at least one credit card in your name. I expect you get offered pre-approved cards and just chuck the applications in the bin, sir. But someone else can fill it in for you and get the card for themselves. That and a recent utility bill would be good enough to prove your name and address were what they said they were.'

'But they weren't!' shouted Neil in frustration.

'Apparently not.'

'And then they bought goods on the Internet and over the phone,' wailed Neil. 'Surely someone would have checked the cards then.'

'The problem with credit cards is that when they were brought in in the seventies, no one imagined that we'd all be ordering expensive pieces of electronic equipment over the telephone. They were never designed for CNP transactions, for the reason that no one had thought of them.'

'CNP?'

'Cardholder Not Present. You're always taking a bit of a risk when you do that, aren't you?'

'How did they do it?' he asked.

'How do you mean, sir?'

'How did they get hold of my details like that? They must have built up a whole file about me. It must have taken them months.'

'They're careful, patient people. I expect someone went through your rubbish,' said the sergeant, with some sympathy. 'Did you put your paper out in a recycling box?'

'Of course I did!' snapped Neil.

'The thieves probably found enough information there to get into your bank account and credit cards and charge all those expensive goods to you. They took out a loan in your name, too, did they? I expect you had an excellent credit rating – that's just what they're looking for.' Neil noticed that his excellent credit rating had been consigned to the past tense. 'And then they'd have had your post redirected, so that you wouldn't see the card statements. I don't suppose you even knew the card companies were threatening to take you to court to recover their money, did you? Better get on to the companies involved and sort it out, sir. Give them the crime report number and they'll cancel the proceedings.'

Neil wanted to drop his head down on to the table and weep. He was already being labelled as a fool, however, so he'd better not give the impression he was weak and neurotic as well.

'Let's hope the worst is over now, sir. We're checking to see if your mail was redirected, and whether they've added your name to the electoral register. Lucky your name isn't too common, isn't it? We might catch a minnow or two, but I expect the main man is long gone.'

'So what am I supposed to do now?'

'Write to all the companies concerned. They'll believe you're a victim, I'm sure, sir. In future make sure you shred any useful papers – anything with your name and address on. I dare say you've got the message by now.'

Neil remembered the woman in the blue suit in Roland Ives's office, who had advised him to do the same thing. He should have listened to her, he realised now. But how many of Foreword's staff had taken her advice to heart and then acted upon it? He'd been careful for a while, of course, but you couldn't think about that sort of thing all the time: he'd had more important matters to claim his attention. He was just unlucky that he had been targeted. It could have happened to anyone. It certainly wasn't his fault, he concluded. It was just a question of bad luck.

Among the thoughts that whirled into and through Neil's head was the memory of a young woman with black hair and eyes, dressed in dark sweatshirt and trousers, going through the bins in the basement at Appleton Court.

Was she the one who had targeted him and stolen his credit rating? He remembered what she looked like, even after several months. She had lots of curly dark hair, and enormous velvety eyes, and small features. She wore an innocent expression and had appealed to him to protect her from the bully in the cashmere coat. But had time added to his picture of her? If someone produced her now, he doubted whether he would be able to pick her out of an identity parade.

Back in his office, he picked up the unpromising manuscript from his desk and hurled it into the waste-paper basket. It clanged in a satisfying way and then shuffled itself like a pack of cards. Too bad. Someone else could put it back in order. He dialled the agent's number.

'Sorry, Beavis,' he snarled into the phone. 'That novel you sent round just isn't for me.' He slammed the receiver back into its rest and then glared at the offending pages. They'd better be sent back to the agent, he supposed. 'Amanda!' he shouted through the open door.

'Yes?' Amanda looked startled at his unusually brusque tone. 'Is something wrong?'

'Send that manuscript back with the standard sod-off note, will you?'

'Don't you want to add a personal note for Mr Kingsley?'

'No.'

Amanda removed the waste-paper basket and its contents and closed the door behind her. Something was wrong with Neil, she concluded. He was usually such an even-tempered man. She'd described him to her mother as sweet-tempered and watched her mother's eyes light up: at last her daughter was meeting eligible men. And if he'd been just a little better-looking, and a year or so younger, she might have agreed with her mother, and fancied him.

That evening, at home, Neil was still fuming. Three beers and two large vodkas on an empty stomach hadn't improved his temper. When he looked in his bathroom mirror, he saw his father's face. He heard his mother's voice in his ear, telling him he was a fool, that he'd never amount to anything, that he was just a miserable little failure.

He hadn't realised how much of his mother's diatribe had remained in his memory. As well as her accusations, he heard his father's sad comments on his failings. 'I thought you'd make something of yourself, Neil. I thought I'd told you never to make the same mistakes as me.'

And I didn't, thought Neil. I made my own, new ones. But I'm just as much of an idiot as the old man. If I'm not careful I'll find myself going down to the corner shop to buy a fistful of lottery tickets. He poured another vodka.

I am a good-humoured man, he told himself. I do not easily lose my temper, or bear grudges. But if ever I meet that dark-haired, conniving girl again, I will tear off her head and feed it to crocodiles. Now, when he saw her face in his imagination, her eyes had reduced in size until they were small and piggy, with a cunning expression in them.

'I knew from the start I shouldn't trust her,' he told himself, forgetting that this was not the case. 'Skinny and undersized. Pale, unhealthy face. Never trust a woman.'

He thought of Cassia, with her long, straight hair and wearing the gloriously expensive cream dress. 'I should never have left her. And perhaps I was a little hard on her, getting her pushed out of her job like that.' But this one, this wicked woman in the cheap tracksuit, she deserved every punishment he could devise for her. All he had to do was lay his hands on her.

As he went to fetch a packet of tissues from the bedroom, it occurred to him that he'd better make himself a sandwich. Eating something might make the room stop swinging from side to side.

The ham sandwich helped. He stopped feeling quite so sorry for himself, and he forgot Cassia, too. Anger surfaced again. He looked around for something to throw at the wall, but the place was as uncluttered and impersonal as only a rented apartment could be. He stamped around for a while and swore, but felt no better at the end of it. Tomorrow he would have to get Amanda some chocolates or whatever it was that fitted in with her current diet, so that she didn't ask for a transfer to someone less temperamental. He could let her edit a mid-list manuscript, too. That would show her he trusted her skills.

Then he ate a second sandwich, sat down with an inch of vodka in a tumbler, and thought about what had happened to him.

At first he had thought he would be liable for it all. The Peugeot 307, costing £16,000. Someone was driving that flash new car around while he had to make do with a two-year-old Honda. He would never be able to pass one of those Peugeots now without wondering if he was the fool who'd paid for it.

And the store cards. Why hadn't they checked his identity properly before issuing someone – *was it that girl?* – with them? Four or five of his favourite London shops, where he spent a modest couple of hundred in cash at Christmas, and she'd clocked up ten thousand in twenty-four hours.

And he was supposed to put it all right himself, which meant days of telephoning and letter-writing. It was all very well for the policeman to minimise the trouble he was in, but he'd heard of cases where it had taken the poor sodding victim *years* to clear his name and prove he wasn't the one who'd spent the money. He saw himself jobless, homeless, living in a cardboard box on the pavement in Cornmarket.

He stared morosely into his glass. It was empty, he saw with surprise. He poured himself another vodka. How did you go about proving that you hadn't spent all that money? Wouldn't there always be a question mark against your name? He might be pitied as a victim, but he would also be laughed at as a fool. Like father, like son, they'd whisper. And his mother's pinched, disapproving face stared down at him. When he thought about it, even through the alcohol fumes he realised it couldn't have been the girl herself who pretended to be him. Even some dozy car salesman might have noticed that Mr Neil Orson should have been a man. She must have sold the information on, or given it to her boyfriend. For some reason the thought of her boyfriend made him angrier than ever. She'd bewitched him with her wild, curling hair. Whether the 'him' concerned was Neil or the boyfriend, was no longer clear to him.

He drank the vodka and looked around the featureless room. He hated it, but he wouldn't be moving to some rose-clad sodding cottage in the near future, that was sure. He wouldn't be ordering new furniture, or calling in the carpet-layers, either. He could forget the ideal cottage garden he had planned, with the white-painted summer house, the pergola, the honeysuckle and clematis, the Californian hot tub. He could forget the kitchen with the Aga and the bedroom with a walk-in wardrobe.

He pulled another handful of tissues from the box, wiped his eyes and blew his nose. Poor little Chloe! What could he do for her now? Sentimental tears dripped from his chin, while the complacent feeling that Phoebe really couldn't expect anything from him now he was in such trouble crept into his heart.

As thoughts of his ex-wife and daughter slipped away, Neil found himself thinking of Umbria – the medieval town on the hilltop, the sky as blue as cornflowers. He had lost these, too, and even before he had possessed them.

He poured another vodka. The bottle, he saw with surprise, was now empty. Hadn't it been more than half full when he had arrived home?

He did have money in his savings account, so he could afford to eat and pay the exorbitant rent of this flat, at least. It didn't seem much of a compensation for the loss of his dream, but it was better than being homeless and destitute, certainly. He'd better check to see just what his situation was.

But by the end of the final glass of vodka he was past thinking about anything at all. He crawled into the bedroom, he pulled himself up on to the bed and fell asleep, still fully dressed and wearing his shoes.

In the morning, once he had found the alarm clock and punched it into silence, he lay in bed for a while, trying to calm his churning stomach by an effort of will. He wanted to get out of bed and pour himself a pint of water to drink, but for the moment he couldn't face moving his head off the pillow. He felt like a church bell, with a large metal clapper bouncing around inside his skull.

Some time later he made it to the bathroom, then the kitchen, and finally into the living room. He was quite relieved that he didn't need to dress, or tie up his shoelaces. He wasn't sure he'd have managed it.

He looked around the living room. Had he really made this mess all on his own? It looked as though he had brought a gang of legless friends home with him from the pub, who had then drunk all his booze and trashed his flat. Maybe he had? He really couldn't remember many details of the previous evening.

He drank another half pint of water, downed a couple of paracetamol, then another couple, and set about clearing up the mess. By the time he'd got the place looking as clean and smelling as fresh as it usually did, he knew that he'd come to certain conclusions the previous night, and had even made a plan of action, but the details were lost in the fog of his hangover. All that remained was a strong feeling of self-pity.

He rang Amanda and told her he'd be in a little late that morning, then made himself a pot of coffee. The coffee helped to clear his head, but reminded him that his stomach was still a bit dodgy. But by the time he left the flat, shortly after ten-thirty, he was looking much more like his usual spruce self. He was a little puffy around the eyes, perhaps, and there was a pinched look to his mouth, but he didn't think anyone at the office would notice.

He did receive one or two comments from his colleagues, however.

'Good party was it, Neil?'

'Got ourselves a tad hung over, have we?'

And Roland Ives stared at him in an unfriendly way when they shared the lift to the fourth floor that afternoon.

So Neil set himself to work to dispel the impression that he was a heavy drinker or an unreliable employee. He contributed several intelligent comments to the afternoon's editorial meeting, and made sure that he was seen taking a couple of manuscripts home with him to read in his own time. One of them was really quite good; he noticed that, once again, Estelle Livingstone was the agent.

The hard work was more effective than the vodka in pushing his financial problems to the back of his mind. He would get back to sorting out the situation at the weekend, he decided.

A couple of days later, taking an early lunch break, Neil was walking through the Covered Market in the centre of Oxford, thinking about cheese. A nice little goat's cheese, wrapped in leaves, perhaps. Or a blue-veined one from France. He'd better not buy anything that made his office smell like a dairy for the rest of the afternoon, though.

And then he thought he saw her. She was waiting at the newsagent's, buying a magazine. She no longer wore a dark sweatshirt and trousers, but a plain navy pullover and indigo jeans, so the effect was similar. Curly black hair. She'd worn a hat last time, but he'd seen enough to imagine how it would look when it was loose. It was the angle of her head as she looked down at the counter that he could swear made her recognisable as the girl who had been going through his recycling box back in Appleton Court.

It was his turn at the cheese stall and he chose quickly, almost at random, paid and walked over to the newsagent's stand. He felt confused and was paralysed by indecision. Maybe it was just wishful thinking, he told himself. Maybe every slightly built, dark-haired girl looked like her. She had been on his mind, and now he thought he saw her wherever he went. But no! It *was* the same girl.

She looked prettier in jeans and pullover. The clothes weren't as baggy as the hooded sweatshirt and he could see that she had a good figure. He remembered the vulnerability in her face, the shy smile she had thrown him while she was being bullied by the man in the expensive coat. And who the hell was *he*, anyway? Neil hadn't seen him before or since that evening and didn't believe he had a flat in Appleton Court. Maybe he was a visitor, but that didn't give him the right to threaten the girl like that.

Just a minute, he thought, and stopped himself. This girl was going through your dustbin. She was probably working for the people who stole your credit rating and ruined your life. She may look like an innocent little thing, but she's a liar and a thief.

She dipped in her purse and looked for the right money. He couldn't really confront her here and now, could he? What if he was wrong about her and she made a fuss? Neil couldn't face a loud argument in the middle of the Covered Market. There was bound to be someone around who knew who he was.

The girl paid for her magazine and turned to leave. Neil looked at his watch. He had forty minutes before he needed to be back at his office. He would forget about buying himself a sandwich at Prêt and follow the girl instead.

She turned into Cornmarket, which was as crowded as ever, then into the High Street. For a moment he thought he'd lost her, but then saw that she had taken one of the narrow alleyways leading off the High Street. He caught up with her just as she reached the door of a restaurant at the foot of the alley.

'Excuse me,' he said, with a resumption of his usual mild manner.

'Yes? What do you want?' She sounded nervous, so Neil

raised both hands as though to show her he meant her no harm. 'I don't know you, do I?' she added.

But even with those few words, Neil was sure. She had quite a distinctive voice, and it wasn't the local Oxford accent, with its long rural vowels, but something sharper, originating in London, he thought, maybe with a background of middle-class respectability, as though she had grown up in a sedate suburb, then run away from home and lived in some poorer part of town. It was true that he didn't really remember her face in detail, but the hair was the same, and so were the dark brown eyes, as though her ancestors were Spanish or Italian.

'I think we met in London,' he said.

'Don't try that old line on me!'

'Wait a minute.'

'I'll be late for work. I haven't got time for this,' she replied, and turned away, as though about to enter the restaurant – Chez Édith, he noted.

'By the dustbins at my flat. Appleton Court,' he added desperately. And then she faced him again and he saw the flicker of recognition in her own face, though she returned to her neutral, uninterested expression almost immediately. 'You took the letters with my details on. You ran up bills in my name.'

For a moment she looked at him uncertainly, as though he'd told her something surprising. But still she didn't answer.

'Tell me your name, at least,' said Neil, and was ashamed to hear the note of pleading in his voice. She had opened the door. 'Who are you?' he shouted.

'*My name is Viola*.' And then she laughed, as though it was a joke. As he stood there, staring at her, she walked quickly into the restaurant, slamming the door behind her.

Neil considered following her inside, but couldn't see how he could get any further without making a scene. Phoebe liked scenes, he remembered, but he'd never really got the hang of them himself.

He walked slowly back to the office, wondering what to do next. *Viola*. Now he remembered that that was the name she had given him in London, too, though he hadn't believed her then.

At least he knew where she worked, that was one good thing. Chez Édith. He'd have assumed she was going to eat lunch, but she'd said, 'I'm late for work.' And that was before she'd realised who he was, so it was most likely true. Was she a cook, a kitchen hand, or a waitress? She had a neat way about her and he fancied the last possibility. He knew her first name and her place of work: he was making progress. He still doubted that the name was really hers. And maybe she didn't work in that restaurant, but had walked straight through and out via the kitchen to escape him. He didn't think so, though. She had been going into the restaurant, he was sure, even before he spoke to her.

Could he come back at two-thirty or so and catch her on the way home? Or did she work evenings, too? He preferred to come back in the evening. He didn't want to gain a reputation for strange behaviour and for disappearing from his office for no good reason. Amanda had given him one or two funny looks since the incident with the manuscript. And he'd had to ring Beavis up and arrange to meet him for a drink in London to make up for the way he had rejected the novel so abruptly.

By three-thirty Neil was feeling the lack of lunch quite keenly. He thought about opening the bag containing the cheese, but didn't want to appear eccentric. He had no knife and plate and Amanda might catch him with a wedge of farmhouse Stilton in his hand and then tell all her friends about it. Luckily it was someone's birthday and he could eat two doughnuts and a slice of chocolate cake without appearing to be anything worse than greedy.

12

Kate was beginning to realise that she and Camilla needed to part company soon if they were to remain friends. Not that Camilla had said anything, but she recognised the signs. Kate was too used to living on her own – and enjoying it – to miss the fact that Camilla was similar. A friend staying for a week or two was fine. Any longer than that and it was as though you had an itch in the middle of your back that you couldn't quite reach to scratch.

And although she had always known that Camilla was a tidy and organised person, she hadn't realised just how pernickety she was. Kate herself was no slouch when it came to keeping her ideas and her work space in order, but she didn't find it necessary to clear away a coffee mug the minute she emptied it. A five-minute wait was acceptable, she thought. But Camilla! Camilla not only tidied away the coffee cups while Kate was still considering whether to pour them both another, she eyed the surface where they had stood as though wondering whether to get out the furniture polish.

It was odd how these habits started to get on your nerves. And she was under no illusions that her own little mannerisms (whatever they might be) were beginning to irritate Camilla in a similar way.

She looked through her address book and made a couple of phone calls but reached only answering machines. She didn't feel that 'Can I come to stay for a couple of weeks?' was a message she could leave on a machine, so she hung up. She even rang Roz, but her line was engaged.

She decided to head into town and stare in some more estate agents' windows. She might see something she liked and buy it on the spot. She was in the mood to do just that.

In fact, halfway down the High Street, she found herself elbow-to-elbow with Faith Beeton once more.

'Still looking?' asked Kate.

'Window shopping,' replied Faith.

'You look a bit glum about it.'

'The sale of my house has fallen through. I'll have to find another buyer before I can make an offer on something else. The one I wanted has been snapped up by a first-time buyer with fistfuls of cash.'

'But you're serious about moving? I thought you were undecided last time we met.'

'I don't always say exactly what I mean,' said Faith in an unusual attack of honesty. 'I'm afraid it's a naughty habit of mine.'

'So you're still in your old house?' Kate remembered that it was situated near St Clement's, within a stone's throw of the city centre. And Faith had a demanding job at an Oxford college. She was probably rarely at home.

'Yes. I've cleared out a lot of accumulated junk, which I suppose is a good thing, and now I feel as though I'm living in a rented place, it's so clean and tidy. What about you?' asked Faith.

'I have the opposite problem. I've sold my house, put my furniture and belongings in store, and now I can't find anywhere I want to buy.'

'That was quick.'

'I found buyers willing to pay above the asking price if they could move in within two months. It seemed a good idea at the time.' She couldn't wait to leave Agatha Street at the time, was what she *didn't* say.

'What's it like being footloose?' asked Faith.

'Haven't you ever tried it?'

'No. I was a dutiful daughter for too many years,' Faith replied, without further explanation. 'I left it too late to be really good at it.'

'Footloose is OK for a while. Gives me a feeling of limitless opportunity. Then the feelings of insecurity crowd in and I want to build another nest. Oddly enough, it's tied up with my sense of identity. If I don't know where I live, how do I know who I am?'

'Very good. You could use that theme for a new novel. How's the career, by the way?'

'Flourishing.'

The conversation looked as though it was coming to a natural end. Faith hitched her bag on her shoulder and prepared to leave. On an impulse Kate said, 'Now that your house is feeling strangely empty, you don't fancy a lodger, do you?' After her stay at Camilla's she quite liked the idea of creating clutter in someone's living space.

'You, do you mean?'

'I need a place to stay for a couple of weeks. I won't take up much room – I just have a couple of suitcases. I'm quiet, house-trained, a non-smoker. And I'd pay rent, of course.' She seemed to remember that academics earned less than you thought they did.

'GSOH?'

'What?'

'You sounded like a Lonely Hearts ad. I was hoping you had a good sense of humour.'

'Definitely.' How could she have survived the past few years without one?

'When would you want to move in?'

'How about this coming weekend?'

'Let's make it Saturday afternoon, then.' Somehow they had shifted into an acceptance of Kate's tenancy of Faith's spare bedroom without any formal agreement. Five minutes later, still standing on the pavement, they had agreed a rent – inclusive, except for the phone bill, which was extra.

'Maybe you'll see the great advantages of my house,' said Faith. 'It would solve both our problems if you bought it, don't you think?'

It was a possibility Kate would keep in mind. They parted, and Kate went back to Camilla's to give her the good news. She had to admit that her friend looked relieved.

'Saturday? As a matter of fact that solves a small problem. A friend of mine's coming down for the weekend. I was wondering where I could fit him in.'

Kate wanted to hear about Camilla's friend, but as usual the other woman merely looked enigmatic and refused to give any details. Kate could never decide whether Camilla had a wild sex life with a succession of young and exciting lovers, or whether her 'friends' were in fact elderly relations who visited, and were visited in turn by Camilla, out of a sense of family duty. She had certainly learned nothing about Camilla's private life while she was staying in her house. Camilla, she was aware, enjoyed keeping her friend guessing.

On the other side of Oxford, Roz's phone was ringing. She stopped swearing at her irreconcilable bank statement and picked up the receiver.

'Hello!'

'Are you all right?'

'Yes, of course I am. Who's that speaking?'

'It's Leda, and you sound more than a little fraught.'

'I'm not surprised. I am suffering from severe stress. I've just been checking my bank statement and I have less money than I expected.'

'I'm sorry about that,' said Leda, sounding cheerful in the face of Roz's bad news. 'But as a matter of fact, in contrast to your situation, I'm just a little better off than I thought I was, so I was going to offer you some work.'

'Paid work?'

'Exactly that.'

'Tell me about it. I'm up for most things, as long as it doesn't involve being a waitress. I'm getting a bit past the stage where I can look winsome while dispensing bowls of soup from a niftily balanced tray.'

'I do need a good waitress, as a matter of fact. But that isn't what I had in mind for you.'

'Which is?' asked Roz cautiously.

'No balancing required, I promise. You know those lovely puds you make?'

'The ones soaked in rosewater and honey and syrup and containing lots of ground almonds?'

'Those are the ones. And the little crispy pastries that you deep-fry – don't they contain pistachio nuts? You gave them to us the Sunday before last when we came to lunch at your place.'

'Best kept for an occasional indulgence, I'm afraid, if you don't want to watch your hips spread.'

'I wasn't thinking of eating them – or not very often – more of selling them.'

'In the restaurant?'

'Exactly.'

'You want me to make trays of little sticky things and bring them over every evening to feed to your customers?'

'Unless you're prepared to make your kitchen comply with the hygiene regulations, I suggest you make them here. You could come over in the afternoons, when the kitchen's not busy. It could be rather fun, don't you think?'

Roz's thoughts were on paying her impending electricity bill rather than on amusing herself, but she said, 'Lots of fun.'

After a certain amount of haggling, which Roz won, having had years of practice in North Africa, they agreed a price.

'And you're quite sure you don't want me to work as a waitress?'

'Good Lord, no!'

Which was reassuring, if not exactly flattering.

'When would you like me to start?'

'As soon as possible.'

Roz glanced down at the disappointingly negative final balance on her statement. 'How about this afternoon?'

'Why don't you come in and make out a list of ingredients? As soon as I've sorted out my suppliers and we've taken delivery, you can make a start.'

'So you don't want me to pop into Tesco's for you? I can probably get most of what I need there.'

'That's not how we do it,' said Leda firmly.

'I'll see you at three o'clock, then.'

'Better make it four.'

When Roz replaced her receiver she reflected that Leda had made a definite statement about who was boss and who was the employee. Oh well, at least employees got paid at the end of the week. She'd insist on that: she really couldn't afford to wait till the end of the month. She'd ask for cash while she was about it.

Back in her restaurant, Leda replaced the receiver and tuned in to what was happening at the table in the window. This was her best table and she liked to think that it gave passers-by the message that Leda's was *the* place to eat, *the* place to be seen. And that was why she'd seated the man in the Italian suit, the good haircut and the manicured hands there, even if he was on his own. His teeth were so white that his smile would be visible all the way to Carfax, she'd thought. But now it looked as if things weren't going quite as well as she'd hoped.

Ellie was a pleasant enough girl, but as a waitress she still had something to learn. That was the trouble with paying the minimum wage, you had to take what you could get. When the place became popular and fashionable she would doubtless be invaded by young, good-looking and competent girls clamouring to work as waitresses, but that time was some way in the future. Meanwhile, she had to make do with Ellie. She was perfectly aware that if she sacked her, Ellie's replacement would be no better at her job, and possibly even worse.

Ellie was flustered. Leda could see Italian Suit was grumbling about his vegetables, pointing into the dish and speaking sharply. Ellie's face was pink and there was a distressing dampness about her eyes. Leda moved in swiftly.

'What seems to be the matter?' she asked, motioning with her head for Ellie to disappear back into the kitchen.

Italian Suit flashed his white teeth at her. 'Just a little overcooked,' he said mildly.

'I'm so sorry, sir,' said Leda, knowing perfectly well that they weren't since she'd cooked them herself. 'I'll replace them for you, of course.'

She brought him the fresh dish of vegetables a couple of minutes later. 'And please order a glass of wine for yourself – on the house.'

She'd make a smaller profit on the meal, but she needed all the good will she could garner. And the two women at the table next to the potted palm looked as though they preferred their vegetables well-done. She'd stick the dish in the microwave for a few seconds and they'd be none the wiser.

'Thank you,' said Italian Suit, flashing the smile. 'Good waitresses must be hard to get.'

'Tell me about it!'

She would schedule a training session with Ellie when the customers had left – if she could persuade the girl to stay a few minutes past her clocking-off time.

That evening, after work, Neil invited Amanda out for a drink at the pub the Foreword staff usually patronised. He considered asking her to join him for dinner, but he didn't want to give her the wrong idea. She was a nice girl, but not quite slim enough for his liking, and it was a bad idea to take up with someone in the same office. You could well find yourself forced to choose between marriage and a new career – at least, that was what he had found when he had gone a little too far with Phoebe.

Amanda was on her second vodka and tonic when he found himself saying, 'I wonder what time a waitress finishes work.'

'Sorry?'

'Just an idle thought.'

'You could try asking the restaurant what time they close,' said Amanda. 'Is she very pretty, then?'

'What? Oh, it's nothing like that. Just someone I wanted to speak to.' He thought about explaining the situation to Amanda.

He could do with some sympathy. But he didn't think it would reflect very well on him at work. He didn't want people to think he was a fool. Better to keep it to himself. He could tell from the expression on her face that Amanda had him down as strange, but probably harmless.

Soon after seven-thirty they left the pub and Neil walked Amanda to her bus stop. The doughnuts from teatime were still sitting heavily on his stomach and yet he knew that he would soon be hungry again. He wondered about eating at the restaurant where the dark-haired girl worked. Viola. He must get used to thinking of her as Viola. There was something old-fashioned about her looks, in spite of her modern clothes, that suited the name. He remembered her, standing by the bins in Appleton Court. She had worn rubber gloves. He could see them now, yellow hands, small as a child's, bright as a doll's. Inside the rubber the skin would be smooth and clean, untouched by the work she was doing. And her clothes were clean, too. Dark tracksuit unmarked by the mess of the dustbins. He thought for a moment of Cassia – so beautiful, so expensively dressed, and with such nasty habits. Viola wouldn't have marked his white leather sofa with a cigarette, he was sure.

What the hell was he thinking about? Viola was a grubby little thief. He must hold on to that thought. But in all honesty he couldn't call Viola grubby. She wasn't grubby at all.

He was quite close to the alleyway, and he strode on down to the door where he had last seen her. There was a price-list attached to the glass. At the bottom it told him that Chez Édith was open for lunch from 12 to 2.15, and for dinner from 7.30 to 10.30; it was closed all day Monday. Today, he was pleased to note, was a Tuesday.

The curtains came only halfway down the window and he could see inside. There were a few early diners, and a waitress taking a couple of menus over to a new arrival. He couldn't see Viola, though. Perhaps she worked in the kitchen after all.

He would go home and prepare himself something light and nutritious from the selection in his freezer, then come back and wait in the dark alley for Viola to emerge. This time he wouldn't let her get away from him.

13

When Barry came round later that same evening, bringing a bottle of single malt whisky with him, Roz told him about her new job offer. Barry was in the kitchen, finding a couple of small tumblers, polishing them on a clean linen tea towel.

'Would that restaurant be "Leda's"? The posh place that's just opened at the bottom of the Woodstock Road?'

'That's it. Do you know it?'

'I popped in one lunchtime, just to suss it out.' It sounded as though he'd popped straight out again.

'She seems to be making a success of it, don't you think?'

'It looks very promising. It could well catch on.'

'I hope she'll find someone else to make her desserts eventually,' said Roz. 'I can't see myself fussing with little nutty, sticky things for more than a month or two.'

'You're a butterfly,' said Barry. 'Just a beautiful butterfly.' He handed her a glass of whisky. 'Water? Ice?' he asked.

'I prefer it neat.' It would help to blot out the memory of her financial shortcomings. 'Here's to Leda's!' she said, swallowing the first mouthful. She was earning money for making her desserts, but not enough to pay off her debts while she was still shelling out for her living expenses. She'd forgotten how expensive life in England could be. And the long, cold spring had pushed up her heating bills. You forgot about things like that when you lived in California or North Africa.

Barry emptied his own glass. The alcohol made him more

expansive, Roz had noticed, and now he stretched his arms out along the back of the sofa and tipped his head back so that he appeared to speak to the ceiling.

'You need a day or two off,' he said. 'How about coming away with me this weekend? We could both do with a break.'

'Sounds appealing. Where were you thinking of going?'

'I'll see what's available that looks like good fun and get right back to you.'

'Just as long as I don't have to look at any ground almonds,' she said.

'Leda's got the place looking right, though, hasn't she?' he said slowly. 'Too many large plants for my taste, but they give the illusion of privacy to the tables. And the food was good. Could have been a little more imaginative, but maybe conventional is what you need in a town like Oxford.'

'I didn't realise you'd actually eaten there. I didn't see you.'

'I was in there at lunchtime a few days ago.'

'So how many points would you give Leda?' asked Roz.

'Eight out of ten.'

'Where did the other two points go?'

'The waitress could have been better.'

'Yes, Leda mentioned that – but good staff are hard to come by, they tell me. What did she do? Spill boiling soup in your lap?'

'Nothing that obvious. I complained about my veg, and she didn't know how to deal with it.'

'That doesn't sound very serious.'

'But in a place like that, where you've only got one waitress apart from the proprietor, she's really important. She's front of house, if you like. Still, apart from that, as I say, it was all pretty good. And the pudding was sensational.' Barry pushed himself off the sofa and took his glass to the whisky bottle. 'Another one for you? No?'

'I don't see how Leda can do much about the waitress situation if she can't afford to pay the best,' said Roz. 'In a place like Oxford, with so many pubs and restaurants for her to choose from, a waitress can walk out of one job on a Monday, and into a new one on Tuesday. She wouldn't want to stand around listening to the boss's criticism of her work.'

Barry was staring into his glass, a smile on his face. 'You know, I may just able to help your friend Leda out.'

'You? How?'

'I'll have to check to see if she's still available, but I do happen to know a girl who'd be ideal.'

'Send her down to Leda's!'

'Like I say, I'll have to check she's free,' said Barry, setting a full glass of whisky down on the table in front of him and sinking back into the sofa cushions.

'Maybe you should do it now.'

Barry got out his mobile, dialled and spoke. 'Holly? Baz here. You still need a job, girl?' There was a pause while Holly answered. 'Right,' said Barry. 'I've got something will interest you. Leda's, at the bottom of the Woodstock Road. I'll get back to you if the owner's interested. OK?'

'Well?' asked Roz.

'She's still free.'

'What's her name? Are you sure she's really good?'

'She's called Holly and yes, I'm sure she's ace at waitressing.'

'Then I'll give Leda a ring and suggest she meets her.' Roz picked up the phone. 'Leda?' she said. 'How are you? How are things going?'

It appeared that Leda had a lot to say about the way her

restaurant was going. Roz allowed her to speak uninterrupted for a while. Then she said, 'As a matter of fact, I believe I know someone who could help you out. Her name's Holly, and according to a friend of mine, she's an ace waitress.'

A minute or so later she put the phone down. 'Send her round at three o'clock tomorrow afternoon,' she said. 'Leda will give her an interview. I hope she's as good as you say she is. Leda's really losing patience with Ellie.'

Barry smiled. 'Let's forget about them. Tell me some of the places you'd like to go at the weekend and I'll see what I can do.'

Lying in bed that night, unable to sleep, Roz reflected that a trip away for the weekend wouldn't really help her finances. It might allow her to forget all about them for a couple of days, though, and that was a good thing. She'd like to be able to talk over her problems with Kate, but she seemed to have disappeared up to London, visiting the new boyfriend, presumably. Certainly she didn't seem to be getting on with finding herself a place to live. Next week, when she got back from her weekend away, she'd give her daughter a ring and ask her round for a long talk. And something would turn up before they actually turned off her electricity, surely.

Just before ten-thirty, Neil – fortified by a stiff brandy – left his flat and made his way on foot through central Oxford towards the High Street. He was a little later than he had intended, but he had become engrossed in rereading the manuscript that Estelle Livingstone had sent him and had forgotten the time. He would make her an offer for it. He would even invite her to come to Oxford again to discuss the matter. She seemed to have enjoyed her last visit. He could promise her another expensive meal and a tour of Foreword's offices. Perhaps Roland would come and shake her hand and make flattering remarks.

He hurried down the alleyway towards Chez Édith, but even as he approached, the lights went out and a couple of figures emerged and walked away, while a third dealt with the locks.

This last was male, he saw, as he reached the door. Viola – *the thief* – could have been one of the other two. The man stared hard at him as he passed, as though believing Neil might be waiting to break into the restaurant. Neil walked smartly past him and followed the two women. They separated when they reached St Aldate's and for a moment he wondered which one to follow. It wasn't difficult. One was tall and bulky and wearing a skirt and jacket, the other was smaller, slighter and wore jeans. He set off after her, moving quietly and keeping his distance so that he didn't startle her. He passed the taller girl and she, too, stared hard into his face. Was there something unreliable in his looks, or was it that he looked like a madman, following this young woman who might – or just as likely might not – be the same one who had been looking through his rubbish bin?

The tall girl turned and shouted, 'Bye, Phil!' At least, that's what it sounded like. Was Viola really her name, after all?

They walked, with twenty yards or so between them, for about ten minutes, down towards the canal, and then Viola turned into a small block of flats. Neil stood for a moment, irresolute. When it came to the point, he felt rather foolish at following her right to her front door at this time of night. If she caught him she might well call the police and accuse him of harassing her. He had no proof that she was the person he had seen, so briefly, at Appleton Court. Who would believe him? As he stood outside the building – it was only three storeys tall – he saw a light come on in a room on the second floor, to the left. He stood for a while longer, wondering whether to walk up the stairs and pound on her door, demanding an explanation or, even better, a confession.

A middle-aged couple walked past him and into the building as he stood on the pavement. They looked at him curiously and for a moment he expected one of them to ask him what he was doing there, staring at their flats. Did they think he was a rejected lover, come to stand outside his beloved's window? They went inside, however, closing the door carefully behind them.

As another long five minutes passed, it gradually became clear to him that if he intended to call on Viola he should have done it immediately, while he was still fired up with anger. He turned and started towards home.

Viola, standing behind the curtain in her sitting room, watched Neil Orson waiting on the pavement outside her flat. She recognised him now as the man who had found her going through his dustbin at Appleton Court. But until he started shouting his accusations, she hadn't realised that he was the man whose bin she'd raided back in London. What the hell was he doing here? Had he been tracking her down all this time? No, she didn't think he had the intelligence for it.

She had handed his details over to Baz and Baz had helped himself to Neil's credit. She felt sorry for Neil, but in a detached way. Poor little Grizzly Bear. Someone's stolen all the honey in your pot and the bees have stung your paws. You're feeling sorry for yourself, aren't you? Well, you shouldn't have been so stupid as to leave your details lying around for anyone to take. It was just asking for trouble.

She'd called him Grizzly to herself, since he looked like a little dark bear. And since she had an excellent memory, she remembered the name on the letters she'd taken and which Baz had bought from her. Neil Orson. They'd really enjoyed themselves, spending his money. They didn't often show off like that, but you had to have a break from the hard work and tedium once in a while, didn't you?

The invitation to the office party had told them that Orson worked for a publisher's, and they had tried to act the part of literary types when they went on their spending binge in Regent Street. That had been fun, talking in a posh voice and having the sort of pretentious conversation that they reckoned bookish people would have. The publisher's address had been in Oxford, she remembered now. The office party had been held at The Randolph. He must have grown tired of travelling down to Oxford every day, sold his flat, and moved here. She'd forgotten about the Oxford connection when she came here herself, but then she'd raked through a lot of bins since Appleton Court.

Well, he might think he recognised her, but he couldn't be sure, not after all this time. He needed to be warned off. She wasn't having him hanging around outside her flat, or outside the restaurant. She could give up the waitressing one of these days, when she had enough girls working for her, but not yet. Maybe a rude message left at his office would put him off. He wouldn't want that happening too often.

She checked the *Yellow Pages*. She couldn't remember the name of his company, but she'd recognise it when she saw it. There were quite a few publishers in and around Oxford, but only two or three with names she had heard of. When she read the name *Foreword* she remembered that that was the one on the invitation. Had he ever gone to the party? She hoped he'd enjoyed himself. It was probably the last carefree evening he'd had before she and Baz had raided his identity.

She'd ring Foreword and check that Neil Orson was still working there. Then she'd leave a message for him. If that didn't work she'd have to think of something more drastic. Baz would help her.

Neil was thinking that he could return at a more respectable time of day. He told himself this as he walked back towards Carfax. That would be far more satisfactory, he thought, as he pulled his jacket collar up to his chin against the cold night air. He knew where she lived, now. She wouldn't escape him. He wouldn't run away like this another time. He would be brave and forceful. He tried to walk briskly and confidently up the broad road, but his shoulders gradually slumped again and he could hear the sound of his own footsteps, shuffling a little, it seemed to him.

He did come back a couple of days later and look again at the flat where he believed the dark-haired Viola lived. But it was a while before he found the courage to climb the stairs and ring her doorbell. He found that it was more difficult than he could imagine, actually confronting someone. He was a man who, after all, had dealt with words, and only words, for a number of years. Words were powerful in his business, especially when written down on paper. Stepping away from the written word back into the real, and possibly violent, world was something that filled him with apprehension.

He would have got round to it faster if he hadn't been so involved in correspondence with the finance houses, just as a crisis erupted at work. He particularly needed to be seen as efficient at this time, and he couldn't take any more time off to deal with his own affairs, so he let them wait. If he was honest, he was happier with inaction. He knew he should check on his bank statements, too, but he had piled all his papers into cardboard cartons and left them in his friend Alistair's barn, along with his three or four precious pieces of furniture. But he did face up to it, eventually.

That was after he discovered what else had been done to him.

Then he was angry enough to have a scene with anyone, let alone a five foot two, slightly built female called Viola.

14

It was the afternoon following Barry's suggestion that Holly should become Leda's waitress, and Roz was up to her elbows in ground almonds and rosewater, when Leda came into the kitchen, accompanied by a pale young woman with limp red-blonde hair.

'Roz, this is Holly, our new waitress.'

'Hi!' said Roz, raising a sticky hand in greeting.

'Ellie's walked out, and Holly will be joining us immediately, I'm pleased to say. She has terrific experience and great references, and thanks for the suggestion, Roz.'

'I'm glad it worked out.'

Leda and Holly, both looking pleased with themselves, left her to her kneading and rolling and returned to the main restaurant.

An hour or so later, as Roz was cutting filo pastry into small squares and brushing it with melted butter, the back door opened and Barry entered the restaurant kitchen.

'Hello,' she said, pausing gratefully from her work. The smell of rosewater was making her feel quite nauseous. 'What brings you here?'

'I've got the tickets,' he said, envelope in hand. 'We're going to Venice. Ever been there before?'

'No – and I've always wanted to. You're brilliant!'

'I'll give you a ring at home to fix the details.'

'Have you heard that Holly's coming to work for Leda, starting today?'

'That's good news. I'm really glad for them. I'm sure it's going to work out well.'

Barry left, and Roz got on with her sticky pastries. She wouldn't care if she never saw another pistachio nut again.

'Hello, Kate?'

'Emma. How are you?'

'I'm afraid that the little problem I was telling you about hasn't gone away. Sam—'

'Junior?'

'Yes. He denies absolutely having done anything to put a charge on my credit card. I know he can be sulky and difficult sometimes, but I think I can tell when he's lying, and I don't believe he is.'

'So it might be one of the others?' asked Kate cautiously.

'I don't know what to think.' Emma sounded as though she was about to cry, and quite unlike her usual brisk self.

'You must be tired, looking after the new baby.'

'Flora's a little gem, but she has had me up at four-thirty every morning this week.'

'I feel a bit guilty asking you this, Emma, but do you think you could remind me of the children's ages and so on? I'm not sure I have them all quite clearly in my head.' Which was another way of saying that she hadn't a clue how many children Emma had (except that it was a lot) or what sexes they were (though they appeared to be assorted).

'I hope you don't want it in writing. I'm not feeling up to facing a keyboard at the moment.'

'Verbally is fine,' said Kate, reaching for a pad and biro.

'Sam's the eldest, and he's just fifteen. Then there's Abigail, thirteen. She's quite sensible, though she does have her moods. Hugo's coming up for twelve.'

'Have I met Hugo?'

'Probably. But he's very quiet, so you may not have noticed him. People do tend to overlook Hugo. Though he is determined, like all of them, and I expect he'll develop moods soon, too.'

Kate scribbled on the pad, balancing the telephone receiver under her chin. 'Go on.'

'Amaryl. You do remember Amaryl?'

'Of course.' Built like a wrestler and with the same aggressive nature, as far as Kate recalled from her last visit to the Dolby household.

'She's just ten. And Tristan is seven. Tristie. A lovely age.'

'Tristie. Yes, I think remember him, too.' No face to match the name came into her mind.

'He looks angelic, with those blond curls, but he isn't, I'm afraid to say. And then there's—'

'If we've reached the under-sevens, I think we can reckon the rest are innocent, don't you?'

'You're probably right about Jack, certainly. We still think of him as the baby.'

'He doesn't mind being displaced by Flora? You don't think he's playing up to gain your attention?'

'I don't think so. He's very superior about Flora being useless at everything he thinks is important. And he and Tristie are good friends. I think if he was going to misbehave he'd throw all his food on the floor rather than look for women with bare breasts.'

Kate glanced at the list with the scribbled ages beside the names. 'I think we can forget about Amaryl and the younger ones,' she said, not entirely sure she had all their names and details down, but confident that they were too young to filch their mother's credit card and use it. 'But it does look as though you'll have to talk to Hugo and Abigail.'

'Oh dear. I suppose you're right. I'll wait until they've finished their homework. If I can catch them before they settle down to their Play Stations we might be able to have a sensible conversation.'

'I'm sure you'll have it sorted out in no time.'

'If I can stay awake that late,' added Emma.

And what if Hugo and Abigail denied all knowledge of the mystery charge? Kate had the feeling that Emma would be back on the phone the next day, asking for further suggestions. *She's got a perfectly good brain of her own*, she thought. *I don't need to battle with her problems.*

'You must think I'm a fool, asking you for help with my children,' Emma was saying. 'But something happens to my mind for the first few months after childbirth. I don't seem able to cope with anything more taxing than how to open a jar of strained spinach. You don't mind my picking your brains, do you?'

This was so unlike the usually self-confident Emma, that Kate spent several minutes assuring her that her time was Emma's to do with as she would, and that she had every confidence in Emma's competence, however recently she had given birth.

'Give me a ring tomorrow,' she said. 'Let me know how you've got on.'

'And what about you, Kate?' asked Emma belatedly. 'Are you still all right for a roof over your head?'

'I'm probably wearing Camilla's patience a little thin. I'm moving on next weekend.'

'I could shift Amaryl and her belongings in with Abigail, if you like, and then you could have Amaryl's room.'

'That's very sweet of you, Emma, but I'm staying with Faith Beeton for a while – you remember her from Bartlemas,

I expect. After that I was thinking of asking Roz if she could fit me into her place for a couple of weeks. I've put all my stuff in store, so I only have two small suitcases with me. But it is a very kind thought, and if I need Amaryl's room, I'll let you know.' The thought of moving a thuggish small child in with her moody teenage sister was not a pleasant one. The atmosphere in the Dolby household could well change from disorganised but sunny to chaotic and stormy overnight. And although Sam and Emma would be welcoming, she could see that the children would view her as an interloper who needed to be shifted out as quickly as possible. But she was touched by Emma's offer. She surely had enough on her plate without taking on a temporarily homeless friend, as well.

'Look Emma,' she said impulsively, 'why don't you take an evening off? Go out with Sam on your own and enjoy yourselves.'

'But I can't—'

'I'm offering to babysit.'

'*You?*' exclaimed Emma unflatteringly.

'Give me a list of their bedtimes, what they eat, and the house rules. I'm sure I'll manage. And you can stay out as late as you like, I won't mind. Don't think you have to be home by eleven or anything.'

'Are you sure?' The idea that anyone would voluntarily take on her entire raft of children was astonishing to Emma.

'Definitely. Think of it as a birthday present.'

'How did you know it was my birthday next week?'

'Just a lucky guess.'

'I'll speak to Sam.'

Kate gave Emma her new address and phone number so that she could ring back.

When she had hung up, Kate thought again about where to go when she moved out of Faith's house. Kind as Emma's offer had been, she hoped that Roz would eventually be prepared to give her house room, otherwise she would have to move further afield in search of a roof. If Camilla's habits had in the end got on her nerves because her friend was so extremely pernickety – quite middle-aged, in fact, Kate considered – Faith appeared to cultivate an appearance of scattiness. She couldn't really be so disorganised, or she would never have got her Fellowship, but Faith liked to present an appearance of who she wasn't, Kate concluded. It was always a little wearing to be around people who were putting on a performance for your benefit, she had found. Apart from anything else, you had to allow them to think you were taken in by it, and this often took a considerable effort on your part.

And for a moment the idea of moving in with Jon Kenrick (on a strictly limited timescale) flicked into her mind.

Up in his room, Sam Dolby was continuing his researches on the Internet.

For *serious* Internet fraud, it appeared that you needed to set up your own merchant company, possibly even your own credit-card processing company. For a sum that was currently outside Sam's reach, but which he could see himself laying his hands on by the time he was twenty-one, you could set up your own bank, apparently, and if you kept the money you made outside the jurisdiction of countries like the US or the UK, they wouldn't be able to get their hands on it, even when they knew that it was stolen.

Cool.

He could begin to build himself a new identity, just for a start. He could stop being Sam Dolby, Junior. Or Little Sam

Dolby. He needn't even be Sam Alexander Dolby any more. He could be someone entirely different.

From downstairs he could hear his mother's voice.

'Supper's ready!'

Then he heard her footsteps on the stairs and her voice calling from outside his door.

'Supper's ready, Sam! And I've made chips.'

Since Emma believed in healthy eating, and the virtues of green vegetables and plain baked potatoes, this was a real concession. Maybe he wouldn't stop being Sam Dolby just yet, after all.

15

In Leda's kitchen, Roz was putting the finishing touches to the dishes of desserts. Leda was sitting at the table, a cup of black coffee in front of her, her feet resting on a stool. Her eyes were closed. This was the quiet time before the customers started to pile in again in three hours' time for dinner. Roz and Leda were on their own, so it seemed a good time for Roz to bring up the subject that had been on her mind.

'How's Holly getting on?' she asked casually.

'She's brilliant,' said Leda, opening her eyes and blinking. Roz had been right that running a restaurant was an exhausting business. 'I meant to thank you for sending her along.'

'I'm glad she's doing so well,' said Roz, relieved. She had taken Barry's word for it that Holly was an ace waitress. Now she could fly off to Venice with a clear conscience.

'She has a tendency to play loud music in the kitchen, but I suppose that's a minor fault in a waitress.'

Oh well, if that was the worst that was happening, thought Roz, she had nothing to worry about.

'Mind you,' added Leda, 'I've hired a woman to help with the cooking, and she looked as though she could brain Holly with her nasty little trannie. I suppose I'll have to speak to her, but I'd hate her to take umbrage and move out on me.'

That evening, Barry came round to Roz's place. As usual, he poured them both a whisky from the bottle he'd brought with him, and relaxed on her sofa.

153

'You all fixed for Friday?' he asked.

'I certainly am.'

'I'll pick you up at eight in the morning, OK?'

'Fine. I'm all set for some serious town-painting.' She turned on some background music and sat in the chair opposite Barry. 'Your protégée is doing very well, you'll be glad to hear,' she said.

'What?'

'Holly – the waitress. Leda's very pleased with her. Except for a liking for very loud music, she appears to be ideal.'

'Loud music?'

'In the kitchen. I imagine it blasts out into the restaurant every time someone goes through the door. But I gather it's a minor fault compared to her virtues.'

'She shouldn't be doing that,' said Barry.

'Really, I don't think it's important.' She was sorry she'd mentioned it.

'Maybe not. Well, shall we find ourselves something to eat, then? How do you fancy Indian?'

Roz fancied any food she hadn't prepared herself and so they left to try the new Indian restaurant in the Cowley Road.

'Kate?'

'Hello, Emma. What's up?' Emma was sounding worried again. She rarely sounded anything else these days, Kate reflected.

'It's happened again.'

Kate wondered which of Emma's problems had repeated itself. 'What has?'

'Another unexplained charge has appeared on my latest credit-card statement. I check them online now, you see, so that I can be sure that everything's all right.'

'I hadn't realised you were getting so competent with Sam's computer.'

'It's time I came to terms with modern technology.'

'We'll have you using a word processor for your books soon.'

'God forbid.'

'So tell me about this new charge.'

'It's from the same company as before and for the same amount.'

'And have you spoken to Sam J and Abigail about it?' She congratulated herself on remembering their names.

'We're calling him Sam Junior these days.'

'Sorry, Emma.' Trust Emma to change a child's name just when she'd got the hang of it.

'And actually it was *Hugo* and Abigail I was going to speak to.'

'Of course. Just a slip of the tongue. Well, have you done it?'

'I shall have to, shan't I?'

'You were only waiting for me to bully you into it. Admit it.'

'You're right. I'll wait until the little ones are in bed and Sam and I and the big ones have eaten and we've washed up. Then I'll tell them I want to have a little chat.'

Kate thought that she'd be exhausted by the end of Emma's evening schedule, but presumably Emma was used to such action-packed days.

'I won't get cross. I won't lose my temper. I'll make sure that Sam is backing me up. I'll be calm and understanding, tolerant and yet firm with them.'

'Good luck.'

'And you're still on for babysitting, are you, Kate?'

'Of course. You haven't told me when you want me, though.'

* * *

Much later that night, when Emma and all her children were fast asleep, Barry drove to a house off the Abingdon Road. He chose the bell labelled *Allen* from the selection on offer and kept pressing it until Holly came to the door. Her hair was a mess and there was a crease in her cheek as though she had just been roused from her bed.

'What's up?' she asked. 'It's bloody two a.m.'

'I told you to keep a low profile,' said Barry, pushing his way past her and into the room. It smelled as though no one had opened a window in here for a week, or changed the sheets. 'This place is a tip,' he said with disgust.

'So what? Is that what you came round to tell me? If so, you can piss off again and let me go back to sleep.'

Barry pushed her against the wall so that she was pinned in a corner, then took her chin between strong fingers.

'Shut up and listen,' he said.

Holly shut up.

'I came to warn you about your behaviour. Do your job. Be a model waitress, I told you. That's what I pay you for, isn't it?'

Holly couldn't speak with his hand grasping her jaw, so she just looked her assent. After another few seconds he let her go. She subsided on to an upright chair while Barry remained standing.

'We understand each other, do we?' he said.

'I do my job. I'm a bloody wonder at it. What do you want? It's not rocket science, is it? I'm only a bloody waitress.' She was nearly in tears, he could hear.

'Forget the music,' he said.

'What music?'

'Don't waste my time with lies.'

'It's only a little trannie,' she said.

'Leave it at home, or I'll take a hammer to it.'

The way he looked at her, Holly knew that he'd take the hammer to her, too, if she argued with him any longer.

'*And* you'll be out of a job,' he said.

'I won't be staying at Leda's much longer in any case, though, will I?'

'No one's suspected anything yet, but you'll want another job when you move on, won't you? Or do you want to try living on your wages for a change?'

'All right,' she said sulkily. And the words covered everything he'd asked for.

When Barry had left, she added, 'Miserable sods.' She could well have been referring to Leda and all her customers as well as to Barry.

Outside in the street, Barry looked at his watch. He wanted to call on Phil, too, but that silly little cow Holly was right about one thing: it was too late now to call uninvited. Phil was a good kid, getting on with the job with no complaints from the management about loud music or anything else, and maybe due for another promotion. He had her in charge of three other girls at the moment. She could take on another three, he reckoned. He'd give her a percentage of the take. Oh well, he'd leave it for now and call round tomorrow night at a reasonable hour to congratulate her on a job well done.

If he'd sent her round to Holly's instead of calling there himself, he imagined that the result would have been the same, but without the unpleasantness. On the other hand, there was something in Barry that enjoyed frightening Holly.

He slid into the driver's seat of the Beamer and drove sedately out to the comfortable house north of the city which he shared with his current companion. He glanced at the speedometer from time to time. Barry didn't believe in getting caught by speed cameras or pulled up by the police for no good reason.

16

It was seven o'clock in the evening and Kate was looking into the freezer, wondering which of the icy boxes she should choose this evening to put in the microwave. The exciting thing about Faith's freezer was the occasional package one came across that had lost any form of identification. You put it into the microwave, instructed the machine to defrost it, and waited to see what would emerge. Haddock in mushroom sauce (made with butter) or an Arctic Roll. One could never be sure what would be on the menu. When she'd visited Tesco's and refilled the freezer herself, the choices would be much more predictable.

Her hand was poised to take out what, from its shape, was probably a quiche, when the front doorbell rang. Faith was out, so she went to answer it herself.

'Jon? What a surprise.'

'I expect I should have rung,' he said, failing to look at all apologetic and following Kate into the kitchen. Her mother had been correct in thinking that Kate and Jon had spent an evening together in London, but Kate had returned to her bed in Faith's house afterwards.

'I'm glad you're here,' she said. 'Will you join me for dinner?' A cloud of condensation had gathered by the open door of the freezer.

'Were you about to choose one of those?' he asked.

'I was. Don't you approve? I'm not entirely sure what's in each of these, but I'm sure it's something edible.'

'Wouldn't you rather come out to eat?' he asked.

Kate pushed the probable quiche back into the depths of the freezer and closed the door. 'You have the serious look of a man pursuing his work,' she told him.

'I thought we'd try the new place at the bottom of the Woodstock Road,' he said, avoiding the implications.

'Leda's?'

'That's the one. I've just heard it's a good place to eat.'

'And that's all?'

'Well, actually, a colleague of mine is interested in various Oxford restaurants at the moment, including Leda's, and I said I'd help him out by eating there and seeing what was to be seen.'

'Roz is working there in the afternoons, making exotic desserts.'

'Roz? Working for Leda's?'

'Oh hell. Is she mixed up in some other scam? I've entirely failed to separate her from the noxious Barry Frazer, I'm afraid.'

'I'm sure this investigation has nothing at all to do with Roz. Really.'

'She's not there in the evenings, anyway.'

'I'm glad. Do you want to change, by the way?'

Kate looked down at her jeans and trainers. Not quite the right attire for Leda's, certainly. 'How much time have I?'

'I've booked a table for eight o'clock, so you have about forty minutes.'

'Help yourself to a drink,' she said. As she went to choose a more elegant outfit she saw he was pouring himself a glass of fizzy mineral water and adding an ice cube. She wondered what it would take to persuade him to stop behaving like a thoroughly responsible member of society.

Thirty minutes later she reappeared. From the expression on his face she'd made the right sartorial choices.

'Now you've finished taking the inventory of what I'm wearing, perhaps you'd pour me a glass of whatever you're drinking,' she said.

'Very effective,' he said, still looking with approval at the fitted velvet jacket and handing over the tumbler. 'You've run out of carbonated,' he added. 'This is tonic, I'm afraid. It's the only soft drink I could find.'

'I'll stock up at the supermarket tomorrow.' Faith was short of a lot of basics and it was the least Kate could do while she was living in her house.

'Are you sure you wouldn't like gin in the tonic?' asked Jon.

'Straight tonic would be delicious,' she said. She had the impression she'd need to keep her wits about her this evening.

'How are you getting on here?' he asked.

'It's all right. It's the usual small terraced house, but you can see they've knocked the two downstairs rooms into one. I don't like the proportions much – this room reminds me too much of a railway carriage.'

'Didn't you mention it was up for sale?'

'You think I should buy it?'

'I just wondered.'

'I'm not sure I could ever stop it from being Faith's house rather than mine. I'd always feel her presence here, looking over my shoulder, forbidding me to change anything.'

He laughed. 'I think that's the novelist's imagination speaking, somehow.'

'If I have to be severely practical, I also think it's rather small, even if it is so central.'

'Yes, I can see it's a bit oppressive. You'll just have to keep looking, won't you?'

As they drove to the restaurant, Kate asked: 'What do you expect to find at Leda's?'

'Nothing, I hope. But it attracts the kind of customers who get their credit-card details stolen.'

'Leda would never do a thing like that! She's an old friend of Roz's!'

'Leda might know nothing about it. It would be one of her waitresses.'

'I think there is only one. It's not a very big place, and Leda herself helps out.'

'I do hope you're right.'

'Are you going to tell me what we're looking out for?'

'I think we should concentrate on having a lovely evening. Someone else will be paying, after all. You can order all the most expensive items on the menu.'

I will, I certainly will, thought Kate. And *two* of Roz's desserts. This was turning out to be a splendid evening.

'I thought you said you weren't interested in the small crooks,' she said as they drove towards the Woodstock Road. 'I gathered that you were interested only in the major players.'

'I'm doing this for a colleague. They haven't got enough staff in their unit to follow up all the information they receive. I just happened to mention I sometimes came down to Oxford and he asked me if I'd help out. In an unofficial capacity, of course. As an observer, as it were.'

'OK. I'll buy it,' said Kate, letting him off the hook. After all, it was unlikely that there was anything illegal about Roz's puddings.

17

Looking back at the whole affair afterwards, Neil Orson calculated that that particular Tuesday was the worst day of his whole life. There were, he admitted, plenty of other days that were in the running for the title, but that Tuesday definitely took the award.

It had started over breakfast, when he was sitting at the kitchen table, drinking the first of three cups of strong coffee and spooning in his muesli. He heard the thump on the doormat that meant his post had arrived and went to pick it up. Neil looked forward to the post. He had never quite lost the childish feeling that there might be something exciting waiting for him.

This morning, however, there were three shirt catalogues and two charity appeals, none of which bore his name, and a business envelope decorated with his bank's logo, which *was* addressed to him.

It was his statement. Neil usually slung statements into a drawer, unopened, but this morning he remembered that he hadn't yet opened the previous one, and that his statements arrived only quarterly. He slit this one open, therefore.

As usual he skimmed through the pages to check the final balance, and at that point he received a very nasty shock. The sort of shock that stopped the blood circulating to his brain and that froze time so that the movement of the second hand on the kitchen clock seemed to arrest and halt.

There should have been more than two thousand in his current account. He couldn't be certain to the last hundred or so, but certainly not less than two thousand. But there was a minus in front of the sum he saw at the bottom of the page. He was overdrawn, and very nearly to the limit that the bank had set.

There must be some mistake. Returning to the first page, he went carefully through all the items. He could see nothing seriously wrong. The mistake, he realised, appeared to be in the opening balance. He needed to look at his previous statement, but it was sitting in one of the cardboard archive boxes, stacked in Alistair's barn, fourteen miles away.

Luckily, Alastair was an early riser. Neil shot out to his car, phoned Alistair from his mobile while driving, and got caught on a speed camera doing fifty through a village. He and Alistair piled the boxes into the boot of the car and Neil drove off, leaving a bemused Alistair standing watching him from the driveway. He was back at eight-ten, unloading the boxes into his sitting room.

He wished he'd labelled them with their contents. It took him twenty minutes before, surrounded now by heaps of old bills and letters, he finally came across the envelope he was looking for. He opened it and looked through it, his hands shaking – and there it was: three months previously, someone had withdrawn five thousand pounds from his account. For a moment he wondered whether he had gone mad and was suffering from amnesia.

No, not possible. He couldn't spend five thousand pounds and not be aware of what he had spent it on. Fifty, maybe. Five hundred, possibly. More than that and there should be something substantial sitting in the middle of his flat sporting a big red SOLD sticker.

This had to be part of the same conspiracy that had robbed him of his credit rating.

He went back to the boxes, scrabbled through the papers and found another unopened communication from the bank. His savings account. It should contain the money from the sale of his flat, and the interest it must have earned, not to mention the money he had put by over the past years. Neil might be scatty about his money, but he still saved against the kind of rainy day that had been visited upon his parents. As he ripped open the envelope, his heart started to race. Someone had emptied his savings account, too.

Neil left the paper-strewn bedroom and returned to the kitchen in a state of shock. He sat down. The second hand on the clock had resumed its movement round the dial. It was eight-fifty-five: past the time he usually left for the office. But he had to contact the bank, and he certainly didn't want anyone from Foreword to overhear him when he spoke to them. He decided to phone in and say he would be in later – he might be reading a manuscript in the quiet of his flat, after all – and then he would ring up his bank and straighten out the mistake.

He made another pot of coffee and studied pictures of shirts while he waited for the time to pass. It occurred to him that at that moment he couldn't afford to buy one of them, not even the nasty blue one with the buttoned-down collar.

Once his personal banker had assured himself that it was indeed Neil Orson who was on the other end of the line, the man found the information Neil asked for quite quickly. The money from his current account had been withdrawn from Neil's own branch of the bank in London. He wasn't known personally to the bank clerk, of course, but he had produced identification – a driving licence and a letter addressed to him at Appleton Court.

'But it wasn't me!' shouted Neil. 'How could you think it *was* me?'

'You did produce adequate identification.'

Neil let that 'you' pass. 'And what about my savings account?'

Apparently, the day following the withdrawal from his current account, he had transferred his savings to an account at a building society which offered a higher rate of interest. Somehow Neil knew that the building society would have no record of him. The funds would be somewhere else, possibly abroad, and in another name. He could see the thief sitting at his computer at midnight and moving money from one account to another with the click of a mouse. *Click*. And there was Neil's money – gone.

It seemed hopeless. How could he prove he wasn't someone who appeared to have even more right to his identity than he did? The thought made his head hurt.

'What did he look like? Have you got a description of him?' asked Neil desperately. But of course they didn't.

'What about the security cameras? Why don't we look at the relevant footage?'

But there was no hope that footage from three months ago would still be in existence. If the pictures of the thief had ever existed, they had been recorded over a dozen times since then, maybe even thrown away.

'You can't expect us to keep hundreds of hours of security footage for that long,' the clerk said reasonably.

Neil wanted to shout that yes, he did expect it. He expected them to keep every tiny piece of evidence that might possibly lead to the people who had stolen his money.

'Why didn't you contact us earlier?' the clerk enquired.

'I hadn't checked my statement until this morning.'

There was a silence at the other end of the line. Neil did not need to be told that he had made a major mistake.

'Come in and see us, Mr Orson. It is a very large sum of money that's missing, but I'm sure we can work it out.'

Eventually he rang off. He drank another cup of coffee and looked at the clock. It was ten to ten. He didn't know how he was going to get through the day, but the last thing he must do was to fall behind with his work. He was completely dependent now on his salary in a way that he had never been before. He had no financial cushion – not even the possibility of a larger overdraft – so he had better make sure that he performed as competently as always. He considered asking Roland Ives for a pay rise, but decided to put it off for a little longer. He must impress him with his diligence and flair first.

He walked to work. The exercise sent oxygen into his numbed brain and helped him to think and plan. Of course it would be sorted out. He would have to report this second crime to the police, then the bank would reimburse him. It would take time, though. The ghosts of his parents looked down at him. He was as inept as his own father. His father had handed his money over to his brother-in-law, and Neil had been robbed by strangers, but the result, at this moment, was the same.

Without money in the bank he felt naked. And *someone had done this to him*. Someone had stolen his life and he wasn't going to let them get away with it. They had stolen the rubbish from his bin. They had watched him. They had found out the minute details of his life and then taken it over. He had to find them and get his own back, the way he had with Cassia. Where could he start?

In his office, he checked his in-tray and wall planner, decided what he needed to do that morning. For a moment he sat with his eyes closed, calming his heartbeat and his breathing. If he couldn't return to normality, at least he could appear to do so.

He looked in his diary. He was supposed to be seeing Estelle Livingstone for a meeting in his office and then take her out to lunch, but he would put her off. He rang her number but only reached her voicemail. He couldn't just leave a message cancelling their meeting, he needed to speak to her personally. She had probably already left London for Oxford, anyway. He left a message for her to ring him back and got on with the first piece of work on his desk, trying to keep his mind off his own problems He kept reminding himself that the bank would reimburse him, but all he could see were the minus numbers at the bottom of his statement.

An hour or two passed and Estelle still hadn't rung him back. Luckily, when he checked his Rolodex, he found the number of her mobile. He caught up with her on the Oxford train. She wouldn't be best pleased at having her lunch date cancelled, but he would make up for it with the size of the offer he made her that afternoon.

Lunchtime was when Neil could be sure of finding Viola at Chez Édith, and he was determined to speak to her. He would pin her against a wall and threaten her with . . . Neil wasn't good at imagining violence, but he knew something appropriate would come to him at the right moment. In the heat of his anger he raced through more work than usual that morning.

By one o'clock he had cooled down a little and reconsidered his options. He could hardly storm into the restaurant and shout at Viola in public. Someone might call the police and have him evicted. He might end up in even more trouble than he was in at present. He would wait for her when she came out, speak to her in private. He had just enough time before he was meeting the Livingstone woman.

'I've rescheduled Estelle Livingstone for this afternoon,' he told Amanda when he passed her desk on the way to the coffee machine. 'Something urgent has come up that I have to deal with straight away. I'll pop out for a snack a bit later.'

Amanda offered to get him a sandwich to eat at his desk, but he told her he'd need a breath of fresh air and would pick up a sandwich while he was out.

'This phone message came for you. It must have come through to the wrong extension because Zoe from Publicity took it down.' Amanda looked as though she was making a big effort not to smile.

'Who's it from?'

Amanda handed him a slip of paper. 'See for yourself.'

The message read: *Stop following me around. And piss off out of my life. Viola*.

'Bad news?' asked Amanda kindly.

'Just someone I used to know,' said Neil stiffly.

'She doesn't sound a very nice person, so you're probably much better off without her.'

Neil groaned. Amanda had never actually heard anyone groan before and it was a sad sound.

'Are you all right?' she said.

'Yes,' he snapped. 'Why do you ask?'

'You're looking a bit pale. I wondered if you were going down with this virus that's going the rounds.'

'No. I'm fine.'

She noticed there was a new air of determination about him. Maybe they'd all misjudged Neil Orson when he first came to work at Foreword. Zoe in Publicity had said he reminded her of Little Bear, but no one would dare to call him that now, she thought, as she watched his rigid back as he marched into his office. Maybe this Viola had been the great love of his life and now he was mourning her loss. He'd be really upset, though, if he knew how the junior staff were giggling about Viola's forthright phone message. It wasn't very kind of Zoe to pass it on to the whole of Foreword.

Estelle Livingstone enjoyed getting out of the office and visiting authors or editors. In truth, her office was untidy and cluttered and made her feel guilty whenever she entered it. She had the constant feeling that something really important was hiding in one of those tottering piles of manuscripts: an undeposited cheque, an inaccurate royalty statement, a manuscript containing a work of genius that some other agent was snapping up at that very moment.

However, she didn't usually leave London and travel to somewhere as far off as Oxford. Especially not twice in the space of a few weeks. It was unfortunate that Foreword Publishing happened to be in that city, though it might have been somewhere really awful, like Birmingham, she supposed. One day they'd come to their senses and move into London, but presumably such a major decision would take them a year or two to finalise. But that nice young editor, Neil Orson, was very interested in a novel by a new client of hers. Big bucks, she dreamed, looking out of the carriage window at the golden fields of rapeseed. Big, big, golden bucks.

It was a pity that the mobile phone had ever been invented. Before its appearance it had been possible to escape all the hassle of the office and forget for a while the demands of unreasonable authors and the conservatism of dismissive editors. Now, although seated in a first-class compartment on a train travelling westwards, she could be reached by anyone who bothered to make a note of her number.

Sure enough, on cue, her phone rang. She thought about switching it off, or pretending that she was in a tunnel. Instead, giving in to habit, she answered it.

'Livingstone,' she said, in the tone that had been known to put nervous young editors off a career in publishing.

'Estelle? It's Neil here.'

'Neil!' She used the tone of voice she reserved for young men who were either good-looking or likely to be useful to her. 'I hope you're not phoning to cancel our meeting. I don't think this train is going to stop until we get to Oxford.'

'Of course I wouldn't cancel, Estelle,' said Neil without conviction. 'I was just wondering whether we could reschedule. Something urgent has come up and it would be much better – for me, that is – if we could meet here at three o'clock instead of eleven-thirty.'

'Of course! No problem. I shall spend a delightful hour or two exploring your city.' Estelle couldn't afford to fall out with an editor, even when he wasted half her day like this.

'In fact, when I come to think about it, perhaps we'd better make that three-thirty,' said Neil. 'I'd hate to keep you waiting.'

Estelle didn't sound quite so pleased with him when she said, 'That's fine. I'll see you later, then. *Ciao!*'

How tedious of him. Estelle tapped her foot on the carriage floor. She was really livid with him and if he wasn't careful he'd go well down in her estimation. It wasn't as if she was wearing the right shoes for sightseeing, even if she wanted to do any such thing. More Oxfordshire countryside slid past the window as she wondered how to spend the hours left unexpectedly free. Who did she know in Oxford who would make amusing company over a light lunch?

There was Kate, of course, but she didn't want to lunch with one of her authors more than once every six months. She hadn't told Kate she was coming to Oxford, anyway. It didn't do to let authors think they were too important. But then, she seemed to remember that Kate had an unconventional mother –

Roz Ivory. They had had several conversations on the phone in the months when Kate had been recovering from the attack in the cathedral. For a while it had looked as though Kate might never get back to work again. But Roz had been very helpful, and she and Estelle had pulled Kate out of her tricky patch.

Did she still have Roz's phone number? She had phoned her originally by mistake, because she was staying in Kate's house while Kate herself moved in with George Dolby. Yet another error in judgement on Kate's part, of course. But then, she seemed to remember, Roz had bought her own house in a different part of Oxford. She checked the stored numbers on her mobile, but didn't really expect to find the one she was looking for. She was in luck, though, when she checked her leather address book. There it was.

'Hello. Is that Roz Ivory?'

It was. And she was free for lunch. Where did she suggest they should go? Roz came up with the name of a recently opened establishment at the bottom of the Woodstock Road. They could have a drink or two first, then indulge in a good gossip over their lunch. And Roz quite understood that it would be better not to mention Estelle's visit next time she spoke to her daughter.

Estelle took a taxi from the station. Once they had driven past the modern concrete building alongside the station, they reached a broad, tree-lined road. She peered through the foliage and saw a lot of ugly grey stone buildings. The famous colleges, she supposed. Not her style at all. Leda's restaurant, she thought as they drew up outside, looked much more promising. Nor did the interior disappoint her, with its dark green walls, white tablecloths and gold-framed mirrors. The wines were adequate, and modestly priced, the food eclectically Mediterranean.

As it was still early for lunch, Roz and Estelle sat with a

bottle of Sauvignon Blanc and some dishes of mézé. Roz was older by a number of years than Estelle, but the two had a lot in common. They chatted about cities they had known, and Estelle added some piquant gossip about the literary world. Eventually Roz said, 'Where's that young waitress gone? I think I'd like to look at the menu.'

The waitress, who had been so attentive till then, had indeed disappeared.

'Holly!' called Roz, glad to show that she was familiar with the staff. But Holly was apparently talking to a friend who had just entered the restaurant, using the front door instead of the staff entrance at the back, noted Roz.

'What an odd couple!' remarked Estelle.

'Chalk and cheese,' commented Roz. For, where Holly was pale-skinned with light golden-red hair and pink, rose-petal lips, her friend was inches smaller, with a mass of curly black hair and dark eyes and brows. Where Holly was plump, her friend was angular.

Roz went to call Holly again but Estelle stopped her. 'It's a very intense conversation,' she said. 'I think we ought to give them a minute or two.'

Roz felt uneasily that this was the waitress she had recommended to Leda, and here she was behaving like the worst of amateurs, but she went along with Estelle's wishes. 'Oh, look,' she said brightly, taking Estelle's attention away from the slow service. 'Leda has a special offer for us.' She handed Estelle one of the cards that stood in a chrome holder on the table. ' "Come to one of our food and wine tastings!" ' she read. ' "Try new food sensations! Taste our Mediterranean wines!" And it's free. All Leda asks for is your name and address. I imagine she'll use them as the basis for a mailing list.'

'It's rather a long way for me to come for a free glass of

wine and a stuffed vine leaf, I'm afraid,' said Estelle.

'Not a bad way of drawing in the punters, though,' said Roz. She glanced across to Holly, to see if she was ready to take their order now, but the two girls were still in heated conversation.

'It's almost as good as a new novel,' said Estelle, following her gaze. 'What do you think they're talking about?'

The dark girl had scrabbled in her handbag and come up with a small grey box that she was urging on to Holly. 'Take it!' she was saying. 'Baz will kill me if you don't earn your keep.'

To Roz, the box looked like the adapter she had attached to Kate's notebook computer before plugging it into the mains. Certainly it was about the same size and shape, though it had no leads that she could see.

'I'm getting pissed off with this,' Holly was saying. 'And you shouldn't have come here now. Why aren't you at work?'

'My shift starts at seven. And I do what I'm told. You would, too, if—'

'Shut up. We've got customers.' They both glanced across at Roz and Estelle, who buried their noses in their glasses and tried to look interested only in each other. Other people's arguments were always so fascinating, thought Roz. It made her understand why a novelist like Kate got to be so curious about the lives of strangers.

'Remember what you're here for,' the dark one said. Roz decided it was time for the waitress to remember what she was being paid for, whatever her friend was saying.

'Holly!' she called again. 'Could you bring us over a menu, do you think?'

Holly pushed her friend into the kitchen, letting the door swing closed behind her. She walked across to Roz and Estelle's table with a professional smile and a couple of Leda's dark green menus.

'Such a smart logo,' approved Estelle, drawing attention to the gold outline of a nubile young woman who appeared to be flirting with a handsome swan. She remembered vaguely that the myth, although classical, was somewhat unsavoury.

'I'll leave you for five minutes, shall I?' said Holly. Roz and Estelle were reading the list of starters and hardly noticed when she left.

Before Holly could retire to the kitchen again her attention was caught by another early customer. She hadn't noticed him come in but recognised him as someone who had been to the restaurant a couple of times before. She smiled, and handed him a menu, remembering that he was one who left a generous tip. The man, who was very tall and wore a dark grey suit, ordered without giving the menu more than a cursory glance, as though he knew its contents by heart, then opened a copy of the *Spectator*, indicating that he didn't wish to be disturbed.

A minute later and he was calling for Holly's assistance.

'What's wrong?' asked Holly. 'Can I help?'

'I've dropped a contact lens. Can you bring more light? Can you find it? I really can't see anything very well without it.'

But although Holly brought the large torch from the kitchen, and she and the customer searched diligently, neither of them could find the lens.

Holly went back to the kitchen with his order. As the door swung open to allow her to pass through, she saw Phil standing in front of her. There was something so arrogant about her, as though she simply didn't care what Holly was doing, or how she was attempting to be an efficient waitress in a place where she was happy, that made Holly see red. Phil was going to spoil all this for her, she saw, and she started to lose her temper.

Without caring what she was doing, or whether she could be heard in the main restaurant, she raised her voice and shouted.

'Now, don't you come round here thinking you can push me around. I'm pissed off with you and Baz both, thinking you can push me around. He doesn't own me. And you're not my boss, either, so you can't tell me what to do. You only work for Baz, same as I do.' Then the door closed behind her and shut out the low buzz of conversation in the restaurant. However, those outside could pick up the two girls' voices, if they listened attentively.

In the kitchen, Holly and Phil stood facing one another. Holly carried on, still furious, still worried that her job was at stake.

'You've got to get out of here. Leda's only popped out to the bank for a couple of minutes to pick up change for the float. I don't want her to catch you here. She'll wonder what the hell we're doing. She's not a fool.'

'Stop making a fuss. You're earning good money, aren't you? And there's hardly anyone out there in the restaurant yet, anyway.' Phil was drawling, as though she wanted Holly to lose her temper.

'Which means the ones who have come in are noticing what we're doing. The customers aren't all stupid,' said Holly, taking the grey box from Phil and slipping it into the pocket of her apron. 'Roz Ivory is in there with some woman down from London. Roz makes desserts for us, and she's an old friend of Leda's from way back. She's knocked around and she may well recognise a skimmer when she sees one for all I know.'

'*And* she's a friend of Baz,' put in Phil. 'So she's probably in on it too. He twisted her arm and she rang Leda to get you this job.'

'How do you know that?'

'Baz told me. He reckons he'll have a waitress in every restaurant in this town by the end of the month.'

'He'll get caught if he's too ambitious.'

'You're scared of *everything*. What got you into this business in the first place?'

'I needed money. I was waitressing at a place in Bristol when I met Baz and he suggested I should work for him.'

'You got a habit?'

'Maybe.'

'You're a fool.'

'I'm a fool if I keep skimming cards in this restaurant much longer.'

'We'll be moving on soon,' said Phil airily. 'Baz never stays too long in one place. And no one's caught him yet.'

'Maybe. But I'm not taking any more risks. I'm going to sort myself out so I don't need to do this any longer.'

'Then you'd better get out of Oxford. Baz won't like it if you give up on him.'

'I don't want to leave. I like it here.'

'If you work here, you work for Baz. Otherwise you have to get out.'

'I'm staying.' Holly was calming down now. 'You won't tell on me?'

'No. It's not worth the bother.'

'You have to leave now. I mean it. Leda really will be back in a minute. And I have to go and take those orders. The customers will be going spare if I leave them alone much longer.'

'You go in. I'll wait for you.'

Holly returned to the main restaurant, patting her pocket to make sure the skimmer was safely out of sight. She took out her notebook and pencil and approached Roz and Estelle's table. But a hand reached out and stopped her. It was the man reading the *Spectator*.

'I need my bill,' he said. 'Immediately.'

'If I could just take the order from the two ladies over there,' began Holly.

'No. I need it now,' he said.

'Very well.' She looked an apology across at Roz, who smiled back at her as though it was unimportant.

The man had already removed two notes from his wallet when Holly returned with his bill. 'This will cover it,' he said, thrusting them into her hand. She saw that he was giving her ten pounds to cover a bill of around eight.

'You've only had your starter,' she said. 'Didn't you like it? Don't you want to finish your meal?'

He didn't bother to reply, but rose from his chair. 'I have no time,' he said as he pushed past her and turned towards the door. To get there, he had to pass close to Roz's table and she looked up to see who was leaving in such a hurry. Their eyes met, and she saw that his were odd: one brown, one grey.

'. . . And then he punched him on the nose,' said Estelle. 'They've been banned from the restaurant ever since, of course.'

Roz joined in her companion's laughter and forgot all about the departing customer.

'All finished?' asked Viola, who was still standing by the back door.

'We'll be really busy in about five minutes' time. You'd better get going.'

'If you insist. But remember what I said.'

'You can go out the back way,' said Holly, opening the door to the yard. This had a very different image from the smart forest green of the front of house.

'Watch it with Baz,' she said, as Viola picked her way through empty crates and opened the back gate. 'I know you trust him now, but that's because you haven't seen what he's really like. He's got a nasty side to him.'

Viola lifted a hand in goodbye, or maybe acknowledging what Holly had just said. Holly watched her leave, then returned to the restaurant. She was just in time: Leda walked through the door just as she arrived at Roz and Estelle's table to take their order.

Apart from the brief interlude with her friend, she appeared to be the perfect waitress that Barry had told her about, thought Roz. She would have worried more about the scene between the two girls, since she still felt responsible for Holly's presence at Leda's, but Estelle had immediately embarked on another gossipy story about two famous authors having a row in a London restaurant that promised to be most amusing.

'Now, I saw someone yesterday eating a very attractive char-grilled feta and artichoke starter,' said Roz, running her finger down the list. 'And perhaps I'll have something fishy to follow.'

'We have some very good monkfish in today,' said Holly.

'Then I'll have that as my main course,' said Roz.

'Perhaps I'll just have a starter and one of those delicious desserts,' said Estelle. Her suit, noted Roz, was probably a size 10, and moving up to a 12 would constitute a major tragedy for her.

'You won't mind watching me eat a main course, though, will you?' said Roz. When you got to a certain age you looked better with a little flesh on your bones, she had always thought. Especially on your face. Estelle would end up looking gaunt if she wasn't careful. She must be nudging towards fifty, after all. Roz helped herself to another olive before ordering the monk-fish as well as the starter.

'We can think about desserts later,' she told Holly.

Holly took their orders out to the kitchen and handed them to Leda.

'Oh, and a few more people have filled in the cards for the

invite to the free food and wine tasting,' she said. 'Shall I collect them up for you?'

'Thanks,' said Leda. 'You can put them in the box over there on my desk. Make sure you suggest to all the customers that they fill one in. I'll send out the invitations next week, I think, to ensure they return with their friends.'

By two-thirty, as the restaurant emptied and those who had jobs to go to returned to their offices, Leda's was nearly empty. There had been another incident, as Leda was busy with late orders and Holly was serving a young couple with their dessert and coffee, when a customer in a hurry had wanted to pay his bill. Roz had gone over to help out – but hardly had she removed the folded bill and credit card when Holly was at her side.

'Here, I'll deal with that,' she said to Roz. 'You don't need to work as a waitress.' And she took the plate away from her.

'Just trying to help,' said Roz.

'You go back to your friend. I'll put the card through.' She reached across to a box on the counter. 'You take him a couple of chocolate mints to keep him happy and then I'll bring him the slip to sign.'

She turned her back on Roz and tapped figures into the machine. As Roz walked back through the door with the chocolate mints she heard the sound of the man's credit card being swiped through the reader.

'I thought we'd appreciate these more than the customer would,' she said to Estelle, setting the chocolates down and removing the gold foil from one of them. 'He's too eager to get back to work to want to eat chocolate.'

Estelle helped herself to the other one.

'There's something funny about that girl, though,' said Roz, chewing thoughtfully.

'Which one?'

'That one,' said Roz as Holly returned with the bill, card and slip for the customer to sign.

'Looks perfectly normal to me,' said Estelle. 'In fact, I was thinking how lucky Leda was to have found such an excellent waitress.'

'I do hope you're right.'

The customer had signed his credit-card slip, checked the amount, given Holly a tip, and left the restaurant, and Holly was just disappearing back into the kitchen.

Now, as the last of the lunchtime crowd returned to their offices, Estelle was killing half an hour before taking a taxi to Foreword's and Roz called to Holly that she could leave if she liked. The only other customer was a forty-something man in a creased grey suit, staring morosely into his coffee cup.

Holly appeared at their table, wearing her jacket. 'Shall I get you more coffee before I leave?' she asked them.

'I don't think so,' said Roz. 'If we need any we'll get it for ourselves.'

'I've brought your bill,' Holly said, putting it on the table next to Roz. 'If you have anything else, you can settle up with Leda.'

'Fine.'

'Bye then,' she said. 'And thanks for your help. I'll get off now.'

Since she now seemed to be the only waitress on the premises, Roz walked across and offered the last customer yet another refill of his coffee cup.

'Might as well,' he said. 'The bastard boss won't be back in his office for another hour, so why should *I* bother?'

Roz proffered milk and cream.

'Pour on the cholesterol,' he said, pointing at the cream jug. 'Bitch of a wife doesn't care if I live or die.' And he spooned in the sugar just to underline the point.

Roz left him to fur up his arteries in peace, returned the

flask of coffee to the sideboard, then placed his bill and a couple of chocolate mints on a saucer and left it by his right hand. Since he showed no sign of wanting to pay and leave, she rejoined Estelle at the corner table next to the fig tree.

'I think I'll have another brandy,' said Estelle.

Roz, who had never really wanted to be a waitress, nevertheless fetched another brandy from the bar and placed it in front of her.

'Won't you join me?'

'I'd better not,' said Roz regretfully. She couldn't even face another coffee, and she didn't think she would ever again enjoy one of her own baklavas after making so many of them.

'Excellent puddings you make,' said Estelle, on cue.

'Glad you enjoyed it.'

'Them,' said Estelle. 'I ate two.'

'Sometimes it's necessary, I've found. What's the problem?'

'A man. Isn't it always?'

'As I get older I find that money runs sex a close second.'

'The trouble is I'm always attracted to the wrong sort,' continued Estelle, not listening, and gulping down her second brandy. 'I should learn from my past mistakes, but somehow *good* men lack something, I find.'

'Danger? The ability to screw up your life?' suggested Roz.

'Sex appeal,' said Estelle.

'Perhaps they need more time to reveal their attractions,' said Roz without conviction.

Estelle's gaze was resting on the crumpled man with the cooling coffee. 'Someone like that, you mean?'

'I shouldn't think so,' said Roz. 'He looks to me as though he's about to be fired.' She left her chair, crossed the room and picked up the plate with the bill and his credit card, then disappeared behind the service door with it.

'Hey!' he called.

'Yes?'

'Bring the machine in here,' he said. He was reaching the truculent stage of drunkenness, she calculated. She brought the card and bill back. 'I don't like it when my card disappears behind those doors,' he said darkly. 'You don't know what's being done to it.'

'Come to the door and watch,' said Roz. 'The machine's attached to the phone line, but I have no intention of doing anything illegal with it.'

So he shuffled across to the kitchen door and watched her every move as Roz dealt with his card.

'OK? It's quite safe, you see,' she said, handing the voucher back to be signed.

The man took his card and the slips of paper and blundered out of the restaurant.

'I don't know what he expected me to do with it!' she said to Estelle as she sat down again. 'And he didn't even leave a tip.'

Neil aimed to get to Viola's flat by two-thirty. This would give her time to return home after her shift ended. He just hoped she wasn't going to go wandering round the shops or visiting a friend. She'd be tired, he told himself. Her feet would be killing her. She'd want to get back to her flat and put her feet up. She'd probably be watching daytime television.

That's what he would do, anyway.

It was possible that she had a lover in the flat, waiting for her. But the flat had been empty the time he followed her there, he was sure of that. There were no lights on until she entered and switched them on.

He wasn't sure what he'd do if she didn't turn up by two-thirty. He really had to be back at the office for three-thirty, when Estelle Livingstone was due to arrive. He could afford to stay until three-fifteen, he calculated, if he took a taxi back to the office. In forty-five minutes he ought to be able to find out what he needed to know.

Amanda wasn't at her desk when he left Foreword. He stopped at a pub on the way down to Viola's flat, ate a sandwich, and then ordered a double brandy to give himself the courage to confront her. When he'd drunk it, he ordered another, just to be sure. Then he walked down to her block of flats. It was nearly twenty to three when he arrived.

To his surprise, the entrance doors were propped open. He had expected some form of security and had worked out a simple plan for persuading another resident to let him in. He crossed the lobby and walked up the stairs, moving quietly, trying to look normal. His heart was thudding. Supposed she denied everything? Laughed at him?

He reached the door on the second floor belonging to the flat he reckoned was hers. He was about to ring the bell (there was no name card next to it), when he saw that the door was ajar. He rang anyway.

Nothing happened. No sound of footsteps. He pushed the door wider and called, 'Hello! Viola! Are you there?' The words sounded ridiculous, even to himself. He dithered in the entrance for a minute or two. Maybe she'd gone out for some cigarettes, or to take her dog for a walk – but, why leave the door open? This was quite a nice part of Oxford, but not a place where you would leave your door ajar when you went out, or even when you stayed at home. He took a couple of tentative steps inside.

He was in a tiny hallway. To his right was another door, closed. In front of him a second door stood ajar. There was a light on. He knocked on that door, too, listened to the silence, and went in.

18

'Kate?'

'Yes, Emma. Have you spoken to the children? How did it go?'

'It was a disaster. Hugo and Abigail both went into their defensive, "you're always accusing me of something" routine. Abigail flounced out of the room and has been sulking upstairs ever since. Every time I go to use the phone I find she's telephoned one of her friends on the extension and they're deep in a discussion about the awfulness of their respective parents. Hugo has glued his headphones to his ears and refuses to listen to a word I say. And Sam Junior won't even let me use his computer any more.'

'So you're not asking me what to do next?'

'Certainly not!'

Kate had the impression that the disarray in the Dolby household was all her fault. 'But you'd still like me to sit for you this evening?'

There was a pause, and then a more conciliatory Emma said, 'Yes. Please. Thank you.'

'I'll see you at seven.'

Estelle arrived at Foreword Publishing on the dot of three-forty, just to show Neil Orson that he wasn't the only one who could keep a person waiting. She wouldn't keep him waiting longer than ten minutes, however, since as an editor he would always be useful. She signed in at reception, pinned her Visitor's Card as unobtrusively as possible to her jacket, and took the lift up to the fourth floor where the senior editors had their offices.

She smiled at Neil's Editorial Assistant, who appeared to be annotating a manuscript, and passed through into his office. Neil rose from behind the desk and walked across to greet her.

'Estelle! Sorry to have rescheduled like this. It's so kind of you to have come. Do come in and sit down. What can we get you? Amanda, please bring us some coffee.'

Estelle was shocked by his appearance. Whatever it was that Neil Orson had had to deal with instead of lunching with her had affected the poor man badly. His face was pale, with a red blotch high on each cheekbone. There were dark rings beneath his eyes and although he was as well-dressed as ever, he gave the impression somehow of being dishevelled. As she leaned across to kiss the air on either side of his face, she caught the whiff of brandy. And then she remembered that she must be giving off fumes of white wine, and brandy, too. But I have a perfectly good reason, she told herself. Anyone who is kept waiting for four hours is entitled to the odd alcoholic drink.

He showed her to the most comfortable seat, an armchair by the window. He sat in another low chair next to her and poured the coffee when it arrived. His hand was shaking, noticed Estelle. She did hope that he didn't have a drink problem. That would be too exasperating, just when she'd found an editor willing to take on at least two of her authors.

She watched him drink his own coffee (black, with three sugars, she noted) and he seemed to pull himself together. He brought out the manuscript she'd sent him and said some very kind things about it. And then he made her an offer. It was considerably more than she had been expecting and she didn't even pretend that someone else was interested. She agreed to pass the offer on to her author immediately on her return to London and get back to him as soon as it was accepted. She expected no difficulties *whatsoever* with her author, she assured him.

They went on to discuss what he and Foreword were looking for in new fiction, and Estelle attempted to shoehorn some of her unsold manuscripts into this mould. Neil's attention wasn't fully on what she was telling him, Estelle felt, but she didn't show her annoyance.

When they finally said goodbye, and Neil had called a taxi to take her to the station, she had the impression that he was relieved to see her go. But that couldn't have been the case, surely?

A couple of hours later, on the way home from the tube station, she stopped off at Oddbins and bought herself a very nice bottle of Pouilly Fumé. She felt she'd deserved it.

Kate Ivory presented herself at Sam and Emma Dolby's front door just before seven o'clock that evening. She might have known it was a mistake to be early: Emma was still in her underwear, wondering what to put on and Sam was endeavouring to keep the children out of her way while she made her decision.

'Where's that tunic top?' asked Kate, flicking through the packed clothes in Emma's wardrobe. 'And your smart trousers?'

Fifteen minutes later, Emma was dressed, and looking only slightly rumpled. Kate had attacked her hair, borrowing Abigail's mousse, styling wax and hairdryer to do so. She had also insisted that Emma remove her comfortable shoes and wear something sexier, even if they did make her feet hurt.

'Wow!' said Sam, when he saw his wife, so Kate knew she'd succeeded in Emma's transformation.

'I've written out a list of their bedtimes,' said Emma, handing across a couple of sheets of A4. 'And also a list of what they should all be doing for the next couple of hours. Make sure that Hugo and Abigail get on with their homework, but don't let them con you into doing it for them.'

'I doubt I could,' said Kate truthfully.

'Flora's fed, bathed, changed and is asleep in her cot. She probably won't wake up until the early hours of the morning. If she *does* wake, just talk soothingly to her, or rearrange her blankets, and she'll go off again. The most you'll need to do is sing her back to sleep. The little ones have eaten, cleaned their teeth and had their baths. You'll need to read them a story and tuck them up in bed. Resist demands for drinks of water – they only do it to get your attention. The older ones may need to be nagged to go to bed at a reasonable hour. They'll try to persuade you it's too early, but take no notice.'

'Fine. I think I'm following all this. What about Sam Junior?'

'He's in his room, playing with his computer. He feels he's above the rest of them and refuses to join in anything. I can't even persuade him to play Scrabble with us these days. But if you could just check that his light goes out by ten-thirty, I'd be grateful.'

'OK. You and Sam get off now. I'll cope. Don't worry.'

'I've left a list of emergency numbers by the phone,' said Emma doubtfully. 'Though you'll probably have to yell at Sam Junior if you need to use one of them. That boy's permanently connected to the Internet as far as I can tell.'

'Probably time to give him his own line,' said Kate.

She was glad to see that Emma looked quite cheerful as she

188

left the house with Sam. When had she last had an evening off, she wondered. Then she turned to the lists that Emma had left her and started to identify those children who were still young enough to be read to at bedtime.

Viola Grant's body was discovered at seven-fifteen that evening by the middle-aged couple who lived on the same floor of the block of flats.

The husband had noticed that her front door was ajar when he arrived home from work at six-twenty. Later, when his wife was putting out the empty milk bottles, she remarked that it was still ajar, and after a short discussion they agreed that they should investigate.

They had seen enough crime dramas on the television to know that there was something very wrong as soon as they ventured inside the flat.

'It was the smell,' Jenny Power said. 'I knew it was fresh blood. We just stood at the door of the living room and looked. We didn't go inside. We could see from there that she must be dead.'

'She'd been dead for some hours, apparently,' said Dan Power. 'I blame myself. I should have taken a look when I first noticed that her door was open, but you don't like to intrude, do you?'

'We're not the sort to push ourselves into the neighbours' lives,' said Jenny Power.

That evening, Leda's had its most profitable session to date.

Word of mouth, thought Leda, fitting another fifty-pound note into the till. That's what it's about. Send out a happy customer and he'll go away and tell half a dozen of his friends about us.

Holly pushed her way past her and through the door to the kitchen. Leda couldn't warm to the girl – it was something about that very pale skin and the impression she gave of being made of strawberry-flavoured marshmallows, soft and yet rubbery. Yet she was a really good waitress. Leda must remember to thank Roz for the recommendation next time she saw her. The girl hadn't even grumbled about the wages; she'd just set about being efficient and ingratiating. No, Leda admonished herself, you really should call her manner 'pleasant'. 'Ingratiating' has a pejorative ring to it. She must have earned herself a small fortune in tips.

She walked through the swing door into the kitchen, where Holly was piling bowls of desserts on to a tray, pausing to make sure they were attractively arranged. Leda touched her lightly on the arm. 'Well done, Holly,' she said warmly. 'You're doing really well.' She believed in encouraging the staff. They worked better if they felt appreciated, she'd always found. And she didn't have to like the girl, after all; she only had to work with her.

By ten o'clock, Kate Ivory was exhausted. Emma's youngest children were really very sweet, and had expressed their delight at her hammy reading of their bedtime books, but Abigail and Hugo had clamoured for help over their homework. She could see that they were both over-dramatising their difficulties and reminded herself that it was just attention-seeking. And anyway, she tried to explain to them, she was really no good at all at science or maths.

Finally she persuaded them to go to bed. She wasn't sure that they actually cleaned their teeth or washed their faces, but by this time she didn't think it mattered. When she'd loaded the dishwasher and cleared up the mess they'd left behind in the large family kitchen, she poured herself a glass of the white wine she found in a box in the fridge and retired to the sitting room. As she sat back in the sofa with her eyes closed, she thought that she had never heard the Dolbys' house so quiet. That at least had to be some sort of achievement. And now she could watch television or listen to some music for half an hour before she had to check on Sam Junior.

At ten-thirty, Kate climbed to the top of the house and approached Sam's door. Sure enough, there was a line of light around the frame. Not having Emma's sensibilities, she rapped smartly and then walked in. Sam, as expected, was sitting at his desk and staring at the computer screen.

'Hi, Sam!' she said.

He looked up, surprised. No one ever walked into his room like that.

From where she stood, it certainly didn't look as though the site he had found was a pornographic one. Which was a relief, thought Kate. She moved across so that she could look over his shoulder.

'Hey! That's interesting!' she said. 'Have you got much more of this?'

'Quite a bit,' mumbled Sam.

'Can I see?'

Sam, who had after all been brought up by Emma to be polite and well-behaved, however hard he attempted to hide it under adolescent rudeness, found it difficult to oppose someone as determined as Kate.

'What got you interested in this?' she asked, looking down the pages he handed her.

'You know Emma's been going ballistic about some un-authorised charge on her credit card?'

'Yes, she told me about it.'

'She's been blaming me for it, I know.'

'No. She believed you when you denied it. I think it's Abigail and Hugo she suspects at the moment.'

'They had nothing to do with it, either. It had to be some kind of scam, so I started to look into it.'

'I hadn't realised that Internet fraud was so widespread,' Kate said. 'The ten quid or so that Emma's been charged looks like peanuts compared to the other stuff you've turned up.'

'As a matter of fact, it's these tiny sums, multiplied a few hundred thousand times, that are the really big earners,' said Sam. 'You see, what you do is, you set up a fraudulent merchant company, and charge people a subscription to something they don't want and haven't asked for. By the time the credit-card companies catch up with you, you've cleared a million dollars or so. Then you close down and start up again under a different name. It's all so slow-moving, you've made your money before they've found you out. And no one wants to blow whistles because we'd all get scared and never use a credit card, or buy stuff over the Net, ever again.'

'What's this about off-shore trust funds?'

'You need a bit more capital than I've got at the moment to set one of those up,' said Sam.

'I'm glad to hear it. Let's have a look at the piece with pictures of golden sands and waving palm trees.'

Realising that he had an appreciative audience for his work, Sam passed across the relevant pages. Kate threw a pile of folders on to the floor and found herself a place to sit down. This is what she read:

Nauru (pronounced *na-oo´-roo*) is the world's smallest republic. It is an oval-shaped blob, some 8 square miles in area, sitting in the South Pacific Basin, about 2,500 miles north-east of Sydney. For about a hundred years Nauru's economy was based on the export of phosphate rock. Now that phosphate mining has wiped out four-fifths of the land area and left the central plateau barren and infertile, the government of this tiny republic is finding other ways of maintaining its prosperity. Nauruans are the richest people in the Pacific, and they want to stay that way.

Health, education and social services are all free. Nauru imposes no taxes: no income tax, death duties, corporation tax. It has signed no income-tax treaties with other nations. In addition, the island has silver beaches, coconut palms and brilliant blue sea. Before you book your one-way ticket to this paradise, however, you should know that foreigners may not purchase land, visas are virtually unobtainable, and no one will answer your letter of enquiry if you apply for one. Oh, and the local transport is terrible.

So why should you be interested in Nauru? Well, you can set up a company there for a few hundred US dollars. It will take two days. No one need know the names of the directors, nor those of the owners, since these details need not even be reported to the Nauruan authorities, let alone anyone else.

It will interest you to know, no doubt, that there are no exchange controls: all major currencies can be deposited on Nauru and then shipped out again, either in the same currency or converted to any other that suits your fancy. And if you set up a trust to own the shares of your company, then none of your creditors will be able to get their hands on your assets if ever you find yourself in financial difficulties, or the divorce court, and there will be no taxes to be paid after your death. Or perhaps you would find it useful to start up your own bank? You could open an in-house bank to deal with your own companies, or set up a finance company to broaden your banking activities. How much would this cost you? About US\$25,000. Peanuts, in other words. And it would take you about two months.

'Do you think I could have a copy of this?' asked Kate.

'Why? Are you thinking of going into the money-laundering business?'

'Not personally. But I may know a man who is.'

Sam pressed the Print key. While they were waiting, he looked at her with more interest than he had shown before.

'You know some interesting people, don't you?' he said.

'One or two.'

'I don't always want to be living this boring life, you know.'

'I hope you're not thinking of taking to a life of crime. Your parents might be quite upset if you did.'

'Sam and Emma are boring.'

'No, they're not. They're . . . they're . . .' Kate had been about to say that they were educated and hard-working and had well-developed social consciences, but she could see that Sam would translate those qualities as 'boring'. 'You wouldn't like it much if they just took off and left you all to fend for yourselves,' she said. 'Or if they lived selfish, self-absorbed lives. You like to open the fridge and find food and a monster pack of Coke inside it. I'm sure your cupboards are crammed with clean, ironed T-shirts and matched pairs of socks. When you go to the bathroom cabinet there's a family-size pack of Andrex.'

'Tesco's Economy,' corrected Sam.

'Whatever.'

'Yeah. I know what you're saying. But I still don't want to turn out like them.'

'I don't suppose you will. But you don't have to throw over all their values to live a more exciting life.'

'Yeah. I suppose.' He didn't sound totally convinced about it. Still, who needed to be respectable and boring at the age of fifteen? Respectability was the Dolbys' family motto and Sam Junior would doubtless grow to see its attractions when he was older. She didn't think Emma had anything to worry about, but she wouldn't be passing this conversation on to her.

She asked Sam to turn his light off within the next fifteen minutes and returned downstairs to her glass of wine. Just before she closed the living-room door, she thought she heard the sound of teeth being vigorously brushed

Sam Dolby and Kate Ivory might have had no more than an academic interest in Nauru's possibilities, but Fabian West is very interested in them indeed.

Fabian West has lost weight during the past few months. His luxuriant chestnut-brown hair has been cut close to his head so that his widow's peak is more pronounced, his eyes appear deeper-set and his nose more thrusting. The fat has dissolved away from muscle and bone, leaving the skin of his face hanging in bloodhound folds. There are deep grooves running from mouth to chin, and his heavy jowls underline the canine impression. His clothes are different, too. Not quite as citified, perhaps not quite as expensive as they used to be, though smarter, cut closer to his slimmer form. His suit is lighter in weight and in style, and makes him look less formidable than the Fabian West of last year. Though his skin is still a clear pink, as though he has just returned from a brisk walk, his eyes have the same dead, unforgiving expression as ever. His nails are manicured, shaped to a shallow oval and polished with a leather buffer. He wears a heavy gold signet ring on the little finger of his left hand.

At first glance you would take him for a stockbroker, or a fashionable dentist perhaps, looking forward to an afternoon on the golf links. But it is always wise not to underestimate this man.

When Fabian slipped away from the mansion in Worcestershire where he had been overseeing the production of forged Euros, he had taken with him a certain amount of capital in the form of easily portable items, designed to be carried in the lightest of luggage in the event of just such an emergency. He still regretted the money invested in the house and grounds. With the increase in property prices over the last year he would have shown a very healthy profit if he had had time to sell it, but he hadn't fancied the idea of a jail term, or even the indignity of a trial, so he had moved away from Lower Grooms and into a less opulent identity, discarding 'Fabian West' like an old glove.

He had moved first to London, changing his name and his appearance. In fact, unless you looked carefully, no one who had known Fabian West last year would recognise him in his current guise. There wasn't much he could do about his voice and accent. He had developed them in his teens and wasn't prepared to ditch the gentlemanly tones, now that they were no longer fashionable, for something cruder. However, he wore dark brown lenses to even out the odd colour of his eyes.

After London, he hadn't stayed in any one place (or even in one name) for very long, leaving a confusing trail of different aliases and addresses behind him, across the breadth of the Midlands. Several of these identities he had subsequently found useful, and had kept. It was always handy to have a choice of bank accounts and credit cards if you needed to disappear in a hurry. He wouldn't get caught by using his 'Fabian West' credit card in a cash dispenser or a motorway petrol station. That sort of mistake was for amateurs.

But now he no longer worried about hiding and moving on. Unless he was unlucky, and by some fluke was recognised by a policeman who had come close to him in the past and happened to have a very good memory for faces, it was unlikely that anyone would trace him to his current domicile. He had bought a small Victorian cottage in a village a little south of Wantage, in Oxfordshire. The village wasn't full of nosy old women or suspicious rural types. The houses were now much too expensive for the locals to buy and most of them were occupied by professional couples who commuted to London or Reading. They had no time or interest in finding out about their new neighbours. These were too busy fitting gas-fired Agas into their remodelled kitchens, and removing their front lawns to provide room for the second Range Rover, to show any interest in a dull, middle-aged newcomer with a forgettable name.

Fabian kept a low profile. He travelled to London or Oxford when he grew tired of the rural views from his windows and wished to spend some money. He still appreciated good food, although he no longer over-indulged himself in it, and occasionally ate in Oxford.

He had put the abortive forgery operation behind him and concentrated on new enterprises. His most recent business dealings promised an even greater reward, and the work he needed to put into them was correspondingly greater. But Fabian had never been afraid of hard work, as long as it resulted in a fatter bank balance and an increase in power over others.

He had, of course, made use of Nauru's facilities. There were around eighteen banks established to service the island's population of approximately 11,000. After Fabian West discovered the advantages Nauru had to offer, the number of banks increased to nineteen. The number of companies incorporated there also increased, as did the number of trusts. Anyone who investigated the properties which Fabian West owned, and indeed those in which he occasionally resided, might well find that they actually belonged to a trust originating in Nauru. Fabian West's name appeared nowhere in the trust's records.

Most of these efforts of Fabian's were aimed at covering his tracks so that even when a crime was discovered, it would be impossible to trace it back to him. He realised that the world was moving on and that some people might consider him middle-aged or, even worse, old. The financial aspects of his new operation he could deal with, but he was having to recruit staff to cover the technical side.

He hadn't been sorry to lose the cruder elements in his organisation that he had been forced to work with before – the heavies who had dealt with people who got in his way. Now, if he wanted to reprimand a rival, or even to remove them from the scene, he didn't need to do anything physical. He could ruin them financially and watch them disappear as surely as if they'd been dropped into a gravel pit with a bullet in their head and a lump of concrete chained to their boots.

Jamie Bates was in his twenties when he first met Fabian West, but he still had an unformed, schoolboyish appearance, and could be taken for seventeen or so. Fabian noticed with approval that he had the pale face, underdeveloped physique and incipient pot belly of the serious computer enthusiast. Fabian liked to employ people who were enthusiastic about their work rather than those who had to be chivvied or cajoled into doing it.

In fact, Jamie had started in his early teens as a hacker, hardly bothering with school and not at all with university, so fascinated was he by the enthralling world of the Internet. *La belle dame sans merci/Thee hath in thrall*. Keats can't have been writing about the Net, of course, but he'd have recognised the zonked expression on Jamie's face after a dedicated night at the keyboard and mouse.

By the time he was in his twenties, Jamie was making a fair living at various Internet scams. It was the latest of these that led him to Fabian.

Fabian was staying in a small flat, at a distance from London, and under one of his many pseudonyms, when the phone rang and a young voice informed him that he had unknowingly entered the Canadian national lottery – and won. The sum Jamie mentioned was 400,000 Canadian dollars.

Fabian West had spent many more years than Jamie in separating the innocent from their money, and he declined to pass on to him the number of his credit card, so that the tax due might be paid (4,000 Canadian dollars was the amount required) and the balance of his winnings then released and sent to Fabian.

He did like the sound of the confident young voice, though, and with a little judicious questioning he found out the extent of Jamie's capabilities – which just happened to chime with Fabian's needs at that time. Before the end of their conversation Fabian had proposed a meeting, and the possibility of Jamie's being offered a job with Fabian's organisation. He had scarcely needed to point out the consequences if Jamie failed to accept the exciting challenge that was being offered to him.

19

Viola's death coincided with an obscenely expensive charity garden party, hosted by a rock star and his Supermodel wife, and attended by every A-list celebrity, so it didn't make the national newspapers. She did make the front page of the *Oxford Mail*, however, with more extensive coverage in Friday's *Oxford Times*.

Few people read the report and remembered who she was. Her neighbours hardly knew her, even by sight, and she seemed to have had few friends. It was inevitable, therefore, that people's attention was drawn to the restaurant where she worked as a waitress. One reporter was heard to remark that it was the best coverage Chez Édith was ever likely to receive. It was also inevitable that the other employees at that restaurant were asked for their opinions and observations by the local press, Radio Oxford and *South Today*. They were also interviewed by the police, but this was less exciting for them.

As a result of these interviews, items appeared under headlines like 'Was Slaughtered Waitress Stalked by Man with Staring Eyes?'. One enterprising press man even persuaded an artist to produce a drawing of the man who had been seen following Viola Grant on several occasions, based on the descriptions given by eye-witnesses.

In the offices of Foreword Publishing, Amanda looked at the drawing and laughed. 'He looks just like you, Neil!'

Neil Orson looked over her shoulder. 'Excuse me,' he said, and disappeared through the door. 'Not feeling very well,' he called behind him.

Amanda was left remembering how he had returned from lunch the day of Viola's death (she checked in the diary – it was the day that he postponed his appointment with Estelle Livingstone), looking just as wild and staring-eyed as the maniac in the newspaper. She mentioned it to Ben from Marketing and Zoe from Publicity while they poured boiling water on to teabags in the staff kitchen.

'I remarked on it at the time,' she said. 'He looked so pale I asked him if he was going down with a virus.' She was enjoying the unwonted attention. General opinion usually judged Amanda to be as dull and virtuous as her boss.

'Always thought there was more to our Neil than met the eye,' said Zoe. 'No one could really be that boring, could they?'

'I wonder where he went at lunchtime,' said Amanda. 'He was supposed to be meeting Estelle Livingstone, but he stood her up. He never did tell me why. Funny, isn't it?'

'Maybe you should ask him. See if he looks guilty. Maybe he'll confess to a life of crime,' said Ben.

'But we're not serious, are we? This is Little Bear we're talking about, after all,' said Zoe. 'He's the man who irons his jeans every morning and dumped a girlfriend because he discovered that she smoked. Harmless Neil.'

'I suppose that's what everyone says about a murderer. You don't imagine that anyone you know could possibly do such a thing. But murderers have friends and families, colleagues and clients,' said Ben.

'He went off to be sick in the loo when I showed him the drawing in the paper,' said Amanda, who wasn't averse to a little exaggeration.

'Maybe we should tell someone about it,' said Ben.

'Like who?' asked Zoe.

They looked at each other.

'The choice seems to be between the police, the newspaper and Roland Ives,' said Ben.

The ten minutes they allowed themselves for a tea break were over, and they returned to their respective offices without reaching any decision about the matter.

Kate Ivory saw the drawing in the paper, too, while she was looking to see what houses were for sale. She showed it to Roz.

'My editor,' she said, pointing. 'That's what he looks like after reading the latest unsolicited manuscript.'

'Really? I thought it looked just like the warden of an Oxford college.' They both laughed. Then Roz picked up the paper. 'I hadn't read this story properly before.'

'A young woman was battered to death in her flat,' Kate told her mother. 'She worked as a waitress in one of those small restaurants at the back of the High Street. No one seems to know much about her apart from that, and they haven't come up with a reason for her murder, either. I expect they'll find that it was her boyfriend in the end.'

Roz was staring at the photo at the bottom of the page. It was only a small one, and looked as though it had been taken from a driving licence or passport.

'I think I saw her the other day,' she said. 'She came into Leda's and spoke to the waitress there.'

'When was that?'

'I forget. But it was the day I met your agent, Estelle.'

'I didn't know she was back in Oxford. Why didn't she phone me?'

'She was having lunch with an editor – maybe your Neil Orson – and he'd stood her up. She had three or four hours to kill, so we killed them together over a bottle of wine and a good meal.'

'Then you toured the colleges and visited the museums together, I assume?'

'I don't think Estelle is very hot on culture. She's better at scurrilous gossip and making heavy inroads into a bottle of Pinot Grigio.'

'I can see you have a lot in common,' said Kate. 'But I do think you should try to remember which day it was.'

'It must have been near the beginning of the week. Leda had enough of my sticky pastries left so I didn't have to slave over ground almonds that afternoon, I remember. Let's say it was Tuesday.'

'In which case you saw Viola Grant, the waitress, just a few hours before she died.'

'Let me read that report again. I didn't take it all in.' When she had run through the account again, she agreed with Kate. 'We must have seen her very shortly before she died. In fact, if she went straight back to her flat after speaking to Holly, we were the last people to see her alive before she was murdered.'

'I think you should go to the police, don't you?'

'No,' said Roz firmly. 'I know nothing about her. I can't help them find her murderer, can I?'

And Kate couldn't budge her. Roz was as obstinate as any of Emma's teenagers. Well, if the police did come knocking on Neil's door, accusing him of being the Stalker, she'd frog-march Roz down to St Aldate's herself. She didn't think it very likely, though. Viola Grant was probably murdered by her boyfriend, whoever he might be. Wasn't that the usual way of it? And anyway, she did see Roz's point. She might waste hours of time down at the police station and it all added up to nothing new.

'What are you doing this weekend?' asked Roz, changing the subject.

'Moving into Faith's house. Had you forgotten?'

'Not really. Do you want me to give you a hand?' she asked as Kate rose to leave.

'That would be kind. There's not much to do, since I have only two suitcases, but you can help to make my bedroom look like home.'

'Are you sure you're doing the right thing, moving in with Faith Beeton?'

'I'll survive. It's very conveniently placed, so near the centre. And since I'm paying rent I can feel independent.'

'Give me a call when you get tired of it,' said Roz. 'I could use a lodger at the moment, too.'

'Thanks.' It was comforting to think that her mother had offered her a room before she asked for it.

Neil Orson bought a copy of the paper on his way home. He opened it when he had let himself into his flat and laid it flat on the table, under a strong light bulb. His likeness stared up at him, maniac's eyes bulging. He read the report that went with the drawing, about the colleagues of Viola's who had noticed him following her that first evening. The drawing was an exaggeration, certainly, nearly a cari-cature, but he had obviously made an impression on them, and they had remembered what he looked like remarkably accurately.

Was it too late to go to the police?

Did they take this sort of report seriously?

Wouldn't it be better to ignore it until something more concrete turned up? Surely no one except Amanda really believed that it looked just like him?

Next day came a further report in the local paper. Jenny and Dan Power had both seen a man who looked remarkably like the drawing of the maniac who was stalking Viola. They had seen him late one night, standing outside the flats and staring up at her window. They had forgotten all about it until the picture in the paper reminded them. They had thought at the time that he looked a little strange and had wondered about asking him what he was doing there. But he had walked away before they had time to do anything about it. And anyway, they hadn't liked to cause a fuss.

You made that bit up, thought Neil. You just walked past me and into the block of flats without giving me a second thought. It was true, he remembered, that they had stared hard at him before doing so.

The Powers added the fact that the man was oddly dressed, in a baggy dark suit, they thought, with a vest or T-shirt underneath, like one of the homeless men you saw drinking British sherry in Bonn Square. Neil remembered that the suit was one his favourites, with a very faint pinstripe, and the polo-neck was grey. He had never tasted British sherry in his life. He was so annoyed that he felt like ringing the paper and telling them how inaccurate the Powers' account was, but conceded that this would be unwise.

There was a note at the bottom of this second report. The police had provided a phone number which readers could call – without even giving their name, if that was what they wanted – and tell them who they believed The Stalker was.

The question of whether to go to the police was becoming more urgent. It would obviously look very bad for him if he was identified and questioned before he did so. But The Stalker was becoming such a solid figure, and one so unlike Neil himself that he was less and less willing to tell anyone that he was the man who had followed Viola and waited for her outside her flat. Once his own identity had been stolen, he argued with himself, it became increasingly difficult to prove who he really was. He wasn't a maniac, or a stalker. He was quiet, good-natured Neil Orson, who always meant to go to the gym and lose the layer of fat around his waist, who allowed strong-minded women to manipulate him and then drop him when they grew bored. He worked conscientiously at his job. He didn't cheat on his expenses. He liked dogs, and spoke to his houseplants, and gave money to buskers. He was a *good* man. But who would believe him now?

Coming from London, where people take it for granted that they are anonymous, Neil had forgotten that Oxford is a small town. The centre, in particular, consists of just a mile of so of crowded streets. Walk up St Aldate's, turn into Cornmarket, then stroll along the Broad to Blackwell's or the Bodleian, and you will bump into half a dozen friends or acquaintances. You will catch sight of the receptionist from your doctor's surgery, the girl who works the photocopier at the office, the retired vicar who lives in the next street to you, the man who fixed your roof last winter. You will recognise the beggars and buskers. You may even know them by name. If your picture – even if it *is* a caricature – is in the local newspaper, someone will recognise you. Someone will telephone the police.

'I don't know his name, but he works in that new office block just past Gloucester Green,' was what the woman in the newsagent's told the police.

Eventually, a policeman will come and check this out,

together with the thirty-eight other reports of The Stalker that the police have received from different parts of the city.

When Constable Mundy, from Thames Valley Police, entered Foreword House, walked up to the desk and asked Valerie Peters, the receptionist, whether she recognised the man in the drawing, she said, 'Mr Orson,' straight away.

'I thought it looked like him,' she said. 'But you never really think it's going to be someone you know, do you?'

'It probably isn't,' said Constable Mundy. 'But we have to check these things out.'

Valerie gave him his Visitor's badge, phoned for Amanda to accompany him in the lift to the fourth floor, and then wondered who to phone first with the exciting news.

'You won't talk about this, of course,' said Constable Mundy while he was waiting for Neil's assistant to fetch him. 'You wouldn't want any false rumours to start flying around, would you?'

'Of course not,' said Valerie. But did she really have to wait for The Stalker's identity to be confirmed before letting everyone know that she had been the first to hear about it?

If Neil was honest with himself, he had been expecting this visit since the first time he had seen his picture in Amanda's newspaper. He had denied the possibility to himself, of course, and now he denied any knowledge of Viola Grant to Constable Mundy.

He composed his face into as bland a mask as possible. He smoothed down his hair just before Amanda showed Constable Mundy into his office. (The Stalker had wild, upstanding hair.) He gave the policeman the comfortable chair and sat down in the other, just as he had when Estelle Livingstone came to the office.

'How can I help you?' he asked. And he made sure that his voice was low and measured and held not a hint of hysteria. He tried to relax the muscles around his eyes so that they didn't bulge, but wasn't sure he was successful.

No, he didn't know Viola Grant. (True enough.) He had never been to the restaurant where she worked. Never eaten there. (That was true, too.) He was new to Oxford, had only lived here for a few months, so he wasn't familiar with St Ebbe's, or the houses and flats along by the canal. Yes, he had been house-hunting, but not in that area.

'And have you sorted out the problem you had when you came in to see us a couple of weeks ago?' Constable Mundy had done his homework.

'I took your advice and I've contacted the bank and finance houses. It's taking time, but it will soon be sorted,' said Neil with far more confidence than he felt. 'Is that all?' he asked, since the policeman continued to sit in his comfortable chair and look at him as though expecting Neil to tell him something interesting. 'I read about the poor girl and I hope you find her killer, but I'm afraid I know nothing at all about her death.'

'Just one more thing, sir. Can you tell me where you were that afternoon, from say, noon onwards?'

'I was here,' said Neil quickly. Then added belatedly, 'It was Tuesday, wasn't it?'

'That's right, sir. And you didn't leave the building at all between what, nine in the morning and five in the afternoon?'

'About nine-thirty until six o'clock or so,' said Neil.

'What about lunch? I suppose your secretary bought you a sandwich.'

'Amanda's an Editorial Assistant,' amended Neil. 'We don't have secretaries these days, you know. I'm not sure she did, actually. I had an appointment here with an agent at three-thirty and I just popped out for a sandwich and a mineral water in the pub at lunchtime. I'm sorry, I'd forgotten about that.'

'Which pub?'

'I think it was called The Old Tom,' said Neil. 'Perhaps they'll remember me there.' But if they did, they could well remember that it was brandy he was drinking, not mineral water, and that he stayed barely ten minutes.

'It's not very near to this office, is it, sir?'

'A brisk five-minute walk. I like to take some exercise at lunchtime.'

If Constable Mundy considered that five minutes was pushing it, he didn't mention the fact. 'Are you a regular there, sir?'

'No. I'm not a great one for pubs.'

'Then I doubt they will remember you.' He looked at Neil for a few moments, and Neil imagined the barman recalling a maniac with wild hair and staring eyes, drinking double brandies and swallowing down a ham sandwich. The thought made him push his hands through his own hair.

'Is that all?' he asked. 'I have a manuscript to edit and I should be getting on with it.'

'For the present,' said Constable Mundy, and left, his face as unreadable as when he arrived.

Neil Orson would have been more worried than ever if he had checked his appearance in the mirror in his executive bathroom: his eyes were staring and his hair, now in need of a cut, was standing up from his head. He looked just like the drawing of him in the newspaper.

Amanda offered to take Constable Mundy back downstairs in the lift. The policeman stood in silence while they were waiting for it to arrive, so that Amanda felt compelled to make conversation.

'I expect Neil, Mr Orson, told you that he knew Viola Grant, didn't he?' She couldn't think why she blurted this out, but it had been on her mind since she read the account of the waitress's murder.

Constable Mundy said, 'Mm,' which could have meant, 'Yes,' or possibly, 'No.'

'At least, everybody was talking about the phone message she'd left for him, so he must have done.'

'Mm?'

The lift was sighing to a halt at the fourth floor, and Amanda waited till they were inside and gliding towards the ground floor before saying, 'The note said: "Stop following me around and piss off out of my life. Viola." And Viola's not a very common name, is it? Not for someone young, anyway.'

'How do you know this Viola was young?'

'Zoe in Publicity took the message and she assumed it was his girlfriend.'

'It's all very vague, isn't it?' said Constable Mundy. 'I think it would be best to keep these ideas about Mr Orson to yourselves for the moment.'

'Maybe she didn't approve of his drinking,' said Amanda, piqued that her information wasn't being taken as seriously as she had hoped.

'Drinking?'

'He came in with a dreadful hangover one morning. Everyone noticed it. And he took me to the pub one evening after work. I'm sure it was an excuse because he didn't want to sit there on his own. I was drinking tonic water,' said Amanda virtuously, forgetting that she had ordered a vodka to go in it. 'But Neil was drinking double whiskies.'

'Sounds reasonable,' said Constable Mundy dismissively. He was so dismissive that she didn't tell him about the state

Neil was in when he came back from lunch that day. And Constable Mundy stepped from the lift, returned his Visitor's badge to reception and left the building.

If Amanda was disappointed by his response to her revelations, she wouldn't have been if she had read the report Constable Mundy put in when he returned to the station.

'Kate?'

'Yes. You found me then, Emma.'

'You sent Sam an e-mail with your latest address, remember? And isn't it time you found yourself a permanent place to live? It can't be good for your work, surely.'

'Or for my character? It's encouraging me to be raffish and irresponsible, you think?'

'You said it, not me.' Emma always managed to sound like someone's mother. Of course, she *was* mother to a large number of children, so she would find it easy to slip into the role. But even if she sometimes pretended to object, Kate found it quite comforting to have such a figure in her life: someone who had high expectations of her, after all. Roz had somehow never filled this role very convincingly, even when Kate was a child.

'Actually, Emma, I'm now staying with someone even more respectable than a headmistress. I've rented a room in Faith Beeton's house in St Clement's. Faith is a Fellow at Bartlemas. She's even Dean of Women Students this year, in charge of the morals of a couple of hundred volatile young females.'

'Don't overdo it, Kate.'

'You're sounding much more cheerful, by the way. Quite back to your old self. Your evening out must have done you good. I'll babysit for you again one of these evenings if you like.'

'Thanks. That would be terrific. But it's more than that. Do you remember our little trouble with the credit-card charges?'

'Vividly.'

'The credit-card company has paid me back for the illegal charges that were put on my account. They believed my story, apparently. They say it's all too common a story. And it had nothing to do with the children.'

'Have you told them so?'

'Oh, there's no need.'

Emma really must learn to talk to her children when it mattered, thought Kate. But she, childless as she was, really wasn't the one to tell her so.

'I'm glad it's sorted.'

'I'm thinking of disconnecting from the Internet. It's full of wicked things out there.'

'So is the world, or so I've heard.'

'Don't be flippant. It's not just the pornography – though that's bad enough – it's all the other material you can find.'

'Like?'

'We all know you can find out how to make a serviceable bomb. I believe you can even download the instructions to construct a nuclear warhead.'

'I think you may be exaggerating.'

But Emma carried right on, ignoring the interruption. 'Sam Junior wanted to order himself fake identification. You know, driving licences, Visa cards, things like that. They say they're "just for fun", but they look pretty convincing to me. Isn't that disgraceful?'

'But even if you un-install your Internet connection, all those things will still be available out there to others.'

'But not to me and my family. Not to *my* children,' said Emma firmly.

* * *

Could she really cut herself off from the outside world and its influences, wondered Kate when she had finished her conversation with Emma. Surely Emma's children would simply take themselves round to a friend's house where the parents were less fussy about what their children found on the Net?

When she saw Faith that evening she sounded her out on the subject of Jon's visiting.

'I dine in Hall on Tuesdays and Fridays,' said Faith. 'Ask him over on one of those evenings, why don't you? Mind you, if you're planning a seduction, you'll have to be quick about it, I'll be home by nine-thirty.'

'It was his mind I had designs on this time, not his body.'

'Please yourself,' said Faith, who apparently had very little opinion of men's brains.

So Kate invited Jon over for dinner and was pleased with the speed with which he accepted her invitation.

'It's so interesting visiting you,' he said. 'I never know what house I'll be invited into.'

'This one's for sale. Do you think I should make an offer for it?'

'It's a bit oppressive, isn't it? Not really your style. And I don't like the proportions of this room much.' Kate was relieved to hear his opinion. There had been subtle pressure from Faith to put in an offer.

After dinner, when they were sitting and talking, expecting Faith back at any moment, Kate brought up the subject of Emma and her problems with the credit-card charges.

'I thought it was just something minor,' she said. 'A ten-pound error that's put right immediately. But I gather there's more to it than that. And the charge recurred another month. Is it something you'd be interested in?'

Jon nodded. 'It could be. Do you remember the name of the company the ten pounds went to, by any chance?'

'No. Only that it was one of those made-up words that mean nothing and that you can't remember. Do you want me to ask Emma about it?'

'I think I'd like to see her about it. Can you give me her phone number? I'll call and make an appointment.'

'Don't scare her too much. She tends to think that one of her family is involved in something that isn't respectable if a policeman turns up at her door.'

'But I'm not a policeman.'

'I keep forgetting that.'

'And this is probably nothing, but I'd like to follow it up just in case.'

Faith returned soon after that and Kate left them together while she made coffee for them all. It was amusing to hear Jon parrying Faith's questions about his work. He was obviously well practised at it.

'I have to get back to London,' he said eventually.

Kate walked with him to his car.

'Can I come back one evening soon?' he asked.

'I'd like that,' said Kate. 'Why don't you give me a ring on the mobile?'

A moment later he closed the car door and pulled smoothly away from the kerb. She hoped that Emma would come up with something useful for him on the credit-card scam.

20

The police arrived at Neil's flat very early the next morning. He let them in wearing only a grey T-shirt and shorts. His eyes were red with lack of sleep and his hair was standing on end, as it usually did first thing in the morning. Like most men blessed with dark, vigorously growing facial hair, he was in urgent need of a shave after his night's sleep.

He let the police into his flat. The leading one showed him a warrant to search the premises and told him that they would be grateful if he would help them with their enquiries, and would he kindly accompany them to the police station. Everyone was very polite.

They allowed him to wash, clean his teeth and dress himself in his faded weekend Levi's and cotton polo-neck shirt. He found, though, that he couldn't face his shaving mirror. He asked if he could make himself a cup of coffee, but they promised him that coffee would be forthcoming at the station.

'What are you looking for?' he asked the officer who appeared to be in charge.

'Can you tell me what clothes you were wearing last Tuesday?'

'What? Let me see. Tuesday. I was meeting an agent for lunch, so I had on my dark blue Armani jacket. I was wearing a black T-shirt under it, and no tie. Oh, and jeans.'

'Where will we find these items?'

'The jacket is hanging in the wardrobe. The T-shirt is in the linen basket. The jeans are folded over the back of the chair.' Neil's brain was starting to work again after its unkind awakening.

The police officer nodded to a colleague who went to collect the items. Neil was driven away in a police car. Luckily dawn was only just arriving and none of his neighbours was up to see him leave.

Later that morning, Constable Mundy again visited Amanda at Foreword. 'I wonder whether you remember what Mr Orson was wearing that day,' he asked her.

'That's easy,' she said. 'Neil's very keen on his appearance, so I usually notice what he has on.' Constable Mundy had seen the red-eyed, unshaven figure in baggy jeans, drinking coffee at the station, but didn't comment on her judgement. 'He was meeting someone for lunch, or at least he should have done, so he was wearing his Armani jacket. It's a bit passé, but he thinks it's still fashionable. It's dark blue. Very plain, very well cut.'

'Do you recall his shirt and tie?'

'He doesn't wear a shirt and tie when he's trying to look like a creative person. He wears a T-shirt or a polo-neck. I think that day it was a cotton V-neck, probably black or very dark grey. And he was wearing jeans. Quite a new pair, I think, but I can't remember what make they were. They weren't his 501s, certainly.'

'You're very observant,' said Constable Mundy, looking slightly stunned at all this detailed information. 'Now, can you tell me whether those are the only items of clothing answering that description that Mr Orson owns.'

'It's the only Armani jacket he owns, certainly. The jeans

were definitely new, and I don't suppose he bought more than one pair. I expect he has more than one of the cotton V-necks, though. Why do you want to know?'

'Just routine. You've been very helpful. Thank you.'

After which Amanda was quite sure that she had been assistant to a murderer.

Roz was surprised when Kate called round, unannounced, the following lunchtime. They always phoned before turning up on each other's doorstep. It was one of their unwritten rules.

'I've brought a bottle of wine,' said Kate. 'It's still quite cold. Would you like me to open it?'

'Why not.' Roz followed her daughter into the kitchen and handed her the corkscrew. 'You don't usually drink at lunch-time, so I assume we're in for a serious conversation?'

'Why do you say that?'

'You have an expression of grim determination on your face. You don't look as though you've come round for a good gossip.'

Kate took a couple of glasses from the cupboard and poured the wine. 'Let's sit down, shall we?'

They sat facing one another, their glasses on the low table in front of them.

'What's up?' asked Roz. 'It looks as though I've done some-thing wrong again and you've come round here tell me off.'

'I hope not. But I'm worried about your friend Barry Frazer.'

'Why?'

'I think there's more to him than meets the eye.'

'You don't usually pussyfoot round the subject like that. Be more specific.' Roz's voice was tight and angry.

'I can't. It's just that I've heard he may be mixed up with – well, with criminal activity, and I don't like to think that you've got yourself involved in it.'

'What sort of criminal activity are we talking about?'

'I don't know exactly,' said Kate miserably, 'but it involves restaurants. He's spent time in Leda's, hasn't he?' Maybe Jon Kenrick had it all wrong. Maybe she had misunderstood him.

'And where did you hear this?'

Kate hesitated. She had told Jon that she wouldn't give away her source. 'It comes from someone who knows what he's talking about.'

Roz stared at her glass for a minute, then drank some of the wine. 'What evidence does your friend have?' she said eventually. 'Am I really supposed to drop a good friend of *mine* on his say-so? What do you think that sounds like?'

'Look, I—'

'It sounds to me like envy. I have a friend who makes me laugh, who takes me to the races, to Venice, to good restaurants, and you want to stop me seeing him.'

'Because he might screw up your life!' shouted Kate. 'Get rid of him!'

'I need more than this to dump a friend.'

'Please. I'm asking you.'

'Leave me alone, Kate. You have no right to make these demands.'

'I was trying to help.'

But her mother refused to be drawn any further on the subject. She insisted on talking about Kate, and Kate's house move. And in the end her daughter gave up and returned home. She'd done her best, but she didn't feel she'd handled the situation at all well.

Later that day, Roz phoned Barry. 'How are you doing?' she asked breezily.

'I'm well. What's up?'

220

'Nothing. Absolutely nothing.' She might have guessed that Barry would see through her casual approach.

'Need to paint another town?'

'Not today.'

'You're sounding very serious.'

'I wanted to ask you about Holly.'

'My waitress friend? She's getting on all right, isn't she?'

'She's getting on very well. Leda is delighted with her.'

'Well then, what's the problem?'

'No problem, Barry. I just wondered why you asked me to recommend her. If she's so good, she wouldn't need a push from me. Leda would have jumped at the opportunity to take her on. And why *Leda's*, if it comes to that?'

'The girl had been out of work for a month or two and hadn't got a recent reference,' said Barry easily. 'I didn't think you'd mind giving her a helping hand. After all, I was vouching for her, wasn't I?'

Roz could hardly say that this was what was worrying her. 'So what was in it for *you*, Barry?'

'You're not getting jealous, are you?' He laughed. 'Holly really isn't my type, you know.'

'No, I'm not jealous. And your affairs are none of my business. But I wouldn't like to think that Holly was cheating Leda in some way,' said Roz. 'She's a friend of mine from way back in our young days.'

'You can stop worrying, Roz. Everything's cool.'

She wished she could believe him. Wished she could believe him about anything at all. And she hadn't even touched on the subject of the murdered waitress. Barry employed Holly, whoever she was ostensibly working for. Holly and Viola knew each other, and Viola was also a waitress. Had Viola been working for him too, or was she jumping to conclusions?

When the two young women were arguing in the restaurant, they had mentioned his name. She hadn't wanted to hear it, didn't want to know what it was all about. Roz admitted to herself that she was getting good at not hearing, not seeing, when it was convenient. Was it time to open her eyes? Phil/Viola had been persuading Holly to do something she didn't want to.

At this point, her reasoning broke down. If it was *Holly* who wanted to break free, then it would be *Holly* that Barry went to visit. If he lost his temper with someone it would be Holly he lost it with, and then battered to death. Why should he be angry with Viola, who was trying to persuade Holly to do what he wanted?

But then she really didn't know very much about Barry Frazer, did she? She had found it amusing and a little exciting to be seen around with him. He dangled his colourful past in front of her eyes like a matador's cloak, but she hadn't wanted to believe he was really a crook. And anyway, it fitted in with the raffish image that she enjoyed having. She had wanted to know nothing about the things he actually did to earn his money, but now it was becoming increasingly difficult to pretend that these were innocent.

Next time Kate asked her about him she might very well tell her everything she knew and let Kate pass it on to her policeman friend. It seemed to her recently that there was a violent streak in Barry. Under the sunbed tan there was possibly a very nasty individual.

21

There were advantages to sharing your living space with another person, Kate had found. For one thing, instead of finding yourself alone with your thoughts in the evening, going interminably round the same problem, you could share it with your friend. Or even with Faith, she thought, unkindly.

'I'm worried about my editor,' she said, as they opened a bottle of white wine, having checked the *Radio Times* and then given up any thoughts of watching the television.

'What's wrong with him?'

'As an editor, nothing. In fact he's ideal. He's going to do wonders for my career, but I have a suspicion that he's got himself mixed up in this murder of the waitress.'

'What murder?'

Trust Faith not to buy a newspaper, or even to read the headlines while she was in the newsagent's buying herself a bar of chocolate. 'Viola Grant, aged twenty-three, battered to death in her flat near the canal last Tuesday. Police seek staring-eyed, wild-haired maniac who is suspected of stalking her during the preceding weeks.'

'What's that got to do with your editor?'

'There's a picture of a man they wish to question and it looks just like him.' Kate brought out the page from the newspaper and showed it to her. 'Given a little artistic licence here and there, it's him.'

'Yes, that's Neil Orson,' said Faith, as though stating an obvious fact. 'Just a minute, let me catch up on the story.'

Kate left her alone while Faith skimmed rapidly through the report in the paper, then answered the questions Faith shot at her when she had finished.

'How do you know Neil Orson?' asked Kate in her turn.

'I told you – I was negotiating a book deal with Foreword. Neil was the person I spoke to.'

'Yes, I suppose he would be,' Kate said resignedly. Faith was moving in on every aspect of her life. 'And what makes you so sure the picture's of Neil?' she asked.

'Because I saw him that day. I was cycling down St Aldate's as he was walking back towards Carfax. I have to say I was quite glad he wasn't going to be *my* editor. I thought he looked to be off his head.'

'How, exactly?' Kate needed to know this. Her future career was intimately involved with this man and his sanity. This question might be selfish, but it was also essential.

'His face was white, and he was walking so fast he had nearly broken into a run. He was bumping into tourists, pushing his way through the crowds. I couldn't believe it was really him, but I had to stop and get off my bike while a car drove out of a side turning, and I had a good look at him, so I wasn't mistaken. I raised a hand in greeting – he might be publishing my novel one of these days, even if he is off his head – but he didn't see me or anyone else, as far as I could tell.'

'How odd!'

'He looked as though he'd learned that moment that his dearest friend had just died.'

'I suppose that could be the case,' said Kate slowly. 'There's only one thing for it – I'll just have to go and talk to him.'

'Is that wise? He might attack you, too.'

'I don't believe he would. And my career will be in tiny broken shards on the ground if he's arrested for murder, even if it is one he didn't commit. I can't see Foreword risking their reputation for one of their editors, can you?'

'I think I ought to come with you,' said Faith.

'No thanks. I'll ring him at the office tomorrow and arrange to see him after work. He and I get on really well. I can't think I'll be in any danger.'

'Let me know when you're seeing him. I'll give you an hour, and if you're not back here by then, I'll ring the police.'

That would do wonders for her career, thought Kate. She could just hear them in publishers' offices all over the country: 'Don't take on the Ivory woman, she'll call in the police if you have an argument with her, and they'll smash your door in and arrest you for GBH.'

'You'd better make that two hours,' she said.

Neil sounded a little surprised, but pleased, that Kate Ivory wished to see him after work that day. She had wondered about meeting him on neutral ground – that would be safer, she knew – but couldn't think of anywhere they could talk without others overhearing, and she was sure this wasn't a story that Neil would want the general public to find out about. If she invited him back to Faith's, Faith would be there, listening and making her sharp little comments. She considered asking him to meet her at Roz's place, but what if Barry Frazer called in? If nothing else convinced her that it was time to find herself a place to live, this did.

In the end, she asked him if she could come round to his flat straight after work. There was something innocuous about the early evening, she always thought. And although she could see that it would be sensible to be frightened of Neil, she really couldn't bring herself to regard him as dangerous. It was something to do with the sweetness of his smile. Anyway, he liked her and wanted to publish her novels. He wouldn't attack one of his authors, would he? And she had her own theory about who had killed Viola, and why.

She certainly wouldn't be ringing up Barry Frazer and asking *him* if she could pop round to his flat for a cozy little chat.

There was little pretence that it was a social call when she arrived at Neil's flat. It was too early to drink wine and too late for tea, so they sat on his hard sofa in his bleak sitting room and got straight to the point. Kate looked around at the bland furnishings. Neil had done nothing to make this space his own. Would she end up in a place like this if she didn't get on and find herself a house to buy?

'What was it you wanted to talk about?' asked Neil. 'You haven't changed your mind about signing with Foreword, have you?'

'Oh, certainly not,' she replied. 'I'm really excited about that. No, I've come about Viola Grant.'

Neil stared at her, his eyes popping, and she could see the likeness to the artist's drawing.

'Why have you come to *me*? I know nothing about her. I've never met the girl. Never spoken to her.' He was gabbling, she noticed. A bad sign.

'Faith Beeton saw you on the day she died, at about the right time, and near her flat,' she said. She didn't add that Faith had seen him in St Aldate's. She thought it was better to let his imagination fill in the detail for himself.

'Faith Beeton? She's as mad as a hatter, you can't believe a word she says. And she can't write fiction,' he added as an afterthought. Kate was strangely elated by this comment. She might be in the presence of a maniac, but at least he wasn't going to publish Faith's novel.

'Look, I don't think you killed Viola. The way I see it is like this,' she said. 'You go out to eat, mostly. You don't come in in the evenings and cook yourself a meal and then sit at that table and eat it on your own. You go out, right? And Chez Édith is quite a nice little restaurant, has a reasonably priced set menu, allows you to take your own bottle of wine, and isn't far from here. So that's where you went to eat, three or four times a week. And there you saw Viola Grant. I know from the photograph of her that she must have been attractive, and you fell for her.'

Neil tried to say something, but she ignored him and carried on.

'You started to follow her around, the way men do when they're crazy about some woman. And then, I reckon, her boyfriend got to hear about it.'

'What boyfriend?'

'I don't know, but she must have had one. He was the jealous type, and thought that Viola was two-timing him – with you – and she laughed at him. Men like that, the possessive, intense kind, can't bear to be laughed at, and he hit her to make her shut up. He didn't mean to kill her, but it all got out of hand.'

'You certainly have a good imagination. I can see why we wanted your books.'

Kate looked at his face. 'You're telling me I've got it wrong?'

'Definitely. If you sit there and keep quiet for five minutes, I'll tell you all about it. I have to tell someone,' said Neil. 'You think you can keep a secret, especially if your whole world depends on it, but sooner or later you have to tell *someone*. I suppose that's why people walk into a police station and confess to a murder. You just have to tell someone.'

Was it only maniacs who repeated themselves like that, wondered Kate, or was it any man who was confused and found himself in an impossible situation? She did hope it was the latter.

'Didn't the police search your flat, and then take you in for questioning? I thought you'd been locked in an interview room for hours and spilled everything you knew into a tape machine.'

'I didn't think anyone knew about that.'

'Word got out, I'm afraid. You were seen going into St Aldate's police station, surrounded by men in blue uniforms.'

'It's not quite the way you described it. They were all very polite when they invited me to come to the police station with them. I did answer the questions they asked me, but I didn't volunteer any other information. If I'd told them the whole story, they'd have been convinced that I was their murderer. They probably still think I did it, but at least they released me without charge. Please listen, Kate. I really would like to tell you what happened.'

Kate shifted in her chair. If her lovely theory about the jealous boyfriend was all wrong, then what was Neil going to tell her? *Had* he killed Viola Grant after all? And if he had, did she really want to hear him confess to it? In spite of admiring her writing, he might decide he had to kill her, too, to keep her quiet.

'Perhaps you should be talking to a solicitor,' she suggested.

'It's possible. But I've committed no crime.'

She wasn't so sure about that. She stood up and moved to a chair a little further away from him. 'I can hear you better from over here,' she said. There was a heavy-looking lamp-stand on a low table a foot away from her right hand. She could pick it up and hit him with it if it became necessary to defend herself.

'That's better,' she said. 'Now, tell me all about it.' She

spoke in the soothing tones that she had heard Emma Dolby use to a young and fractious child.

'I got back to my flat that evening,' he began. 'This bloody, characterless flat that I shall now probably have to live in for the foreseeable future, until my finances are sorted out. I sat down on this hard beige sofa, poured myself a whisky and wondered what the hell I should do.'

'I think you need to start a bit further back in the story,' said Kate.

'You're right. Well, I ran – I *fled*, you could say – from Viola's flat. That must have been when Faith saw me. I don't remember walking back up St Aldate's. I just knew that I had to be back in the office, looking sane, for the meeting with Estelle Livingstone. Do you think she noticed anything?'

'She hasn't mentioned it.' But then, she hadn't mentioned to Kate that she was meeting Neil Orson, nor even that she was coming to Oxford that day.

'I gave her a larger advance than she was expecting on a manuscript. That probably distracted her. I had to have quite an argument with Roland about it afterwards, but I managed to swing it.'

'Lucky author,' said Kate, wishing it had been *her* manuscript that had been sitting on his desk that afternoon. 'I think you still need to go back a stage or two in the story.' Reversed time sequence was all very well in a literary novel, but it was deeply irritating in a real-life narrative.

'I should start at the beginning,' he said. He paused for a moment as if he wasn't sure where the beginning was, then continued. 'It all began a few months ago while I was still living in London. That's where I met Viola Grant. You're right in that: I *had* met her. I did know who she was, though I didn't know her surname.

'It was after midnight and she was going through the rubbish bins belonging to the block of flats where I lived. Appleton Court.' He spoke as if this ordinary London flat was his dream home. Compared to this rented one it might well have been.

He went on to tell Kate about the devastation wrought upon his life by that small event, whose significance he had completely overlooked at the time.

'I thought she was looking for valuable objects that had been thrown away by rich idiots like me. In fact, that's what she was doing, but not in the way I thought. She didn't expect to find a discarded diamond cuff link. She found something much more valuable: the keys to my bank accounts and credit rating. And as well as my money, she stole my life. It was as though she walked into my shoes and became *me* – a shadow self.'

'A *Doppelgänger*,' suggested Kate.

'Only *I* was the double,' said Neil. 'She, or her boss, was the real Neil Orson.'

'It seems a very sophisticated crime for Viola to commit. She was only a waitress, after all.'

'Someone else was behind her, of course, but I have no idea who. That was one of the things I wanted to ask her when I went to her flat. I wanted to get even. She had to pay for what she'd done. I don't let people get away with things,' he insisted. 'I'd end up like my father – utterly broke – if I did.'

'So she had to pay with her life?'

'Of course not.'

'But you went to her flat that lunchtime,' prompted Kate.

'Just after lunch. Her shift ended at two, I thought. Maybe two-fifteen. I went to her flat, arriving at two thirty-seven.'

'You're very precise.'

'I looked at my watch. I had to be back at the office, remember, to meet Estelle. I couldn't be late, not after leaving her to stew for hours. God knows what the woman did with herself!'

'She had lunch with my mother,' said Kate. 'That's how I knew you weren't in your office when Viola was killed. You'd cancelled an appointment at short notice, which is hardly typical behaviour for you.'

'I'd discovered that morning that someone had emptied my bank accounts, the savings account as well as the current. It was the last straw. I had nothing left! Yes, I know that the bank will give me my money back eventually, but that doesn't stop me from feeling gutted at what's been done to me. Someone's walked in and fingered all my personal details. Can't you imagine what that feels like? I was sure it was *her* – Viola Grant. I wasn't going to let her get away with it. You were right that I'd seen Viola in Oxford, and recognised her, and followed her. It's just that it wasn't for the reason you supposed.

'I had a couple of double brandies in a pub to get my courage up, and then I went down to her flat to confront her. And there was the first odd thing: the main doors were open, and so was the door to her flat. I rang the bell anyway, and when there was no reply, I walked in. I found her in the sitting room. At least, I assumed it was her.' His voice grew hoarse, remembering. 'The person lying there had dark hair like hers, and she was wearing jeans, which Viola often did. But her features were unrecognisable. Whoever killed her did so in what I can only describe as a frenzy. He must have been a madman. Or perhaps it was someone else who had been cheated out of their life by her and wanted to get their own back, wanted to make her suffer the way *they* had.

He paused. 'I knew quite well that *I* could have been the murderer. *I* could have done it. If I had arrived a little earlier, if I had asked her questions about what had happened to me, and if she had laughed in my face, if she'd made fun of me, I could imagine myself doing just that to the girl.'

He stopped, and Kate watched his face from her seat across the room. Would he really have done it? She thought he had too much imagination to make a murderer. It was surely more difficult to perform such a violent act if you could imagine so clearly what the results would be.

'I don't think so,' she said, when she'd considered it. 'At least, you might have started to hit her, but I don't believe you could have carried on. Suppose you'd cut her lip, say.' Neil winced. 'You'd have been horrified, just as you are now at the suggestion. You'd have seen that trickle of blood and you couldn't have carried on. You're too aware of the consequences of your actions.'

Neil looked slightly more cheerful. 'That pale skin, it would have shown every mark,' he said.

'There you go, then,' said Kate.

'And yet, that afternoon while I was talking to the Livingstone woman, the thought came to me at odd moments that perhaps I *had* done it. It was like a scene from a film that screened itself inside my head, an alternative version of reality: I arrived five minutes sooner, Viola had opened the door and I beat her up. I hit her until she died.'

'You don't really believe that's how it was. You can't even remember what you hit her with, for example.'

'I could have blanked it from my memory. These things happen to people, don't they, when they've done something so horrible they can't face up to it?'

'I don't think so,' said Kate, hoping that her confidence in him was justified. But, somehow, the more Neil talked, the more she believed in his innocence.

'Why did I go there? That's what I keep asking myself. What did I think I would achieve? She wasn't going to confess to stealing my life. That was just one of my fantasies. She was much tougher than me, I know that now. I was wasting my time. If only I could turn back the clock!'

'It's really not doing you any good to keep going over the "what ifs",' said Kate.

Neil wasn't listening. 'And why, *why* didn't I call the police? I was halfway up St Aldate's before it even occurred to me. I'd always thought of myself as a solid, law-abiding citizen, after all.'

'Or you could have called an ambulance,' said Kate, who had been thinking just that.

'It was too late – that much was obvious. The girl was definitely dead.'

How can you be so sure, wondered Kate, but she didn't voice the thought aloud. Neil was wracked with enough guilt as it was. He didn't need to wonder if a thread of life remained, and whether Viola could have been saved if the ambulance crew had arrived in time.

'What will they think?' Neil was saying.

'Who?'

'The police. I'm sure they'd believe that only someone who was guilty would run away like that.'

'Or someone who was frightened.'

'I've just been hoping that they'll never know I was there.'

'What do you mean? Surely you told them what you've just told me.'

'No way! I stuck to the story I'd given them before. I was in my office all day, and just went out for a sandwich at lunchtime.'

'But they must know you were lying.'

'How?'

'Did you touch anything?'

He thought for a moment. 'I must have touched the front door when I went in. And I used the door handle to go into the sitting room. But I don't think I touched anything else after that. I certainly didn't touch the body.'

Then how could you be so sure she was dead?

Neil's face was looking pinched and much older as he went back over the scene in Viola's flat.

'I thought I was going to be sick,' he said. 'My mouth was full of acid and my stomach was heaving.' He raised his fists to his mouth as though repeating the actions of that moment. 'I forced myself to relax, and to think. The only thing I could think of was to run away. Bloody pathetic, wasn't I?'

'I don't know how many of us would be brave and resourceful in those circumstances,' said Kate. 'Do you think anyone saw you going in, or coming out again?'

'I don't think so. I'm not the sort of man you notice.'

But Faith noticed you, thought Kate. You certainly looked like a maniac fleeing from the scene of the crime when she passed you in St Aldate's.

'Even if they did,' Neil was saying, 'my description would fit any one of a thousand others. And I wasn't away from the office for any longer than a quick lunch would have taken.'

'So your secretary—'

'— Assistant.'

'So your assistant wouldn't have noticed anything unusual, either.'

'Apart from the fact that I postponed my meeting with Estelle because I had something urgent to take care of. No, I don't think she noticed anything odd. I behaved perfectly normally when I arrived back at the office.'

Neil was obviously proud of the way he had carried on as if nothing had happened. Kate wasn't so convinced that neither Amanda nor Estelle had noticed anything different about him.

'If you touched the door you did leave fingerprints,' she said. 'They must have found them.'

'But they haven't got them on file,' said Neil. 'They won't know whose fingerprints they are.'

'Didn't they take your prints when they took you in for questioning?'

'Oh,' said Neil, remembering.

'So they *do* know you were there.'

'You think they'll come back and arrest me?'

'I imagine they're looking for more evidence that you killed her.'

'There isn't any.'

'Apart from the fingerprints, you don't think Viola had anything in the flat to connect you to her?'

'She was hardly likely to keep notes on her victims. And she must have passed the stuff she stole from my bin to the man she was working for.'

'It could have been a woman. It wasn't necessarily a man.'

'Does that make a difference?' Kate thought that a woman was less likely to beat another to death, but she didn't say so. 'She wouldn't still have my bank statements or whatever around in her flat.'

Again, Kate wasn't as sure of this as Neil appeared to be. All it needed was a slip of paper with his name and address on and the police would be round, banging on his door again early one morning. Even if the address was Appleton Court, London SE1, they'd soon know it was him.

'They searched your flat. They took you in for questioning. They released you. That must be because they didn't find the evidence they're looking for. But that's not to say that it doesn't exist, even if you didn't kill her. I imagine they don't yet know you have a motive.'

'You're not absolutely sure of my innocence, are you?'

'Of course I am. I wouldn't be here if I thought you'd killed Viola. But if the police discover that Viola's the one who stole your identity, then that's going to give you a motive in their eyes.'

'In fact, it wouldn't have been Viola who used the details, would it?' said Neil. 'She'd have raked through my rubbish and then handed over the proceeds to her boss. She'd probably forgotten all about me a few days later. She wouldn't even remember my name or address. As a matter of fact, it's the name of her boss I really wanted to find out.'

'If you're right, then her boss would probably like to find you, too,' said Kate.

'Why? He'd keep out of my way, surely?'

'He's just lost one of his team. Probably a valued member of the team, at that. He'll be as anxious as the police to find out who killed her. In fact, he'll want to get to the murderer *before* the police.'

'You don't think her boss murdered her, do you?'

'Why should he kill Viola if she was making so much money for him?'

Neil stared at her, comprehension dawning. 'You mean he'll think that *I* did it. And he'll come after me to get his revenge.'

'You may convince *me* of your innocence – you may even convince the police. But I think Viola's boss is going to be a much tougher judge.' And that's if he gives you the chance to tell your side of the story, thought Kate. He might take his revenge first and look for proof of your guilt afterwards.

'The important thing is to make sure no one finds out I'd been in Viola's flat,' said Neil, ignoring the fact that his life could well be under threat. 'The police aren't going to tell the press something like that, are they? The neighbours say they saw me outside her flat, but no one else knows I went inside. As long as I keep out of the limelight and concentrate on my work, I'll be fine.'

'As one of your authors, I'm all in favour of that,' said Kate. 'But—'

'I've got a lot of ground to make up if I'm ever to get my foot back on the property ladder,' said Neil, expressing his over-riding concern.

'And what about the one who's still out there, the man who stole your identity?'

'I don't suppose I'll ever find out who he is now,' said Neil.

'I think you're going to have to try,' said Kate. And if she wasn't going to need to look for a new editor, she'd better help him in his search.

Away from Neil's flat, she checked her watch – it was eight-fifteen – then dialled Sam Dolby's number from her mobile.

'Yeah?'

'It's Kate here. I was wondering whether you'd continued with your researches into credit-card fraud.'

'Might have.'

She took this for a 'yes'. 'Can I come and talk to you about it? And about identity theft, too?'

'What makes you think I know anything about that?'

'Last time I was in your room I had to remove a folder labelled *IDENTITY THEFT* in black marker pen from the chair before I could sit down.'

'Right.'

'So?'

'You want to come over now?'

'Yes.'

'All right.'

Sam answered the doorbell himself, so Kate avoided having to explain to Emma what she was doing in her house. Emma, she well knew, would be tucking up the last of the little ones, and making sure that the older children had completed their homework.

They went straight up to his room. Sam handed her a page headed *Thieves could steal your identity and you wouldn't even know it was happening*.

'Is this the sort of thing?' he asked.

'Yes. Now, you've been doing research on this kind of fraud, so you need to fill me in on the details. As far as I can see, there are two different scams that have been going on, happening to people I know. First of all there were the small, recurring charges put on to your mother's credit card. The money was refunded by the credit-card company, but I'd like to know whose pocket it went into. And then, secondly, there's my editor, Neil. A few months back, he caught someone going through the rubbish in his bin at his flat in London. Some weeks later, credit and store cards were taken out in his name and huge bills were run up. Someone took out a loan in his name, too, to buy an expensive motor car. And then he found that yet more money had been removed from his bank accounts.'

'Cool.'

'Not from Neil's point of view, I can assure you. Now I can see that he should have kept a better eye on his bank accounts,

238

but I think he's the kind of man who's actually afraid of those envelopes that turn up from the bank, and just slings them into a drawer without opening them. What I want to know is, who did it to him? Would it be the same people who put the charge on Emma's credit card?'

'Basically,' said Sam, sounding, did he but know it, remarkably like his father, 'you have two different organised gangs here. The one that targeted your friend Neil would be based in the UK, maybe just a region of it. The bin-divers go looking through trash, or the green box that Emma puts out, and take anything they can use to establish an identity. That means old bank statements, credit-card statements, utility bills, details of your employment, stuff like that. If you have the basics, you can find out the rest. Banks tend to ask the same questions when you ring them up, like "What's your mother's maiden name?" Well, you can find it out, can't you? All that stuff's public knowledge. You can get a copy of a birth certificate, of a driving licence, even.'

'You can?'

'These are skilled operators.'

'And then they just help themselves to the victim's money?'

'And his credit rating. The banks and the finance companies pay in the end, of course.'

'So why don't they do something about it? Why don't they stop it?'

'They try. They've set up their own anti-fraud unit, but the criminals are always at least one step ahead.' Sam sounded as though he admired the criminals more than the plodding investigators in their wake. 'And the cost ends up in the charges on your bank account,' he added.

'What about the others, the ones who targeted Emma?'

'Now these are the international operators. They take small

sums from millions of people in lots of different jurisdictions. That means countries, really,' he added kindly. 'That makes it just about impossible for any one agency to catch up with them. And unless the finance companies get together, they don't even realise how widespread the problem is. They just give someone like Emma her ten quid back and forget about it.'

'Where do they operate from?'

'Could be anywhere. Could be Nigeria, could be a Caribbean island, could be Oxford. But the money's probably moved to a dodgy bank on an offshore island eventually. It helps if you own the bank, too, of course.'

'This has been an education, Sam. Thanks.'

'That the lot?'

'There's just one more thing. What have restaurants got to do with it?'

But at this moment they both heard Emma's voice outside the door. 'Sam! What's going on? Have you got a friend in there with you?'

Sam and Kate looked at one another. Kate shrugged, then opened the door. 'Hello, Emma.'

'Kate! What are you doing here?'

'Would you believe me if I said that Sam was helping me with my homework?'

'If you mean that he's been finding material on the Internet that will help you with your next book, then yes, I would. But I thought you were quite capable of doing that for yourself. Why ask Sam?'

'I haven't got a computer at the moment. Mine's in store and Faith keeps hers at college. I'd use the one at the library, but it's closed for the night.'

'Well, I'm glad that Sam could be of help,' said Emma.

'I'd better be going now,' said Kate, taking the hint. 'Bye, Sam. Thanks a lot.'

'Cheers,' said Sam.

Although the police hadn't lost interest in Neil Orson, they now had the preliminary forensic reports following the search of his flat.

Neil Orson's fingerprints matched two of those that had been found in Viola Grant's flat. This indicated that he was lying when he said that he had never been there. Whether he lied because he had killed Viola, or because he was frightened, they didn't yet know. No trace of Viola Grant's blood was found on his clothing, however. The person who had battered her to death must have been spattered with her blood; it would have been on their skin, and possibly in their hair, too. The witnesses who had seen the wild-eyed man fleeing through Oxford that Tuesday afternoon had not mentioned seeing blood, and although everyone agreed that his shirt was some dark colour and therefore wouldn't show up the blood as white or pale blue might, still someone should have noticed something, even on grey or dark blue.

Viola Grant's blood had been found in the basin and waste pipe in the bathroom. Three hairs had also been found in the basin which did not match her DNA. They didn't belong to Neil Orson, either, indicating that someone else had been in Viola Grant's flat.

They didn't rule out the possibility that Neil Orson might have had an accomplice who had done the actual killing, or that he might have paid someone to kill Viola for him – or simply to teach her a lesson that went tragically too far.

22

'I wasn't sure at first about having you to stay here,' said Faith, 'but now I've got used to having someone else about the place I'm really enjoying it.'

'You are?'

'Yes. First of all there's your mysterious boyfriend, the one who turns up for brief visits and then disappears off again. He looks like a policeman, the brooding, I-have-a-secret-sorrow type of policeman, but you tell me he isn't. So I suppose he must work for one of the security services, or perhaps he's a tax inspector.'

'Neither of those,' interrupted Kate.

'You're just gullible! And whenever I'm dining in Hall you and he get together for intense, secret conversations. At least, I think that's what you're doing. You're looking too cross to be having a really satisfactory sex life. Right?'

'You're exaggerating – Jon called in just once – not to mention turning my friends and family into characters in a melodrama.'

'It's what I'm good at. One day it will make me into a brilliant novelist. And then there's your mother, the redoubtable Roz who, having retired from her raffish travels, appears to have transformed herself into a gangster's moll.'

'I told you my worries about Roz because I thought you'd make intelligent suggestions about what I should do.'

'Oh, no. I don't give advice,' said Faith airily.

'Actually, now that the subject of Roz has come up, I think I'll be moving in with her soon.'

'You think she needs protection from someone?'

'Herself, mainly. But yes, I am rather worried about her. She thinks she's invincible, indestructible, but no one is, are they? She may need my help.'

'I didn't think that you and she got on very well.'

'That's in the past. We're the best of friends these days. And anyway, Faith, I've found a house I like. I've made them an offer.'

'Really? Whereabouts?'

'Jericho. Convenient for city centre, rail station, cinemas, theatres and buses. What could be better?'

'Congratulations. I wonder how I missed it?'

'Would you mind if I moved out quite soon? I'll pay you to the end of the week, of course.'

Kate escaped to her room and picked up her mobile phone. 'Roz? I'm glad I found you at home. Are you still in need of a lodger? I will pay whatever rent you need if I can move in more or less immediately.'

'Do you need help with your packing?' asked Roz.

'That's all right – I can manage on my own. And by the way, I've made an offer for a house in Jericho.'

'Excellent news!'

Kate was getting good at packing up her few clothes and belongings, stowing them in her car and driving across town to new lodgings. She wrote out a cheque for Faith, handed over an expensive bottle of wine and a bunch of flowers, then completed the transfer to Roz's house, which was less than a mile away. In half an hour she had unpacked and made herself at home in Roz's spare room. Her mobile rang while she was doing so.

'That was the agent,' she told Roz. 'The owners have accepted my offer.'

'Brilliant! When can I come and look at it?'

'Soon!'

Once she was settled, and Roz was busy in the kitchen knocking up something for their supper, she pulled out her mobile again and rang Jon Kenrick.

'Do you fancy another trip to Oxford?' she asked when they had exchanged greetings.

'Where are you living at the moment?'

'I'm back with Roz.'

'Is that wise?'

'Definitely. I shall keep her on the straight and narrow now I'm here.'

'You sound excited, as though you have things to tell me.'

'Yes. The first thing is that I've made an offer on a house and the agent phoned ten minutes ago to say that the owner had accepted it.'

'That's brilliant. I'm really pleased for you. And what's the other news?'

'It's exciting, too, but I need another one or two pieces to complete the puzzle.'

'And you think I can provide them?'

'Actually, I'm pinning my hopes on a fifteen-year-old schoolboy for that.'

'I'm tied up for a day or two, but I could come down on Friday evening, if you like. Why don't you find a pub on the river where we can go for a meal.'

'I know just the right place.' And she gave him Roz's address and instructions on how to find it.

* * *

'I'm full of plans for the new house,' she told Roz as they sat down to eat that evening, balancing plates on their knees in front of the television.

'It will take two or three months before you can move in, won't it? You're welcome to stay here for a while yet,' said Roz, switching channels to her favourite soap. 'Just as long as you let me watch *EastEnders* in perfect silence.'

There was no sign of Barry, Kate was relieved to notice. Maybe Roz had given him the push. She wouldn't start asking about him on her first evening, though. It would be a bad move to begin her stay with a row. On the other hand, while Roz was immersed in the soap, she could get back to her friend Sam.

The Dolbys' phone line was engaged and remained so for the next half hour. Either Sam was busy on the Internet, or else one of the girls was chatting to a friend. Either way it could be hours before the line was free again. Kate retired to the kitchen to do the washing up.

Some time after nine she tried the Dolbys again and this time she was in luck. 'Could I speak to Sam, please? Sam Junior, that is.'

'Is that you, Kate?'

'Yes.'

'I'll give him a shout, but I have to warn you that he doesn't always respond.'

But Kate was in luck. Sam came on the line a couple of minutes later. 'Yeah?'

'You didn't get a chance to tell me what was happening in the restaurants.'

'Oh, that one's easy. Everyone knows that. Skimming.'

'You'll have to explain.'

'You have a little machine, slips into your pocket, can read the strip on a credit card, right? So you give your card to the waiter, he takes it out of sight, puts it through the reader so that you pay your bill, then puts it through his skimmer and swipes it again. Takes your details. Details get transferred to a computer and then to a blank card. Someone pays fifty quid for it, uses the new card, stuff gets charged to your account.'

'And they do this in restaurants?'

'Restaurants are full of people with money to spend, aren't they?'

'True.'

'And garages. It happens in garages sometimes, too.'

'But the people with the machines aren't acting independently, surely?'

'It's a whole organisation. Someone has the computer, the skimmer and the decoder, and the technical know-how. He has restaurant or garage workers on his payroll. He gives them the skimmer, pays them a percentage and does the business with the blank cards.'

'Sam, you're a star.'

'Cheers.'

She rang off, thinking about what he'd told her. It didn't have to be a waiter, of course. It could be a waitress. Like Viola Grant. And what about the girl who worked at Leda's? Was that what Jon was doing when he took her to dinner there? She went back into the living room. *EastEnders* had finished and Roz was leafing through a magazine, looking bored.

'I brought some wine with me,' she said. 'Shall I pour us a glass?'

'Good idea.'

When she'd placed the glasses on the table, Kate said, 'I was thinking about Leda's – the restaurant where you work.'

'Yes?'

'Do you know the waitress at all?'

'Holly? I know her in passing, not particularly well. Why do you ask?'

'Have you ever heard of skimming?'

'Yes. That's when they put your credit card through a machine, transfer the details to a blank card and then charge stuff to your account.'

'Right. You don't think it's happening at Leda's, do you?'

'You think Holly's on the take? Has she got the brains for it, let alone the technical know-how?'

'She could be part of a much larger organisation, working for someone who lends her the skimmer and pays her a percentage.'

Roz was silent.

'What's up? You've thought of something, haven't you? What is it?'

'When Leda first opened the restaurant she was having trouble finding a good waitress. Barry told me he knew of someone and suggested Leda should take her on.'

'Holly?'

'Yes, that's right. At the time I thought it didn't ring true. Why should he find a really good waitress for Leda when he didn't even know her? I don't think Barry's that altruistic, do you?'

'I wouldn't have thought so.'

'And there's more. You say that Holly could be part of an organisation. Well, the day I was in Leda's for so long, when I was lunching with Estelle, Viola Grant came into the restaurant to talk to Holly.'

'That was the day she was murdered.'

'Yes – and she and Holly were having a long, loud argument. Holly wanted out of whatever she was involved in, and Viola was warning her against it. I heard her say that Barry Frazer would object.' Roz lifted her glass and drank down half the contents.

'Skimming. They must have been talking about skimming,' said Kate.

'If they were, then it would seem that Viola was the one who gave out the skimmers and collected the data. Do you think she was behind the whole organisation?'

'Or Barry was – *is*,' said Kate. 'If he was placing Holly in Leda's restaurant, then he must have been the organiser, don't you think?'

'You could be right.'

'You've got to break with him. You can't go on seeing him. He's not just a chancer, he's a criminal.' Kate was getting excited again.

'I'll think about it.'

'And I think you should tell me everything you remember from that lunchtime at Leda's. It sounds as though the things that were said and done then were the cause of her death, just an hour or so later.'

Next day, while Roz was out, the house agent rang Kate on her mobile. A larger offer than hers had been received for the house in Jericho. Would she care to better it?

'You want me to enter into an auction? I'm not sure I wish to do that,' said Kate, furious. On being told that an extra thousand or two on the asking price would do the trick, she told them, 'I'll think about it and get back to you later today.'

It was true that she could afford it, just, but she hated the feeling that she'd been gazumped. After lunch she went for a walk around town, to check out any new properties on the market and mull over her decision.

*   *   *

It was in the early afternoon, when Roz had returned from making desserts for Leda, that her doorbell rang in the insistent way that heralded the arrival of Barry Frazer.

'What's up, Barry?' Roz had never seen him looking so nervous. His shirt was creased, the knot of his tie was not quite centred, even his hair looked as though it needed a cut. For the first time in their acquaintance she could see the Essex lad underneath the careful accent and handmade shirts. He pushed past her and into the house.

'Are you on your own?'

'Yes. My daughter's out at the moment. She'll be back later, though. She's just gone out for a quick walk.' Somehow it seemed wise to let him know that she wouldn't be alone in the house for long. She hadn't liked what she'd learned about Barry Frazer from Kate.

'I'll be gone by the time she gets back. I've just come to say goodbye, really.'

'Where are you off to?'

Barry didn't answer the question. 'Why don't you make us a pot of coffee?'

As Roz took the cafetière from the cupboard and poured in the coffee, she heard Barry going upstairs. She might not have heard him at all, but he hadn't learned to avoid the tread that always creaked. Perhaps it was because Kate had warned her about him that she noticed then that, instead of going into the bathroom he went into the spare bedroom, the one that Kate was now using. She followed him upstairs, avoiding the creaking tread.

'What the hell are you doing in my daughter's room?' she asked.

Barry was reaching up to the top of the wardrobe, pulling

out a box. 'Just collecting my gear,' he said. He held the box protectively against his chest. 'I thought this was the spare room.'

'What gear?' asked Roz sharply. 'Why didn't you ask my permission? You haven't been using my house to store drugs in, have you?'

He grinned, the old Barry, confident that his charm would win her over. 'Nothing like that. You know me, I don't touch drugs,' he said. 'I didn't think you'd mind if I left this little box up here where no one would think of looking for it.'

Roz knew that though it might be true that Barry didn't use drugs, he wouldn't be averse to selling them to other people, not if there was money in it for him.

'There are just a few papers I left for safekeeping,' he was saying. 'I didn't tell you about them before because I thought you'd be happier not knowing they were there.'

Roz felt anger creeping through her. It was an unfamiliar sensation for her: she usually took what life threw at her in her stride. 'What papers?' she asked.

'Nothing very much.' He opened the lid of the box and showed her. Apart from papers, there appeared to be a number of blank credit cards and some computer disks, also a small plastic box with a groove down one side.

'So I was right. You've been running a skimming operation.'

'Better not to jump to any conclusions,' said Barry.

'I'm not a fool. I know what that is: it's a skimmer. You swipe a credit card through it and it takes a copy of the information so that you can make up a fake card with the cardholder's information. I suppose you had Holly using one for you at Leda's.'

'Don't worry about your friend Leda. Holly wasn't stealing from her or anything like that. She's done her no harm.'

'She could have put her out of business!'

'I think maybe I should be going. I've got a friend picking me up in his car in five minutes.'

'And why have you got to leave in such a hurry? Are the police on to you? I'd like to know whether they're likely to arrive at my door in the early hours of the morning, clutching a search warrant.'

'Don't worry. No one's on to me. And I don't think the pigs will come looking for me for quite a while yet. I've covered my tracks too well for that.'

They were back downstairs in the hall. Barry looked at his watch, which was still wafer-thin and gold, she noticed. He wasn't down to his last pennies, then.

'Can't we sit down?' he asked.

'If you must.' She wasn't strong enough to throw him out physically, even if she wanted to.

As they sat down in the living room, Roz heard a key turning in the front door lock. Barry didn't appear to notice, though. It must be Kate, returning earlier than expected. She hoped she'd hear their voices and leave them alone. Light footsteps crossed the hall and entered the kitchen.

'Who's that?' asked Barry suddenly.

'Kate. Don't worry, she won't disturb us.'

The footsteps went upstairs, a door clicked shut, and the house was quiet again.

'Are you running because of the girl, Viola?' asked Roz.

'No. Why should I do that?'

'You might run if you were the one who murdered her.'

'I wouldn't do that. She was making a fortune for me. I wouldn't kill that off, would I?'

Barry's logic convinced Roz where protestations of affection for the girl wouldn't.

'If you really want to know, I made a big mistake and targeted the wrong man,' he went on. 'Viola picked up some details for me in Worcester and I borrowed a lot of money from the accounts of a man called Karl Church. How was I to know that wasn't his real name?'

'Did he get his revenge?'

'He had his own operation going. He'd opened a bank on an offshore island. He set up a website telling potential customers what he had to offer – and it was just what I was looking for. Once you'd set up a trust fund – managed by his bank, of course – no one could get their fingers on any of your money. Not your ex-wife, not the Revenue, not your creditors. And no questions asked as to where the funds had come from. You didn't even need to use your own name. It meant that you could transfer money from the punter's account to the offshore bank without anyone ever seeing you. You didn't go into their bank and demand the money at gunpoint, you did it by a click of your mouse. All gone!'

'And?'

'He must have known it was me pinched his money. He's got his contacts and his own experts. He's a powerful man. He waited until I'd transferred just about all my wonga, and then he nicked it. The whole sodding lot.'

'And you can't get it back?'

'It could be anywhere by now. In Hong Kong or Moscow, for all I know. Who do you suppose I should complain to?'

'What are you going to do now?'

'Take the money I have left and disappear. That man will come after me, you can bet. I don't suppose he's satisfied his revenge is complete yet. I'll use one of the other identities I've set up. At least I'm an expert at that – he'll have trouble tracing me this time. And then I'll have to start again.' He stood up.

He was starting to acquire broken veins across his cheek-bones, Roz noted. He wouldn't last long as a suave conman if he went on drinking the way he did.

There was the sound of a car drawing up to the kerb outside Roz's house. Barry picked up the box he had taken from on top of Kate's wardrobe. Roz followed him out to the front door.

'Who was he?'

'Who?'

'The man who's after you. What's Karl Church's real name?' she asked, just before she opened the door.

'Fabian West,' he said.

'I'm sure I've heard that name before.'

'Well, keep clear of him. If he comes looking for me, lock your door.'

'And how would I recognise him?'

'You needn't bother about that. If he turns up here, you'll be dead before you can open the door.'

Barry walked through the door and Roz watched him walk towards a car parked a few yards away.

'Fabian West,' repeated Kate.

Roz shut the door as Barry climbed in the car. She didn't see who was driving and she didn't want to know. The car pulled away again and Roz turned to look up at her daughter. Kate was standing at the top of the stairs, looking down at her.

'Was that Barry?' asked Kate.

'Yes. And he was leaving.'

Kate walked down the stairs and followed her mother into the sitting room. Roz picked up the two glasses and took them out to the kitchen.

'Shall I make tea?' asked Kate.

'Please.'

'When you say "leaving", do you mean for good?' asked Kate, putting the kettle on to boil.

'Yes.'

'Thank God for that. Do you want to tell me about it?'

'Not really. You wouldn't want to know the details. But he's being pursued by someone even nastier than he is, apparently. Therefore he is unlikely to return.'

Kate noticed that her mother, too, looked relieved that Barry had disappeared out of her life. Roz was obviously glad to see the back of him.

'I must give you something towards my keep, by the way,' said Kate. 'I can't expect you to feed me as well as giving me a roof over my head.'

'That's all right,' said Roz.

'I insist.' It seemed to Kate that her mother was in fact happy to take the cheque she wrote out for her. 'I'm a *successful* novelist now,' she said as she handed it across.

Kate made tea for both of them and they took their mugs through to the sitting room.

'From what Barry was saying,' said Roz slowly, 'I think he could have been the person responsible for what happened to your editor.'

'He stole Neil's identity and cleaned out his bank accounts?'

'I don't know for sure, but he did say that the waitress, Viola, the one who was murdered, was working for him. And I think he operated in London before he moved into the provinces.'

'It could have been him, I suppose, but I bet there are hundreds of people out there doing the same thing.'

'From something Barry said, I got the impression that they had their own areas and nasty things happened to trespassers on their patch.'

'Do you know where he's gone?'

'No. I didn't ask – I didn't want to know. And I didn't ask what name he'd be using in future, either.'

'I can understand that. But I imagine that Neil would be interested in knowing, even if you're not.'

'There's no point. Fabian West has done to Barry what Barry did to Neil. And since the bank where he deposited his funds was not a reputable high street one, but some institution belonging to Fabian West, then no one's going to pay his money back. In Barry's terms, he's broke. I expect he still has a gold watch or two to his name, but his wonga's all gone.'

'Wonga? Where *do* you learn these words?'

'It's a technical term meaning "money", I believe.'

Kate laughed. 'Did you find out why Fabian West had it in for Barry?'

'Barry took material from a flat that belonged to West in Worcester. He was using a different name and Barry didn't realise who it was.'

'I imagine that Fabian West couldn't expect the bank and finance houses to reimburse him, either. He wouldn't want anyone looking too closely into his sources, would he?' asked Kate.

'And someone might have recognised him. I imagine they all have *his* photograph hanging on the office wall,' Roz said flippantly.

'They'd know him by his odd eyes,' said Kate.

'What do you mean?' Roz stared at her.

'One is grey, the other brown. Though I suppose he wears coloured contact lenses to disguise them.'

'Then I saw him that lunchtime in Leda's.' Roz had lost her smile.

'Are you sure?'

'A very tall man. One grey eye, one brown. And he dropped his contact lens. He was making a fuss about it. Shortly after that, he paid his bill in a hurry and left. I'd nearly forgotten about it.'

'It's got to be Fabian West!' Kate said excitedly. 'Do you think he knew about Viola working for Barry?'

'It's a bit far-fetched, isn't it? And anyway, Viola doesn't work at Leda's. Holly does.'

'You said she was visiting Holly.'

'A coincidence, surely.'

'But she was murdered an hour later,' Kate pointed out. She put down her tea cup. 'A pity you didn't get his address.'

Roz sprang up from her chair. 'My God! I think I might have done. I'll have to go and check. I'll be back in about half an hour.'

The front door clicked shut. While she was out, Kate phoned back the house agents and made a new offer on the property in Jericho.

Roz returned in under half an hour.

'Leda hadn't thrown this away, luckily,' she said. 'I found it in her desk. Here,' and she handed across the card that the *Spectator*-reading customer had filled in for his free wine-and-food tasting.

'How did you know which one it was?'

'He used a real fountain pen, not a biro. And look at his prissy handwriting. This one has to be him.'

'You're sure?' Kate demanded.

'Positive.'

Kate hoped Roz was right. If she wasn't, some innocent citizen was about to have his door bashed in. She picked up her mobile and dialled Jon's number again.

257

'Jon?'

'Kate, I'm in the middle of something, could I call you back?'

'No. You need to know this immediately. I have Fabian West's address and phone number. At least, it's where he was living on the day that Viola Grant was murdered.'

'Are you sure?'

'Yes.'

'Brilliant. You'd better give it to me.'

So Kate read out a forgettable name and the address of a cottage in a small village south of Wantage, in Oxfordshire.

'Hold on,' said Jon. She heard voices in the background as he appeared to be giving instructions to a colleague. 'Right. That's being dealt with. You won't tell anyone else about this for the moment, will you?'

'No. And I'll gag Roz if that's what you want.'

'It might well be necessary. But tell me how you got hold of this address.'

'He filled in a promotional card last Tuesday offering him a free meal. He wrote this name and address on it.'

'Why didn't you let me know sooner?'

'I've only had it for about thirty seconds. Barry Frazer mentioned his name, and when I told her about the odd eyes, Roz remembered a customer in Leda's restaurant. She drove over there to see if the promotional card he'd filled in was still there, and it was.'

'That's a relief. I thought you might have kept it to yourself for a while.'

They both knew that that's what Kate had done once before, giving Fabian West just enough time to leave before the police came knocking on his door.

'And by the way, I believe he's your murderer,' Kate added.

'What makes you say that?'

'Barry Frazer stole his identity – one of his identities – by mistake and nicked large sums of money from him. Viola had been working for Barry.'

'I think I'm following this.'

'Well, Barry wouldn't have emptied out West's bank accounts, would he? He thought he was someone called Karl Church, apparently. West must found out who had ripped him off and he went after Barry. But he found Viola. At least, that's what I believe happened.'

'Fabian West doesn't usually kill people. He gets others to do it for him.'

'He could have been out of control. You'd be pretty angry if someone took over your identity, wouldn't you? And Fabian wouldn't risk claiming his money back from the bank, like any honest citizen, would he?'

'I'll pass the information on. If they pick up Fabian West, it's one of the things they could look into. If he's charged with murder he won't get bail and it will give us a chance to sort out some of his dodgy financial dealings. Mind you, if he's convicted of murder, we probably won't bother wasting our time on him any longer. We'll just move on to the next problem.'

'Can you still come down to Oxford tomorrow evening?'

'Yes. I'll bring some wine with me. If we get our hands on Fabian West we'll have something to celebrate.'

23

After dinner the next evening, while they were all feeling mellow with good food and excellent wine, Roz disappeared into the kitchen, saying, 'If you two are going to be talking about Emma Dolby, I'll get on with the washing-up. I find that woman so irritating that I prefer plunging my arms into hot detergent rather than listen to yet another sad story of her life.'

'Emma's all right really,' said Kate, 'but I would like to hear the end of her story. Did you go to see her?'

'Yes,' Jon said, 'and she was very helpful, not least because she is so patently honest. You don't have to wonder whether she's hiding something.'

'So what did you find out?'

'The charges on her card were part of a much bigger operation. I did recognise the name of the merchant company who had put it there, and it was one that had been interesting us. Do you want me to explain how it worked?'

'Sam Dolby has already done that.'

'Well, Fabian West was behind that particular version of the scam. He's using his bank on an offshore island and the processing company he's set up to charge small sums to millions. It's the card companies who lose in the end, since they reimburse the victims.'

'How many cards did he charge?'

'About three quarters of a million.'

'And how much did he make?'

'About fifteen million pounds.'

'What! Really – do you mean it? I wonder how much of it Barry stole from him.'

'And some of the charges would be recurring, for as long as he could get away with it. The twist on this particular version of the fraud was that the charges were apparently for subscriptions to pornographic sites. The argument was that people didn't want it to be thought that they'd visited such sites, so they just paid up. It was particularly embarrassing for them if it happened to be a company credit card they were using.'

'Go on.'

'The money was paid into various accounts in West's own bank in the Pacific, and was then moved out again, and we simply don't know where to. I don't suppose we ever will. Presumably they're funding enterprises of his all over the world.'

'And how did Emma come into this?'

'We checked the transaction back and it confirmed some of the facts we already had in our hands.'

Kate recognised that Jon was being vague on purpose. This was a long-term investigation of his, after all, and he wouldn't want Kate or Emma to pass on any of the details.

'The credit-card people paid back the money she'd been charged, luckily. With all those children of hers, she needs every penny.'

'How many children has she got? There were shoals of them swimming around the house when I visited her.'

'I've never quite managed to get them all to stand still in one place to be counted.'

At this point, Roz returned, bringing a tray containing mugs and a cafetière. 'I hope you've finished your conversation.'

'Yes. You're safe from Emma for a while.'

'Have you told Jon about the house in Jericho?'

'Yes. They've accepted my second offer and promised that they will consider no others.'

24

At his desk, Jon Kenrick was downloading a copy of a document that had been sent to him, unofficially, from a colleague in Oxford. He read it through and then filed it. He wouldn't be passing on its contents to Kate, although he knew that she would be interested in them.

St Aldate's Police Station, Oxford, 19 July 2002

Transcript of interview with Fabian West

It was pure coincidence that I was in Leda's restaurant that lunchtime. Well, perhaps not exactly coincidence. I knew the sort of place those scum – excuse my choice of language, but it is accurate! – liked to work. They picked on prosperous places with a young, fashionable clientele.

You know what the young are like: their favourite meeting-places come and go. One week they're all eating Italian, the next it's Thai, then something they call Fusion. They have no real taste, no sense of national identity – excuse me again, I am off on one of my hobby horses, riding it away into the sunset, if you let me. These are the sort of young people who glance at their credit-card statement, don't bother to check it properly, and then send off the minimum payment. Every few months their limit will be raised by a finance company which is only too pleased to have customers willing to pay their exorbitant rates of interest. Enough!

As I say, I could see that this was the sort of place where Barry Frazer and his minions would be operating, and so I took a table at Leda's and kept my eyes open. Where there are fools like those customers there will be wolves willing to prey upon them. At least in that restaurant I knew the food would be edible. I had been there a couple of times before and even if I found out nothing new, I would enjoy my meal.

Yes, I mentioned the name of Barry Frazer. I was looking for him because I knew he had stolen my money. No, I hadn't reported it to the police, nor to the bank. Why should I? Would you have found him for me? Would you have recovered the substantial sums he removed from my accounts? No, of course you wouldn't! And you would have come peering into my affairs with your beady eyes and your magnifying glasses. I would have been answering questions from your tame accountants and the Inland Revenue for years.

I knew Frazer was operating in this area, among others. Of course I did. I had people looking for him, but that didn't mean I couldn't keep my own eyes open, too. It was wrong of me, stupid of me, to be doing so, but it was *my* money he had stolen. A very substantial sum. And no, I do not wish to be more specific. He had stolen the identity I had set up for myself so carefully in Worcester, too. You have no idea how that makes one feel, have you? I felt *violated*. Yes, I will put it that strongly. As far as I was concerned, this was *personal*.

Very well, to get back to that Tuesday.

I arrived early, nearly one of the first in the restaurant. I sat unobtrusively in a corner, reading a magazine. Which magazine? I hardly remember at this distance of time. It would have been one of the older, more conventional periodicals, of that you may be sure. I arrived early because at that time the staff would be off their guard. They have recently arrived for their shift, you understand, and have not yet moved from their easygoing off-duty selves to the role of buttoned-up professional. Not that the staff at Leda's was extensive. There appeared to be only one waitress. The proprietor, the eponymous Leda, did most of the cooking. And then there was another woman who provided desserts and who helped out as necessary. She was there with a smart-looking woman friend and they appeared to be lunching as normal customers.

The waitress looked innocent enough. A tall, pallid girl with that light red-blonde hair that is particularly offensive to those who love beautiful things. Pale pink skin. Very pale blue eyes and colourless lashes. Not fat, but soft-looking, as though she never took any unnecessary exercise. But she was deft enough, and an attentive waitress.

However, just after she had brought me my starter of whitebait, the brown bread and butter, the little bowl of tartare sauce (out of a bottle, I fear – I could taste the acetic acid), her attention was removed from her customers by the arrival of her friend. At this point I learned that my pallid waitress was called Holly and her friend was called Phil. This cannot have been her real name and I learned later that she was called Viola. A much prettier name, don't you think?

There was immediately something so sharp, so knowing, about this second girl that I buried my head in my magazine and listened to their conversation. She was pretty, if you like that kind of thing: lots of dark curling hair and flashing brown eyes. She gave the impression of energy – of energy that might be unleashed at any moment and cause fireworks to explode overhead. But I am being fanciful. No, she looked as though she would grab any opportunity if she saw an advantage in it for herself. I suppose she was one of those who have no moral sense whatsoever.

Within a minute or two it became evident that Viola had brought a new skimmer for Holly. Her previous one had ceased to work – there was some story about an accident to it that I didn't believe, and I doubt that Viola did, either. What I understood was that Holly no longer wished to be associated with such criminal activity and was making excuses to break away. But the other girl, Viola, could see no good reason for giving up. And then she spoke the name of her employer – of Holly's employer, too, I suppose. Now this was a name I *did* recognise. Barry Frazer. I had suspected that he was their employer, but this was my confirmation.

Yes, this was the man who had stolen money from my account in Worcester. I am not usually careless, but when I was moving around after the collapse of the business deal I was involved in last year, I became so: I may have thrown out a letter or two that had not passed through the shredder; I may have pushed a bank statement into a black plastic bag without first tearing it into small pieces. I was thinking about evading the hounds who were pursuing me, not of the rats who were picking up the scraps I had discarded in my wake.

But this year, with my new enterprise established and bringing in a profit, I had the time and the motivation to track the man down. You may think he was just a petty criminal, that the theft of a single one of my identities was something I should put behind me and forget. But forgiveness is not in my nature, I am afraid. And the theft of even one of my identities diminishes me, as I see it. He could not be allowed to get away with it. As I have already mentioned to you, I was angry.

Fortunately I had Jamie, dear Jamie Bates, to help me. I gave him the name, Barry Frazer. I had also discovered that

Frazer was running an operation covering the western part of England, with occasional forays into London. He had a large staff – if that is what you call them. I'm sure he had bank clerks on his payroll, as well as bin-divers and waitresses in many fashionable restaurants. The man was an entrepreneur, and quite efficient, but not on *my* scale, and he shouldn't have attempted to steal from me. Doubtless he was unaware who Karl Church really was, but ignorance is no excuse. No one steals my money and gets away with it.

To return to my story: I considered staying in the restaurant until it closed and then following Holly and persuading her to tell me where to find her principal. Then it struck me that it was possible that she didn't know where he lived, that the Viola girl was the go-between. Certainly Viola appeared to be more familiar with him and his whereabouts. She also appeared to be higher in the hierarchy than Holly. I might waste my time sitting around, then following Holly, only to find out that she didn't know where he lived. The man might be alerted to my interest in him and simply disappear. I knew he was capable of such a thing.

So I decided to follow Viola. *She* certainly knew Frazer and must be acquainted with his address, or at least with a method of communicating with him. The proof was that she was passing on the new skimmer to Holly.

I knew that Viola was waiting to continue her argument with Holly in the kitchen, so I had to act quickly, before she left the premises and disappeared into the Oxford streets. So I called the waitress and asked her for my bill. She was surprised that I was eating only my first course, but I made some kind of excuse and told her that I was in a hurry. I paid her in cash, and left, without considering the two major errors I had just committed.

First, I had dropped a contact lens on the floor and had failed to find it. And second, I had filled in a card with my name and address, applying for an invitation to a food and wine tasting. Stupid of me, I know, but it's one of my little weaknesses. I have never been able to pass by those plates of cubed cheese or sliced sausage in the supermarket. I suppose we all like to take something and give nothing in return. Someone put the two items together and you know the rest.

I hurried out of the restaurant. I was just in time. I could hear through the kitchen door that Viola was leaving. Holly was angry with her and she was departing through the back entrance. I left by the conventional way and waited for her to walk up the alley and join me in the Woodstock Road.

She and Holly were too angry with one another to notice me going out after her, and two other women customers were calling for Holly's attention. I knew Viola's type: she was too arrogant to look behind her and wonder who might be following. Even if she realised that I was there she would assume that her sex appeal was the cause. But I don't think she did notice me, in any case.

She walked rapidly, back towards Carfax and then down St Aldate's. The streets were crowded with lunchtime shoppers and the tourists and foreign students that afflict the city at all seasons of the year. Goodness knows why they come! They seem unaware of Oxford's history, of her architecture and culture. They eat at McDonald's and point their cameras at anything over fifty years old.

I'm sorry, I went off at a tangent for a moment. To return to our business. I caught the impatient tap of Viola's feet as she was held up by yet another crowd of French schoolchildren or Spanish teenagers. These young people seem to imagine that they own the very pavements and that the local inhabitants are most unreasonable to wish to pursue their legitimate business along the thoroughfares.

We weren't more than fifteen minutes or so, however, in arriving at the flat where Viola lived. The outer door was kept open, at least during the day, I assumed, and I followed her inside and up to the second floor. I may be a big man, but I can be exceptionally light on my feet. She glanced down the stairwell once, but I pressed myself against the wall and she failed to see me.

Once she had let herself inside I waited a couple of minutes – I didn't want her to think I had been following her. She had a spyhole in the door and I arranged my face into something bland and unthreatening. I believe I even smiled. She opened the door cautiously but she had no security chain and I merely pushed it wide and stepped inside. She was a small girl, although wiry, and couldn't resist someone of my height and weight.

I do regret what happened next. I must confess that I lost my temper. I know that I am a passionate man, but I have learned to control those passions. But I suppose that forces kept so strictly under restraint must be overwhelming when they eventually break through – like the eruption of a volcano – a force of nature that nothing can control. Is that what they all say: 'I couldn't help myself?' I apologise for being so predictable.

To begin with I simply asked her for Barry Frazer's phone number and address.

She laughed at me. 'Why should I give you those?' She had quite a refined accent, but I believe it was learned rather than original. 'Bug off!' she said rudely.

I hit her.

'That's why,' I said. I was still fully in control of my feelings at this point.

Have you noticed that people with that vivid colouring, especially women, have an obstinate streak? There was blood on her lip and a red patch on her cheekbone that would turn into a bruise, but she sneered at me.

'Why don't you try offering me money instead?' she said. 'I might just answer then. You'd have to give me lots and lots of money, though, wouldn't you?' She was implying that I wasn't rich enough to buy her. And she stood there defying me. But I can be obstinate, too, and I had reached the point where I no longer felt like offering money for the information I wanted.

I remember how it felt when I looked at my bank statements and found that all the funds I had deposited in those two accounts had been removed.

'But you came into your own branch, Mr Church, and drew the money out in person,' the Personal Banker had the effrontery to tell me.

'How did you know it was me?' I asked, reasonably enough.

'You had perfectly adequate identification. A driving licence with your photograph and signature, according to our records.'

And so, as I told you, Frazer had robbed me not only of my money but of my identity. Yes, I know that I've already taken my financial revenge. Frazer won't ever be able to get his hands on what he thinks of as *his* money. It is no longer in Nauru. It has been transferred to . . . No I'm not telling you where.

As I say, Frazer had to pay now for stealing my identity. Or one of them – but he wasn't to know that at the time. He probably knows better now. It all came down to the fact that Frazer had to pay for the pain he had caused me, and this little chit of a girl knew where he was. The one thing I cared about now was that she was going to give me this information.

I looked around the room, knowing that she must have an address book somewhere. It was a colourless, cheap place, with a sofa and chair picked up from one of the second-hand shops in St Clement's. She had pinned up a couple of posters on the wall to brighten it up. A Georgia O'Keeffe, as I remember it, and something erotic by Mapplethorpe. She had placed some pink flowers in a blue vase, too.

I couldn't see what I was looking for, though, and there was nowhere obvious for her to have put it away – no desk or table. The flat looked as though she used it only for sleeping or perhaps for watching late-night films on the television.

'Your friend, Barry Frazer, stole something valuable from me,' I said.

'Your wallet? Money? Your credit card?' she sneered. There was nothing I could put my finger on exactly, but I sensed she was laughing at me.

'Money, certainly. But also my identity. And now I want payment for them.' I was still under control, you notice, even under such provocation.

You think I should have seen the absurdity of what I had said? What is my identity, after all? I have had so many of them over the years that I hardly remember which is the real me, if such a thing exists. He stole *one* of my identities, and *some* of my money. But the feeling of powerlessness, of frustration, of having been *invaded* and taken over were as acute as if I had had only the one, like any ordinary man.

Remembering the theft of myself, the hollow space somewhere inside, I felt the anger surge up again.

'You *will* tell me where he is,' I said, louder this time. And I hit her again.

273

Her head lolled to one side and she may have lost consciousness. I was aware only that she knew where to find Frazer and that she wouldn't tell me where he was.

What is it about a victim that makes us want to join in with the aggressors rather than fly to their aid? I have never believed that story about the Good Samaritan. He would have searched through pockets to see if the thieves had left anything behind for him and then, disappointed, would have delivered another punch or kick to the figure on the ground. Perhaps this is something *you* know about? No?

While she was standing there, defying me, the girl had a chance that I would spare her. Once she lay there, the marks of my fist livid on her pale skin, the brute that is inside every man took over. You think I'm a psychopath? I don't believe I am. I am just an ordinary human being who found himself in an extreme situation.

Pity and compassion didn't come into it. I wanted answers and if the girl wouldn't give them to me she would pay for her silence.

By the time I realised that she would never tell anybody anything ever again, there was a lot of blood, and much of it was on me. I don't suppose I'd been there more than ten minutes. She was only a small, slightly built girl, and in spite of her obstinacy she didn't take long to die.

As I stood there and looked down at her broken, unrecognisable body, I felt the anger draining away. I was left feeling empty. If anything, I wanted to rest, I was so exhausted. Yet some vestige of self-preservation remained. I knew I had to get away. She might have invited a friend round, or some neighbour might have heard the noise we'd made and come to investigate. I needn't have worried, it turned out: she was not the kind to have friends, let alone invite them to her flat. And the neighbours were all at work, and in any case quite uninterested in anything that happened around them. I had to get out of this stasis and think. I needed a plan.

This may seem strange to you, but this was the first time I'd ever actually killed someone and I wasn't used to having to hide the consequences. I probably didn't do it very well.

I looked down at the mess on my jacket and trousers and realised that I couldn't simply call a taxi and leave the flat. I'd have to clean myself up.

There was a full-length mirror in the wardrobe in the bedroom. I looked at myself carefully, then set to work. First I washed my face and hands and rinsed the front of my hair. I took off my jacket and waistcoat and looked in the mirror again. I didn't look so bad now. My hair wasn't as neat as usual, but the splashes of blood on my dark trousers were hardly noticeable. The waistcoat, which I wear at all seasons of the year, had protected my shirt. I thought about sponging the blood off my trousers but decided that would merely draw attention to their soiled state.

When I had reduced my appearance to as near normal as I could manage, I folded my jacket inside out, placed the waist-coat inside it, found a supermarket carrier bag in the kitchen and bundled them into it. I carried the bag under my arm and left the flat. No one had seen me arrive, I was sure. I glanced at my watch: I had been in the flat for less than half an hour.

This was a street where there were people around during the working day. I walked a hundred yards or so, then used my mobile to call a taxi. I asked him to take me to the railway station, then waited until he had left before taking another cab to the place where I had left my car.

Although I was shattered by my ordeal, I pride myself on the fact that it did not take me long to recover from it. It is a mark of a fine athlete, I believe, that after strenuous exertion he rapidly returns to his resting state of a strong, slow heartbeat, unlike those of us who are less gifted physically. My talents lie in the mental, rather than the physical field, of course, but the analogy is valid.

By the time I arrived back at my house my own breathing was back to normal and I was thinking calmly. I saw no reason to panic. Why should you connect me with Viola's death? There was no obvious link between us and no one, as far as I could tell, had seen me enter or leave her flat. Of course, this was before I knew about the clever things you could do with my carelessly scattered hairs. I'm sure if I had consulted Jamie on the subject, he would have known all about it. As it was, I preferred to keep this particular matter entirely to myself.

I soon disposed of the suit I had been wearing. I had an incinerator in the garden, which would have dealt with it adequately – though I certainly didn't want the neighbours noticing that I was burning something odd. The smell of burning wool – so nauseatingly pungent, don't you find? – might well draw unwelcome attention. The sitting room had a solid fuel burner which would deal with the problem more discreetly. I took a pair of scissors to the suit – a robust pair that I found hanging on a hook in the kitchen, not the ones I use on my fingernails – and I burned it in small pieces. I mixed it in with the logs that I usually burn. The aroma from the latter would disguise the smell of the former, or so I hoped. The weather was warm, certainly, but not so hot that some heating would seem eccentric. Old houses are always cold and damp, in my experience, and need airing, even in summer. The black-bellied stove would do the job nicely.

Once I had the fire burning to my satisfaction, and the fragments of my suit distributed among the logs, I went to take a bath. I felt dirty all over and needed to scrub myself clean. When I looked at my hands I was sure I could see flecks of dried blood underneath my fingernails.

I thought I had done quite well in the circumstances, but of course I had forgotten about your modern forensic science. I suppose every petty thief knows about DNA samples and such-like these days, but I come from an older generation and those things are mysteries to me. It is, after all, the first time I have ever committed such a violent crime. I know now that the two or three hairs that I left in the bathroom basin were enough for you to extract my DNA. The blood which transferred itself to the upholstery of my motor car, now invisible to the eye, is identifiable as Viola Grant's. Even the shirt and shoes, which bore near-invisible spots of blood, can be forced to link me to the crime.

I did make some effort to flee the country, I'm afraid to confess. I have a substantial trust fund on a Pacific island called Nauru. I quite fancied the idea of spending time on a silver beach, under a brilliant blue sky, admiring the waving palm trees. Unfortunately, I was unable to acquire the necessary visa. I wrote to the relevant Nauruan authorities. I telephoned, even. I truly thought that they would welcome my financial expertise in their efforts to create a post-phosphorus economy. But no one replied. You may think that you can now lay your hands on my funds in that Pacific republic, but that will not be possible. My money is quite safe and will be waiting for me when I am eventually released.

A statutory life sentence for murder, you say? Ah, well.

Don't think, however, that you will build a case against me involving my Internet dealings as easily as that in which I am accused of the murder of Viola Grant. When you try to follow my financial affairs, you will find yourself involved in years of work. If you sort out the painstaking detail and *do* send the file to the Crown Prosecution Service, your troubles will not be over. Supposing that it ever comes to court, do you believe that any jury will ever understand your evidence and your arguments? The case will collapse, you will look like fools – again – and I will walk away free.

But not, I understand very well, from this other *débâcle* with the girl, Viola Grant. I do try to use her full and correct name, you notice. It is the least I owe her.

Yes, you may take my statement away and have it typed out. Please ask the typist to pay particular attention to her spelling and punctuation. I wouldn't wish to be thought an illiterate as well as a criminal.

And when I do sign it, which of my names would you like me to use?

25

A few days later, Jon and Kate met again, this time in London. They'd been to a film they both wanted to see, and then had a meal. The weather was at last warm and they were walking back through Covent Garden and down towards the Strand.

Jon asked, 'Do you like the sea?'

She looked puzzled. 'Swimming, do you mean? Sailing?'

'No. Just the sea. The grey pebbles, the noise of the surf on stone, the far horizons. The horizontal lines of it. Cities are made out of verticals and right angles. Rural England is a series of soft curves. But the sea, and the sky above it, are drawn in horizontal lines.'

'Why do you ask?'

'I've always loved the sea, felt at home there.'

'Is that where you grew up – in some seaside town?'

'No, but the first time I was taken to the shore I knew that that's where I belonged. It wasn't a beach full of holidaymakers and ice-cream vans, but a long expanse of estuary, empty except for the sea birds and waders.'

'I like it, of course,' said Kate. 'But I can't say I have your passion for it.'

'I've bought a little place down in Sussex.'

'A cottage by the sea?'

'It's small enough to be called a cottage, but "cottage" summons up visions of thatch and stone walls and roses round

279

the door. This was built between the wars from red brick and tile. You have to know it well to understand its charms.'

'Like the best kind of people,' said Kate.

'I'm glad you see it like that. I was wondering whether you'd like to spend a few days there. With me.'

'Yes,' said Kate. 'I think I would.'

'I know you've just bought a house, and want to get settled into your own place, but I thought it would make a bit of a break for you.'

'The answer's still yes. We're not completing the sale for another six weeks.'

'That gives us plenty of time, then. And I have a small boat.'

'I enjoy rowing.'

'Not quite that small.'

'When were you thinking of taking this break?'

'How about next Thursday, say for five days?'

'Sounds fine to me.'

'Good. That's settled.'

'I'm glad I'm moving. I think I'm going to enjoy living in the new place.'

'That's drawn a line under the past, then. You'll be able to move forward in your life.'

'I'd like to know what's happening to Fabian West first. Did you find him? Has he been arrested?'

'Yes, to both those questions. The police are still waiting for the results of the DNA tests, but they're pretty sure that the hairs belong to him. And they found some bloodstained clothing in his house. He'd destroyed his shirt and the suit he was wearing, but he'd forgotten about his shoes. If the blood matches Viola's, he'll be charged with her murder.'

'It's nearly over,' said Kate. 'Fabian West was behind the killings in Agatha Street. Even though he won't be charged with those murders it sounds as though he'll be found guilty of Viola's, and then he'll be sentenced to life imprisonment. I've left Agatha Street at last. I've been free and footloose for a few weeks, and now I've found a new place to live and I'm ready to settle down again. I can start to forget about the tragedies and get on with my life.'

'And your editor is no longer suspected of murder, his money has been returned to him, and he is a now wiser man, so your career can flourish, too.'

'How did you know about Neil?'

'I hear these things on the grapevine.'

'I can see I shall have to keep my thoughts to myself in future.'

Headline hopes that you have enjoyed reading OXFORD PROOF. We now invite you to sample Veronica Stallwood's next Kate Ivory mystery, OXFORD REMAINS, available soon in hardback.

I was six years old when my father died.

You would think that after all these years the events of that night would have faded from my memory but they are still lurking there in all their colourful detail, waiting in ambush like the pirates in my childhood dreams. One reason for their tenacity is that I think in images rather than words (which is strange when you consider the importance that words have had throughout my adult life).

It is all so clear to me, even now.

'Wake up!'

My mother's voice pierced through the layers of sleep, her hoarse words stirring the air close to my ear and interrupting my restless dreams. I was dreaming of breakers pounding harshly against a hostile shore, of a fragile craft, whipped by wind and rain on to the rocky teeth of a storm-lashed cove, while I strove vainly to save her helpless crew. For I had espied two figures in the boat, mouths agape with soundless cries for help, white hands fluttering in supplication. But, valiantly as I strained against the inertia of sleep, my limbs refused to obey my will, and my voice, like theirs, was drowned by the screaming of gulls far above my head.

'Wake up,' my mother was saying. I remember her rasping

whisper and the way she kept repeating the same phrase, 'Wake up!' as she shook my shoulder. I was a heavy sleeper in those days and, besides, I was loath to abandon the boatmen to their watery fate, and so I fought against her efforts to waken me. At that moment those two unknown people in the boat were so much more real to me than my mother and father. Why was it necessary to wake up in the middle of the night to join my parents' shadowy world when I was needed so urgently in my own vivid one?

'Get dressed. You have to get dressed and come downstairs.'

'Why?' If I had been fully awake I would never have dared to question my mother's orders like that.

'It's your father,' she was saying. 'You have to help me.' And then, most worrying of all, she added, 'I don't know what to do.'

Her words made me feel as though all responsibility for the family were being heaped upon my inadequate shoulders. How could I possibly bear such a burden?

My eyes were open by now and I was struggling to sit up in bed. My mother had switched on the light, a bright central bulb that shone straight into my still blinking eyes. She was sitting on the edge of the bed, very close to me, so that I could smell the mixture of *Ysatis* and fear that oozed from the soft folds of her body.

As I blinked, her face came into focus, too close to mine. And now I could smell, too, the wine on her breath and see a thin red arc painted on her lower lip where the wineglass had rested.

'Get dressed, like a good child! You can do that, can't you?' I sat and watched as she took the pile of folded clothes from the chair and placed them beside me. And then she left the room.

I forced myself to sit up in bed, to swing my feet out from under the blankets and over the side into the cold winter air, for there were no heated bedrooms in our household. I pulled on the school clothes I had removed just a few hours before. Perhaps it wasn't the middle of the night after all, for at that age I would have been in bed at seven, well out of the way so that my parents could enjoy their evening meal in peace. I would have been asleep by seven thirty.

My eyelids kept sliding closed, I remember, and I had to thrust my chilled feet into recalcitrant socks. Then there remained only my shoes, and I fumbled them on, but couldn't quite manage to tie the laces. I hoped that no one would notice.

I stumbled out of the bedroom, then awkwardly descended the stairs and pushed open the drawing room door. This was not my territory. I only ever entered this room by invitation. It was my parents' place, kept free of childish things.

'So you're here at last,' said my mother. She sounded odd, as well she might, I realise now. 'Go over there.' She indicated the chair on the opposite side of the fireplace. The logs had burned down so that only the heart of the fire still glowed red, and the room was turning chilly. 'What can you see?'

And so, obediently, I approached the silent figure in the red velvet armchair which was reserved always for my father. He was sitting there now but his shoulders were slumped and his head lolled to one side. The skin around his mouth was tinged with blue.

'Father?' I enquired, but he didn't reply. I stared at him while he in his turn stared at the floor close to my feet. My own eyes followed his gaze towards my school shoes with their trailing laces. And then I saw that in my haste I had put them on the wrong feet. They looked so peculiar, with the toes pointing quaintly east and west, like a clown's, that I couldn't help myself from breaking into laughter.

The laughter rebounded from the high ceiling and echoed around the striped walls as though it existed quite independently from me, like the laughter of a stranger. I stuffed my hands into my mouth, for I was desperate to stop the terrible sound, but still it hiccuped out through my fingers.

I can still see the scene reflected in the mirror of my memory: me with my hands over my mouth, mother's white face staring at me with disbelief, and, impervious to us both, the silent figure of my father. By then, of course, I realised he must be dead. There could be no other explanation for his disregard of my unseemly behaviour.

I looked again at my mother, but all I could see was the blood-red arc of her lower lip and the expression of something that might have been satisfaction in her eyes.

Oxford Mourning

Veronica Stallwood

When novelist Kate Ivory first meets Dr Olivia Blacket, an academic at Leicester College, Oxford, the atmosphere is far from amicable. Olivia refuses to show Kate the fascinating material she is researching, even though it concerns the same esteemed literary figure that Kate is writing about. Determined to nose out the scandals that could provide her with a best-seller, Kate discovers a darker side to Dr Blacket. What are the strange obsessions that haunt her? What is her relationship with Kate's boyfriend Liam? And most of all, who would want to murder her . . . ?

Liam's name heads the list of suspects, but Kate knows that several others were in the vicinity of Olivia's rooms at the time of her death, including a bizarre 'family' of civilised squatters – four men guarding a blank-faced girl. As Kate is drawn into their circle, she struggles to understand a complex web of overlapping lives, and realises that, before she can unravel the truth, her own beliefs and values will come into question . . .

'Stallwood is in the top rank of crime writers' Mike Ripley, *Daily Telegraph*

0 7472 5343 9

headline

Oxford Shift

Veronica Stallwood

Joyce Fielding is missing. She walked out one afternoon into the streets of Oxford and just disappeared. And now, Kate Ivory has been hired to find her. Joyce is a sober, respectable widow in her sixties and there is nothing at first glance to explain her disappearance, so Kate consults her own mother, the irrepressible Roz, to help solve the puzzle.

It isn't long before Kate, following Joyce's trail, discovers a dead body. The police may think that Joyce is a criminal and Kate an interfering amateur, but Kate realises that Joyce has unwittingly walked into danger, and that the hunt for the missing grandmother is a race against time . . .

In her usual iconoclastic style, Kate threatens to bring chaos to the annual carol service in Oxford's cathedral before she finally brings the real murderer to book.

'Novelist Kate Ivory snoops with intelligence, wit and some nice insights' *The Times*

'One of the cleverest of the year's crop [with] a flesh-and-brains heroine' *Observer*

'Irresistibly readable' *Financial Times*

0 7472 6009 5

headline

Oxford Shadows

Veronica Stallwood

When the flying bombs terrorised London in 1944, anxious mothers sent their children away to the peace of the countryside to escape the danger. Oxford and its surrounding villages appeared to be havens of safety, but dangers other than bombs menaced some unlucky children – and for ten-year-old Chris Barnes, the result was death.

Over fifty years later, novelist Kate Ivory, searching for wartime love stories as material for her latest historical romance, uncovers Chris's tragic tale. Amongst the piles of old papers in the attic of the house she shares with her partner, George, she finds the child's diary and drawings, and, in an old newspaper, a haunting photograph of a face she cannot forget. But one thing remains unclear – why he died so young.

Never able to resist a mystery, Kate determines to find the truth, but the knowledge comes at a price – the boy's death appears to implicate George's family – and Kate is faced with an impossible choice . . .

'Novelist Kate Ivory snoops with intelligence, wit and some nice insights' *The Times*

'Stallwood is in the top rank of crime writers' *Daily Telegraph*

'One of the cleverest of the year's crop [with] a flesh-and-brains heroine' *Observer*

0 7472 6844 4

headline

Oxford Double

Veronica Stallwood

Writer Kate Ivory has new neighbours on either side of her terraced house. On one side lives Jeremy Wells, a diffident, charming Oxford academic. On the other lives Laura and Edward Foster, who are intent on enjoying every moment of their retirement. None of them seems likely to become embroiled in serious crime, nor to be its victim. So when the Fosters are shot in what looks like a contract killing, the explanation must be a case of mistaken identity.

But Jeremy begins to behave rather oddly. First he leaves dubious messages on Kate's answering machine, then he asks her to take a mysterious package to his colleague at Bartlemas College. And when he insists Kate helps him to go into hiding, she asks herself the question: If an unassuming Oxford academic has been leading a double life, is it possible the Fosters did too? Either way, with both of her neighbours out of the picture, it's up to Kate to uncover the truth.

Don't miss Veronica Stallwood's other irresistible Kate Ivory mysteries:

'Stallwood is in the top rank of crime writers' *Daily Telegraph*

'One of the cleverest of the year's crop [with] a flesh-and-brains heroine' *Observer*

0 7472 6845 2

headline

Now you can buy any of these other books by **Veronica Stallwood** from your bookshop or *direct from her publisher*.

FREE P&P AND UK DELIVERY
(Overseas and Ireland £3.50 per book)

The Rainbow Sign	£5.99
Deathspell	£5.99
Death and the Oxford Box	£5.99
Oxford Exit	£6.99
Oxford Mourning	£6.99
Oxford Fall	£5.99
Oxford Knot	£6.99
Oxford Blue	£5.99
Oxford Shift	£6.99
Oxford Shadows	£5.99
Oxford Double	£5.99

TO ORDER SIMPLY CALL THIS NUMBER

01235 400 414

or visit our website: www.madaboutbooks.com

Prices and availability subject to change without notice.